Praise for

PHILIP R. CRAIG's

incomparable

MARTHA'S VINEYARD MYSTERIES

"Reading Philip R. Craig is armchair traveling at its finest."

Alfred Hitchcock's Mystery Magazine

"Nicely crafted mystery that is worth spending some time on."

Knoxville News Sentinel

"Craig just keeps getting better."

Chattanooga Times

"Reading [Craig's] books is like a pleasant holiday, visiting old friends (his recurring characters) and enjoying a popular resort area, all without leaving the comfort of your favorite chair."

Los Angeles Daily News

"Craig vividly portrays the island mystique."

St. Louis Post-Dispatch

"It wouldn't be summer without a new Martha's Vineyard mystery."

Boston Herald

Other Martha's Vineyard Mysteries
by Philip R. Craig

VINEYARD ENIGMA
VINEYARD SHADOWS
VINEYARD BLUES
A FATAL VINEYARD SEASON
A SHOOT ON MARTHA'S VINEYARD
A DEADLY VINEYARD HOLIDAY
DEATH ON A VINEYARD BEACH
A CASE OF VINEYARD POISON
OFF SEASON
VINEYARD DEDCEIT
DEATH IN VINEYARD WATERS
A BEAUTIFUL PLACE TO DIE

Coming Soon

A VINEYARD KILLING

PHILIP R. CRAIG

VINEYARD FEAR

A MARTHA'S VINEYARD MYSTERY

(Originally published as *Cliff Hanger*)

AVON BOOKS
An Imprint of HarperCollins*Publishers*

This is a work of fiction. Names, characters, places, and incidents are products of the author's imagination or are used fictitiously and are not to be construed as real. Any resemblance to actual events, locales, organizations, or persons, living or dead, is entirely coincidental.

AVON BOOKS
An Imprint of HarperCollins*Publishers*
10 East 53rd Street
New York, New York 10022-5299

Published by arrangement with Charles Scribner's Sons

Map illustration by Aher/Donnell Studios
ISBN: 0-06-059444-6
www.avonmystery.com

First Avon Books paperback printing: May 2004

Printed in the U.S.A.

10 9 8 7 6 5 4 3 2 1

For my grandchildren,
Jessica and Peter Harmon,
who live with their parents in the Colorado mountains
far, very far, from *Martha's Vineyard*
and the singing sea.

"There are always many more disordered states than there are ordered ones."

Stephen W. Hawking
A Brief History of Time

"Though lovers be lost love shall not;
And death shall have no dominion."

Dylan Thomas
"And Death Shall Have No Dominion"

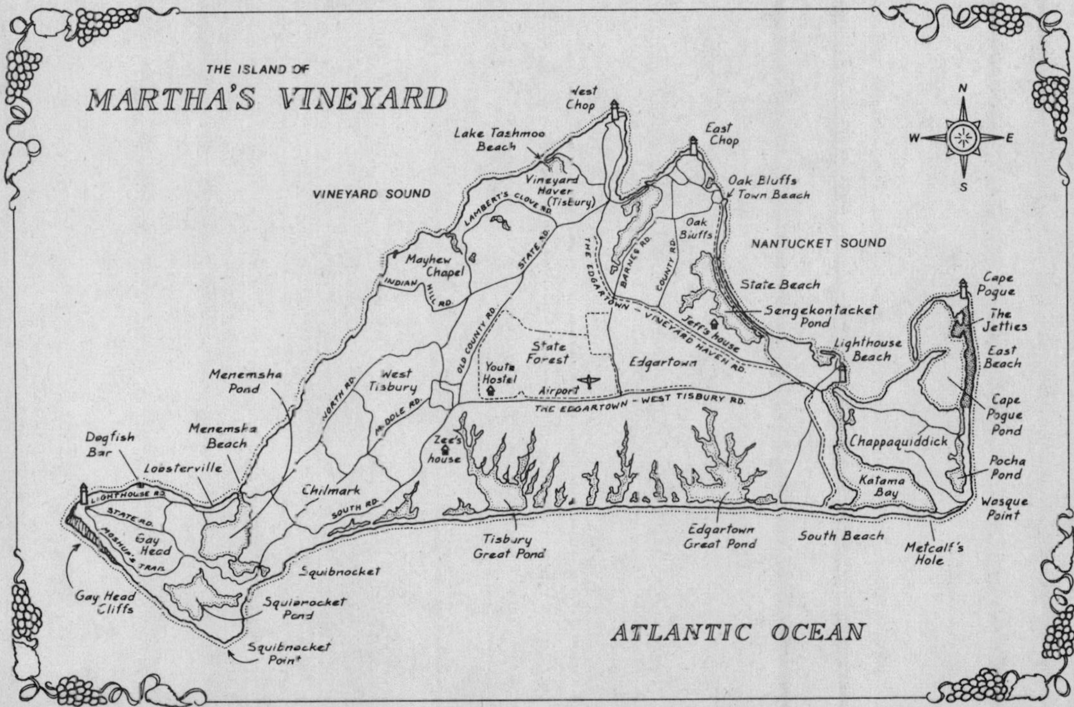
THE ISLAND OF
MARTHA'S VINEYARD
N
W
E
S
VINEYARD SOUND
NANTUCKET SOUND
ATLANTIC OCEAN
West Chop
East Chop
Lake Tashmoo Beach
Vineyard Haven (Tisbury)
Oak Bluffs Town Beach
Oak Bluffs
LAMBERT'S COVE RD.
STATE RD.
BARNES RD.
COUNTY RD.
THE EDGARTOWN - VINEYARD HAVEN RD.
Jeff's house
State Beach
Sengekontacket Pond
Mayhew Chapel
INDIAN HILL RD.
OLD COUNTY RD.
State Forest
Youth Hostel
Airport
Edgartown
Lighthouse Beach
Cape Pogue
The Jetties
East Beach
Cape Pogue Pond
Chappaquiddick
Pocha Pond
Katama Bay
Wasque Point
Menemsha Pond
West Tisbury
NORTH RD.
MIDDLE RD.
THE EDGARTOWN - WEST TISBURY RD.
Zee's house
Dogfish Bar
Menemsha Beach
Lobsterville
Chilmark
SOUTH RD.
LIGHTHOUSE RD.
STATE RD.
Gay Head
MOSHUP'S TRAIL
Squibnocket
Gay Head Cliffs
Squibnocket Pond
Squibnocket Point
Tisbury Great Pond
Edgartown Great Pond
South Beach
Metcalf's Hole

VINEYARD FEAR

▪ 1 ▪

The first time, I thought that I'd just been involved in a near-miss accident. The second time, I thought I'd almost killed myself. The third time, I realized that someone wanted me dead. I couldn't imagine why. But then many a murder victim probably has a look of surprise on his face.

If the bluefish hadn't gone north early or if the bonito had arrived on time, maybe none of it would have happened to me, but late July found the waters around Martha's Vineyard so barren of fish that it seemed the usually fertile sea was dead, and I worked the beaches in vain. I didn't have any better luck fishing from the *Shirley J.,* either, partially because the midsummer winds were fluky and weak and an eighteen-foot catboat is none too swift in the best of conditions. Unlike the power boats, whose speed was not dependent upon the winds, the *Shirley J.* was slow to get out to the shoals and just as slow returning home, and I had little daylight fishing time between going and coming back. Not that it would have made much difference, since the shoals were almost as empty of fish as the shore and the guys in power boats weren't doing much better than I was in the *Shirley J.*

I was bored and eating the early summer's catch out of my freezer instead of fresh stuff out of the sea.

Of course I could have been eating shellfish. Martha's Vineyard, and Edgartown in particular, has some of the East Coast's finest shellfishing ponds, after all. I could have had clams, quahogs, mussels, or maybe even some oysters, in spite of the truism that you're really only supposed to eat oysters in months with an "r" in their names. The "oysters are mushy and tasteless in warm months" theory is not necessarily gospel. I've eaten good Vineyard oysters in the middle of the summer.

But I didn't want any shellfish. Eating shellfish bored me.

Everything bored me. If I hadn't been bored, I never would have gone across Vineyard Sound to America, and if I hadn't done that, then . . .

The real problem was not the lack of fish. I had gone fishless before. The problem was that Zee had left the island for a month. I had learned about this plan for the first time in the spring, when we were down on Wasque Point on a very brisk May morning waiting for the bluefish to arrive.

Zee, wearing her waders, a sweater, a hooded sweatshirt, and her topsider jacket, did not look like her normal slender self. Her apparent bulk did not fool me, though, because I knew what she looked like in warm weather. She and I had been alternating between making casts out toward the light buoy to the south of the point (one way to determine which way "straight out" is, when it's too dark to see anything) and coming back to the truck for its meager warmth, and coffee from my large, stainless steel thermos jug.

I was as bundled up as she was, because it wasn't yet sunup and the southwest wind, blowing in from the sea, was cold. Moreover, the heater in my ancient, rusty Toyota Land Cruiser was none too good and you had to wear a lot of clothes to keep warm anytime the air was chill, even if you weren't going fishing.

When Zee came up to the truck, I would usually go down and make my casts, just so one of us would have a line in the water most of the time. Sometimes, though, we were both in the cab at the same time, drinking coffee and listening either to the C and W station from Rhode Island, which for some reason I can pick up well on Wasque, or to the classical station over in Chatham.

Gradually the sky lightened in the east, most brightly just to the left of where Nantucket lay right over the horizon, and then the sun inched into sight behind low clouds and climbed until it was a huge orange-red ball of fire coloring the sky and setting the ocean momentarily aflame. I put my rod in the spike on the front of the Land Cruiser, and dug out the slingshot I'd made from a piece of leather and two thongs. I picked up some choice pebbles from the edge of the surf. I smiled at Zee.

"Watch this."

I put a stone in the sling and whipped it down the beach.

"You see that? I hit that tree dead center."

I threw another stone. Zee got out of the truck.

"I used to do this when I was a kid," I said. "Yesterday I was reading Samuel again; you know, the part where David and Goliath are promising to feed each other's flesh to the birds of the air and the beasts of the field, just before David does Goliath in, and I remembered making these things, so I made this one. Nifty, isn't it? And I haven't lost the old skill either. It must be like riding a bicycle."

"There's no tree there," said Zee.

"Use your imagination," I said. "Watch this. There! I got it again. Great, eh?"

"You're a sick man, Jefferson."

"If you'll just call some fish in, I won't have to do this. Wow! Another hit! Ah, I have the golden touch! You want to try?"

"No. Put that away, and have some coffee."

"I used to make slingshots out of forked pieces of wood and strips of rubber from old inner tubes, too, and later I had a BB gun. Ah, this brings it all back." I grinned at her, put away the slingshot, snagged my coffee cup from the dashboard, and watched the birth of yet another day. There is no prettier place to see it happen. Zee leaned on the truck beside me.

"How did you manage to become such a saint, after such a violent childhood?" she asked.

"Moral vigor," I said. I waved at the ocean. "I have a hunch that just at the exact moment when I finish this coffee and walk down there and make my cast there'll be a fish out there waiting for the plug to hit the water."

"Sure," said Zee. "I think that's about the tenth time you've made that prediction this morning."

"I was just practicing before. This time I mean it."

"I'm going away for most of August," said Zee.

I drank my coffee.

"I'm going to a women's conference up in New Hampshire."

"You don't have to tell me where you're going."

"I thought you might want to know. It's a conference on 'Women in the Health Professions.' "

Zee was a nurse. "It's probably a good time to go," I said. "The fish will be going away and you'll get to miss the August People." Some of the island cops say the August People are more trouble than either the June People or the July People.

"I've been thinking about going to medical school," said Zee.

I hadn't heard that before. I finished the coffee and held the cup in my hand, looking at the rising sun. "You'd make a good doctor."

"I haven't decided yet. That's one reason I'm going to the conference."

I was still surprised about the medical school idea. "It must be some conference if it lasts a month."

"There are two conferences, actually. The medical one and then another one about women's lives. Some of the same people will be at both of them. Then I'm going to just take some time off and be by myself for a while. Maybe I'll even go see my folks."

"Sounds good," I said.

"I'm going to make a cast," said Zee. She took her nice eleven-and-a-half-foot graphite rod out of its spike and walked down to the silvery-red water. The waves weren't too big, but the water was chilly if you let it splash up into the front of your waders. Zee walked the receding water down, made her long, straight cast, and stepped back before the next wave hit the beach. Out toward the whitecaps in the Wasque rip I saw her Roberts hit the water.

I looked to the west. A couple of trucks were coming along the beach. One of them looked like George Martin's Jeep and the other looked like Iowa's pickup. They were planning to hit the rip two hours before the turning of the west tide. Not a bad idea. Zee and I had arrived four hours before the turning and had nothing to show for it. So much for the Early Bird theory. As I looked west, I heard Zee yell and turned to watch a huge swirl surround her plug. A bluefish, sure as taxes!

"Get on there!" encouraged Zee, slowing her reel.

Another swirl, but no hit. Zee inched the plug in. A Roberts is about as good a surface plug as I know. It catches fish sometimes when nothing else seems to do. Zee flicked her rod tip and the Roberts jumped a bit at the end of her line. The bluefish took another whack at it and missed again.

"Come on!" said Zee, encouragingly. Another swirl. Her rod bent. "There!" She jerked up the rod tip to set the hook and the Roberts flew through the air. "Damn!"

I grabbed my rod and made my cast as I reached the surf. Zee's plug was back in the water and sure enough there was another swirl right on it.

"Look at that!" cried Zee. "There he is again! And again! He can't catch it, the rascal! Come on, fish, catch it!"

But the fish did not catch it. He swirled and flashed and hit it with his nose and chased it all the way into the surf, but he never got it.

Meanwhile, about two turns on the reel in from the end of my cast, I was on. I felt the hit, set the hook, and heard the reel sing.

"Get him!" Zee grinned at me and made her second cast and a moment later we were both on, rods bent, lines cutting through the water.

They were fighters, and they walked us down the beach before we got them in. Nice ten-pounders, just up from the Carolinas. We were carrying them to the Land Cruiser when George and Iowa pulled up beside us and got out. There was a passenger in Iowa's pickup. A woman.

"Perfect timing," said George, taking his rod off his roof rack.

"What's that Madieras person doing here?" said Iowa. "Women belong in the kitchen, not out here catching us men's fish."

"I left a couple for you," said Zee, "but you won't catch them by standing around complaining."

"All right, all right," said Iowa, getting his rod and following George down to the surf. "Getting so a man's got no place to call his own. Damned women are everywhere. I thought I told you not to bring her out here anymore, J. W."

"Just because your wife's too smart to hang around listening to you grouse all day doesn't mean I have to forsake the company of the fairer sex," I said.

"Nothing fair about Zee," said Iowa, making his cast. "She's caught a lot of fish that rightfully belonged to me. Whoops! On, by Gadfrey!"

And he was. And so was George. And moments later, so were Zee and I.

As I brought my fish in, I looked at the passenger sitting in Iowa's pickup. She was a youngish woman, one I'd not seen before. Several fish later, the young woman was out of the pickup, getting a closer look at the action on the beach.

"My niece," yelled Iowa over the sound of the surf. He took a fish off his plug and gestured all around. "Gerry, these characters live off the fish they steal from me. That's George, that's J. W., that's Zee. She's the worst of the bunch. Everybody, this is my niece, Geraldine Miles. Visiting from Iowa City. Brought up all wrong. Doesn't know a damned thing about fishing. Trying to teach her how to live right!"

The woman smiled and Iowa was headed back to the surf.

"Gangbusters," said Zee an hour later.

The fish had gone, but we'd gotten our share and the five of us were standing by the trucks drinking George's coffee since Zee and I had almost finished our own before the fish had hit.

"Not bad, not bad," Iowa said. "Even a woman could catch 'em today."

Zee pretended to peek into his fishbox. "How many did you get onto the beach? One? Two? A bent rod doesn't mean a thing. They don't count until you land them, you know."

"You're hard," said Iowa. He had at least ten fish in his box and was feeling good.

Geraldine Miles drank coffee with us, smiled, and was quiet. She moved in an unnatural, awkward way, as though some of her bones hurt. She was a pretty woman about Zee's age, with brownish hair and a milky skin. At first I thought that she was shy. After a short time, though, I suddenly realized she was more troubled than shy. I studied her when she wasn't looking and decided that her smiles were more polite than real, that she was trying to be happy rather than actually being happy. The fact that she'd gotten up in the wee hours to come to Wasque with Iowa when she knew nothing at all about fishing suggested two things: that Iowa, who normally went fishing alone or with his dog or very occasionally with his wife, Jean, who did not share his fanatical love of surf casting, was trying to get his niece occupied with things other than those troubling her, and that she was agreeable to such distractions.

Maybe she had come to the island to escape problems at home. I knew something about that, having come to live on the island for the same reasons several years before. Now I felt a sympathy for her, but had my own desire for distraction. Zee would be away for the last month of the summer, and I wasn't really up to thinking about that yet.

"I see you hauled the *Mattie* and put her back in again," said George. "Kind of early, isn't it? John Skye doesn't usually come down until the middle of June."

John Skye was a professor at Weststock College who hired me to keep an eye on his house and boat in the winter and to get both ready for his arrival for the summer. If you're going to live on Martha's Vineyard year-round, you take jobs like that. The *Mattie* was his big old wooden catboat. She floated at her stake in the harbor all winter and sometimes I had to chop ice away from her hull. In the spring I hauled her, painted her bottom and topsides, and dropped her back in. An old wooden boat will last forever if you keep her painted and in the water. Haul her out and put her in the barn, she'll dry up and fall apart.

I looked away from Geraldine Miles. "I got a call from John," I said. "Seems that he's making his house and boat available to a professor he works with. John does that sort of thing sometimes. If he's not here, he'll let other professorial types use his place. This guy and some students are coming down to the island to do a study of some sort. Everything's got to be ready and waiting for them."

"More for you to do now, but less to do later," nodded George.

"When are they coming?" asked Zee.

"Next week. They'll be here about ten days, I guess."

"And then John and Mattie and the girls will be here." Zee was fond of the Skyes.

"I don't think so. According to John, Mattie and the twins are going out to Colorado for the summer."

"There's no ocean in Colorado," said Iowa. "There's no bluefish. Why would anybody want to go there?"

"There's no ocean or bluefish in Des Moines, either," Zee reminded him.

Iowa was a retired high school superintendent. "Yeah," he

said, "but I was smart enough to leave Iowa as soon as they'd let me go! Well, I suppose they can't fish for trout out there in the Rockies. That way the trip won't be a total waste of time."

"Not everybody likes to fish," said Zee.

Iowa's eyes widened. "Is that a fact? I never knew."

"John came from out there someplace," explained George. "Grew up on a cattle ranch before he came east. Mattie and the girls went out there to meet his mother after he and Mattie got married, and the three of them fell in love with the place."

"The twins are horse crazy," added Zee. "And they love the mountains."

"Well, the mountains are okay . . ." grumbled Iowa.

In the warming morning sunshine, Geraldine Miles pushed the sleeves of her sweatshirt up, then caught herself and pulled them down again, but not before I saw the bruises on her upper arms. Her eyes flicked around and met mine. She looked away.

"Not a bad choice of summer vacations." said George. "The mountains of Colorado or Martha's Vineyard. Too bad you can't be both places at once."

"Maybe they'll split the season," I said. "Half out there, half here."

"The perfect solution," said Zee. "I'd love to go to Colorado someday."

"The Vineyard will do for me," I said, wondering if that would still be true if Zee went off to medical school. How long did medical school take? Four years? And then there'd be a residency. How much longer would that be?

"Well, I'd like to go out there," said Zee.

"Good idea," said Iowa. "I'll be glad to help, if you'll just leave right now and stay away from my bluefish till the derby's over this fall. Now lemme see if I've got any money here . . ." He pretended to dig in his pocket.

Geraldine Miles smiled and the rest of us laughed. But I

was wondering if Zee was developing a sugar foot. Was the wander-thirst on her? Was the island giving her cabin fever? First she was going to New Hampshire and now she'd like to go to Colorado.

As things turned out, I was the one who went to Colorado. I nearly died there, in fact.

2

Martha's Vineyard is verdant island surrounded by golden sand beaches. It lies about five miles south of Cape Cod and lives off its tourists. Ten thousand year-round islanders play host to a hundred thousand summer visitors who bring in the money which oils the island's gears. The year-rounders labor mightily in the summer, some working two or three jobs, some renting out their houses and summering illegally in tents or shacks; many then go on unemployment during the winter.

Island wages are low and everything else is expensive, but summer jobs are sucked up by college students who are looking for vacation jobs with access to sea, sun, surf, and sex, and who don't really care if they actually make any money before returning to school in the fall. More serious workers come from overseas, legally or illegally, and live wherever they can while working as hard as they can, since even low Vineyard wages are better than they can earn at home.

Day-trippers come across from Cape Cod, take tour bus rides, buy knickknacks mostly made in Asia but sold with Vineyard logos in island souvenir shops, and go back to America having done the island in half a day. Other summer visitors come for their week or two of escape from the real world. The harbors are filled with yachts, and there are great summer houses owned by the people who come for the season.

John Skye was one of the house owners. He owned a part of what had once been a farm. The house had been built in the early 1800s, in the time before the island economy became dependent on tourism. In those days, islanders, like most coastal people, generally tried to make a living by combining farming and fishing, two of the toughest jobs imaginable. Tourism, by comparison, offered easy money, so when the island economy turned in that direction, farmers' sons and daughters left the farms for the towns and, years later, John had bought his house, outbuildings, and land pretty cheap.

Before I knew him, he and his first wife had come down every summer from Weststock, where he taught things medieval at the college. When she had died, too young, he had missed a season and gone instead back to southwest Colorado, where his people still lived. The next summer he was back on the island where, a year or so later, he and I had met on the beach and, in time, I became his caretaker, charged with closing his house in the fall, keeping an eye on it over the winter, opening it in the early summer, and caring for the *Mattie.*

The *Mattie* wasn't the *Mattie* when I went to work for John. She was the *Seawind.* She became the *Mattie* when John married Mattie, whose young husband had left her a widow with twin daughters when he drove his motorcycle into a tree at a high rate of speed.

And now Mattie and the girls had fallen in love with Colorado and John had a dilemma: where to spend the summer? Out by Durango, near the mountains they all loved, or on the island they all loved?

"If Colorado had an ocean, it would be no problem," John had said on the phone. "If they could just flood everything east of the divide, or maybe all of Texas, I could live out there for the rest of my life, but . . ."

"Everybody's got problems," I'd said.

"Except you. You've got it made, J. W."

"Who's this guy you're sending down, and when will he be here?"

"Jack Scarlotti. He'll be down May 25. He's our current

hotshot junior faculty member. Sociology, Poli-Sci, or some combination of both, I think. Anyway, he's very dashing, very intense, very bright. The ladies all love him. Not a bad guy, actually. Teaches a grad seminar. Wants to take the whole class down to the island for a week so they can do field research among the locals, before the summer people really get there."

"The island as a laboratory. Natives living in isolation from the mainstream. That sort of thing?"

"I think that's it. Something like the deafness bit, maybe."

Presumably because of inbreeding, a lot of up-island people once suffered from a type of deafness. Some medical or academic type had studied the phenomenon and his conclusions had been written up and had attracted a good deal of comment.

"The politics of isolation," I said. "Professor Scarlotti's students do the legwork and write papers and he puts it all in a book with his name on it and uses it as a required text in all of his courses."

Skye laughed. "Spoken like a true scholastic, J. W. Where'd you learn about that trick?"

"From listening to you and your academic buddies at those cocktail parties you throw."

"I'll have to advise my colleagues to talk less about our trade. They'll give away all of our secrets. I'm going to have Jack come by your house for the keys. Then you can take him over to the farm. Is that okay? I'll let you know what boat they'll be coming on."

"Okay."

"I think you'll like him. He's a good guy even if he is a whiz kid. I understand there'll be about ten grad students with him, both sexes. They should all fit in the house if they don't mind sleeping double. I want nothing to do with deciding who sleeps where, by the way."

"I'll make sure the place is clean, that there are sheets and blankets and water and lights, and that the fridge has bacon and eggs and bread waiting for them. I'll show him where the A & P is, too. Can this guy sail?"

"He says he can. If he wants to go sailing, you can show him the *Mattie* and where the dinghy is on Collins Beach and where the oars and oarlocks are in the barn."

"No problem."

"I'll have him leave the keys with you when he leaves. I'll be down in the middle of June."

"That'll give me time to clean the place up again. What do you mean, you'll be down? What about Mattie and the girls?"

That's when I learned that Mattie and the girls were going to Colorado to stay at John's mother's ranch.

"So you'll be living the jolly bachelor life, eh?"

"That's an oxymoron. The bachelor life is not the life for me. I have a theological crisis whenever Mattie has to be away. Sleeping alone in a double bed is evidence that there is no God."

"Why don't you just go out to Colorado with your wife and avoid this existential predicament?"

"I thought you of all people would understand. Bluefish, my boy! Clams! Quahogs! I haven't had a fresh bluefish since last summer. I haven't had mussels. I haven't had a clam boil. I haven't had one single littleneck on the half shell. Life is not always easy, you know. We have to face tough choices."

"Well, my favorite woman is right here, so I don't have to choose between her and fish."

"You're a lucky man."

A few days later, when Zee told me about her New Hampshire plans, I didn't feel so lucky, but at the time I could not but agree with John.

John's house was off the West Tisbury Road. In the wintertime, when the leaves were off the trees, you could catch a glimpse of the ocean from a couple of his upstairs windows. If some developer had gotten hold of it, he probably would have called it Ocean View Farm, or some such thing.

In preparation for the arrival of Dr. Jack Scarlotti and his band, I turned on the water and electricity, made sure there were no leaky pipes and that the toilets all flushed, and vacuumed and dusted the house, including the fine, big library where a few thousand of John's books tended to slow me down a lot as I examined titles and fingered through pages when I should have been working. I made sure there were blankets and sheets in the linen closets, opened screened windows so the place could air out, turned on the bottled gas for the stove, mowed the large lawn, and checked the barn and fences for needed repairs.

Behind the barn the grass was high in the field where the twins kept the horses that wintered at a farm up toward Chilmark. The horses would stay at that farm this summer, I reckoned, since Jen and Jill would be in Colorado with their mother instead of here. I liked the twins although I simply could not tell one from the other. I realized to my surprise that I would miss them. Was I becoming a sentimentalist?

I unlocked the tack room, where the twins kept their saddles and other riding gear and grooming supplies, enjoying, as always, the smell of leather and oils and the scent of horsehair and sweat that gets into tack, and the smell of hay and grain that is usually mixed in with it. Everything was fine, so I locked the door again and went back to the house, closed the windows, locked up, and went home. As I drove I saw Geraldine Miles walking slowly toward me on the bike path that paralleled the road. The bike paths on the Vineyard are popular with walkers and joggers, and Geraldine was limping along with an intent look on her face. In the warm spring air, she wore long pants and a long-sleeved sweatshirt. I considered offering her a ride, but changed my mind. She was walking because she wanted to be walking. I drove past and she never glanced at me.

On May 24, I got another call from John Skye. Jack Scarlotti and company would be coming over the next day on the one-fifteen boat from Woods Hole.

I went to the A & P and bought juice, instant coffee, bread, oleo, bacon, and eggs. As is customary on Martha's Vineyard, I paid a lot more for the food than I would have on the mainland. Such is the price of island living. All businesses overcharge and claim that it's because of the cost of bringing in supplies on the ferries. The overcharges are, of course, much greater than the freight costs, but it is a convenient lie shared by the businesses, and islanders tolerate it because they must. Once the state sent down a Consumer Affairs official in response to complaints about unjustifiably high prices. The official agreed that island prices were outrageous and had little to do with freight costs, but could find no law against the practice of overcharging and went back across the sound to America, never to return. Some people were disappointed, but no one was surprised.

I put the food in John Skye's refrigerator and went fishing.

At home again, I filleted the fish on the metal-topped table behind the shed in back of my house and threw the carcasses into the trees. As long as the wind blew from the southwest, the scent of rotting fish would blow away from the house. Within three or four days, the bones would be stripped bare by insects and birds and there would be no smell at all. Blues, like people, are biodegradable.

I set one fillet aside and put the rest in my freezer, then celebrated with a bottle of George Killian Red. George Killian Red is a product of the Coors brewery. Coors beer ("brewed with pure Rocky Mountain spring water") may be a bit overrated, but George Killian Red is a good beer that I enjoy.

My peas were ready, but there was also some asparagus coming up, so I picked that and managed to get it back to the house without eating it raw, proof that I have a will of iron. Asparagus out of the garden is so tender that it really doesn't have to be cooked at all, but on the other hand, a bit of butter doesn't hurt it. I put it in a pan with a little water and cooked it in the oven while I fried up the bluefish fillet, and made a sauce of horseradish, mustard, and mayo. In the fridge I had the last half of a loaf of bread I'd baked the day before (you always eat at least a half loaf of fresh bread as soon as it comes out of the oven), and in a bit sat down with another George Killian to a supper better than what anyone else I knew was eating. A Vineyard meal, the gift of the earth and sea. I wished that Zee was sharing it, but she was at the hospital on the four to midnight shift, alas. I managed to eat everything by myself.

The next afternoon at two-thirty I heard cars coming down my long, sandy driveway. Not too many cars come down my road, but these were right on time. The one-fifteen boat from Woods Hole gets into Vineyard Haven at two o'clock. It should take about a half hour to get your car off the ferry and down the road to my place. Dr. Jack Scarlotti could apparently read a map, because here he was with his students.

They were in two station wagons which stopped in the yard. I was pulling weeds in my garden and was glad for an excuse to stop. Weed pulling is not my favorite pastime. Car doors opened and people got out. Ten people in their twenties. The eldest came toward me. He was one of those dark-haired, dark-eyed, tight-skinned people who almost glitter with intensity.

"Mr. Jackson?" He put out his hand. "Jack Scarlotti." His grip was quick and firm. He gestured at the people with him. "My students." A girl with glasses was hovering directly behind him. "My teaching assistant, Bernie Orwell."

Bernie Orwell thrust out a hand and we shook. Her palm was soft and a bit damp. "How do you do?" she asked.

I thought she looked tired. "I do reasonably well," I said.

Another young woman, slim and attractive, stood beside Scarlotti. He did not introduce her. I looked at him. "I'll get your keys for you. Then I'll take my car and let you follow me out to John's place. If one of your crowd wants to ride with me, I'll point out the post office and some other places you might want to know about."

"I'll do it," said Bernie Orwell. Although her voice was without expression, she was quick to serve, which was maybe one reason she was his teaching assistant instead of just another student.

"Good enough," said Scarlotti. "Interesting place you have here," he added, looking at my house with a studious eye.

"An old hunting camp. I put in heat, water, and electricity. Otherwise it's about the same as it was eighty years ago when it was built. You'll find John's house a good deal more civilized."

I got the keys and gave them to Scarlotti, then pointed Bernie Orwell to my rusty Land Cruiser. The other girl climbed into the front seat of the station wagon driven by Jack Scarlotti. The station wagons got themselves turned around and followed me out to the highway.

"A station wagon train," I said to Bernie Orwell. "Does that make me a station wagon master?"

"What? Oh. I get it." She smiled a distant metallic smile. She was older than most people wearing braces, but I guess it's never too late to straighten your teeth. Hers didn't look too bad. She glanced back at the following cars.

We drove into Edgartown and I pointed out the post office, the drugstore, the liquor stores, and, when we finally got past the normal traffic jam in front of the almost brand-new A & P, the hardware store down by the park.

"We call this Cannonball Park because of those stacks of cannonballs in it," I said. "It's got cannons, too, as you see, but they're the wrong size to shoot the cannonballs. Don't ask me why."

"Very well, I won't."

"That way's downtown," I said, pointing, "but we're going this way." I turned up the West Tisbury Road and drove until I got to John Skye's driveway. The station wagon train followed me down to the house.

"So this is his place," said Bernie Orwell in her dull voice. "He liked to talk about it."

Scarlotti and the students emptied out of their cars and looked appreciatively at John's farm. After seeing my place, they realized how well off they were here. Bernie Orwell went to Scarlotti's side.

"I know where all the stores are. We'll need to do some shopping. I'll make a list and get right back to town."

"Let's look at the house first, Bernie," said Scarlotti, smiling.

She shrugged, and flicked a glance at the other young woman. "Yes. Of course."

A tired dog, but one still willing to please.

I climbed back into the Land Cruiser. "You know where I live and my number's in the book. If you need me, let me know. I can fix most of the things that might break while you're here."

"Thanks."

"Do you know about John's boat?"

"I know it's moored in the Edgartown harbor somewhere. He said we could use it."

"If you decide to go sailing, contact me and I'll show you the boat and John's dinghy."

"I doubt if we'll have time for sailing, but if we get our work done and the weather's good . . ."

I drove away and didn't see any of them again until, two weeks later, the station wagons came down my driveway and Jack Scarlotti handed me John's keys and drove off to catch the ferry back to America.

That afternoon I went up to John's house to clean up the mess. I found what I expected to find: overflowing trash barrels behind the house, breakfast dishes still in the dishwasher (which had been John's none-too-romantic-but-greatly-appreciated last year's birthday gift to Mattie), a lot of beer cans stacked on the back porch, and a very large pile of dirty linens which had been stripped from the beds. I also found three stray and unmatched socks and, behind the kitchen table, one earring. I opened windows to air out the house and spent the morning cleaning up. I washed several loads of linens in the machine and hung them on the solar drying line, vacuumed the house, washed the dishes, and made a run to the dump (once a favorite shopping spot where fine and useful stuff could be found and taken home for further use, but now an efficient and expensive recycling facility where all lumber had to be cut into short lengths, glass and paper and plastics had to be separated into colors and grades, and it cost you money for every barrel of just-plain-rubbish you deposited).

When the linens were dry, I folded them and put them away in various closets, and decided that John's house was back in shape. I checked the barn and that, too, was fine.

I closed the windows and loaded the beer cans into the Land Cruiser so I could take them to a liquor store where I could get a nickel apiece for them, thus adding a bit to the meager Jackson coffers and cleaning up the environment at the same time. Then I took a last turn around the house to see if I had missed something. I had.

Upside down in the flowers at the side of the front porch was a small green knapsack. It looked to me as if it might have been knocked off the porch when the gang was stacking stuff outside to be loaded into the cars. I got it and opened it up, looking for some ID. Inside were a variety of items: a zipped plastic bag containing lipstick, face powders, tiny bottles, and brushes; a Swiss army knife; pen, pencils, and notepaper; some Kleenex; cigarettes and matches; a plastic 35mm container with a bit of white powder in it and another film container with some pills; two books.

I wet a finger and tasted the white powder. Hmmmmm. I decided not to try one of the pills. I looked at the books. One was a book of social theory. Inside the cover was Bernadette Orwell's name. The other was a journal. I opened it up.

Its first entry was almost two years old and had to do with what Bernie Orwell had been doing that September day at Weststock when she began her senior year. She also wrote about how she felt, which was not great. I flipped pages shamelessly. A few entries later, Bernic was very happy with her courses and particularly happy because she was in a Medieval Literature class with Dr. John Skye, "a wonderful, wonderful person."

Lucky John. I wondered if he knew in what favor he had been held. I flipped ahead. If John hadn't known earlier, he surely knew later. Bernie wrote of lingering in his classroom, of seeing him in his office, of thinking of him at night. Bernie waxed up and down in her moods. No surprise, considering her film containers. Powder up, pills down was my guess. I found myself uncomfortablc rcading Bernie's secret words, but not so uncomfortable that I stopped reading. Instead, I flipped far ahead in her journal.

Last fall. Graduate school. Hot and heavy thoughts of Jonathan, who had not only become Jonathan instead of Dr. Skye or plain old John, but who, according to Bernie, was "so beautiful and brilliant" that she "trembled at the very thought of his touch." Good grief! So people really did write stuff like that. I wondered how anyone could think of John Skye as beautiful. Feeling suddenly like a voyeur, I closed the journal and returned everything to the backpack.

I went inside and phoned Weststock and asked for Bemie Orwell's address. They said they didn't give such information out. I got Jack Scarlotti's number and called that, but no one answered. I phoned John Skye. He obviously would know. But John said he'd get the address from the registrar and call me back. I found a beer in the fridge and drank it while I waited and wondered why John had told me he didn't have the address at hand. When John called back, he gave me an address in New Jersey, but said the registrar had been unclear about her Weststock address.

I scribbled a note to Bernadette Orwell and told her where

I'd found her backpack and the earring in John's house, and that he'd given me her address. I put the note in the pack with the earring (which, after all, might actually have been hers and certainly was of no use to anyone else), and packaged everything up. I took the package to the post office on my way home, and sent it parcel post, thus robbing Uncle Sam of the first-class postage he would have required of me had I told him of the note inside. It's hard to hold your own against the government, but I try.

That evening as I was eating crackers and bluefish pate, the phone rang. It was Bernadette Orwell calling in a panic from Weststock.

"I'm terribly, terribly sorry to interrupt you, but . . ."

"Relax. I found your backpack."

"What? You did! Oh, thank you . . . !"

"It had fallen off the front porch. I got your address from John Skye and sent everything to New Jersey. I didn't know your Weststock address."

"Oh! I just changed apartments . . . Well . . . Thank you! Thank you! My journal was inside . . . I've always kept a journal. Oh, I hope . . . You didn't . . . Oh, dear . . ."

"Don't worry," I said, "I don't read other people's journals. Only a real crumb would do a thing like that."

"Oh! Well, thank you again. You have no idea how worried I've been . . ."

"Think nothing of it," I said. Bernadette was in Weststock and her cocaine and pills would soon be in New Jersey. Everybody has problems. One of mine was being a real crumb sometimes.

▪ 3 ▪

I was wrapping smoked bluefish for my illegal markets when the phone rang. The Commonwealth of Massachusetts and the town of Edgartown insist that people who sell processed fish to restaurants and other purveyors of food should have very expensive and sanitary facilities to prepare that fish, but I prepare my smoked bluefish in my kitchen and smoke it in a smoker made out of an old refrigerator and electric stove parts salvaged from the dump long ago, before the environmentalists seized control of the world. I maintain that if I've never poisoned myself or the guests at my table, my food won't poison anybody else either. Happily for me, some fine establishments on Martha's Vineyard agree with me and are glad to buy as much of my illegal smoked bluefish as they can get. Why not? It's the island's finest, after all.

It was mid-June and John Skye's voice was on the line.

"Just got down. Place looks fine. How are the fish running?"

"They've been up around Cape Pogue for the last couple of days. Not too big, but lots of them."

"The little ones are best. Have supper with me. I'll feed you my catch."

"Sure."

"Zee working nights? No? I'll give her a call. Maybe she can join us. All my own women are out west. Bachelorhood is no kind of life, my boy; you've got to have women around if you want to be happy. I'm going fishing. You want to come along?"

"Sorry. Delivery day."

"Ah. See you about six."

"Yes."

On the way to John's farm, I saw Geraldine Miles walking on the bike path. Her pace was longer and she was moving more easily than when last I'd seen her. She was young and her body was healing itself. Her face looked better, too. There was some color in it. I liked the way she looked.

At six, I parked my ancient, rusty Land Cruiser beside John's brand-new blue Jeep Wagoneer. John came out of the house, shook hands, and helped me take three cases of liquor from his Jeep and put them in the Land Cruiser. On Martha's Vineyard, booze, like all other commodities, is vastly overpriced, so when our friends come down from America they bring our orders for life's essentials with them. John handed me his receipt for the liquor and I paid him in cash. A deal. I found a bottle of Moselle in one of my boxes and followed John back into the kitchen, where I put the bottle in the freezer for a fast chill.

He took two glasses and a half gallon of Stoli from the same freezer, sloshed dry vermouth around in each glass and tossed it out, then filled the chilled glasses with icy vodka and dropped two olives in each glass. He handed one glass to me. The perfect martini.

"Cheers."

"Shalom."

The vodka was smooth and cold as a mortician.

"Damn fine."

"Sit."

We sat and looked at one another. I tried but failed to see him as beautiful. He was fiftyish, a bit over six feet tall and short on hair. He was developing a slight belly that embarrassed him not at all; he held that it was emergency rations in case of atomic attack. When not on the island, he lived in Weststock where he was a professor at the college, specializing in literature written in European languages not spoken for at least a thousand years. He had once told me that one of the things he liked about his work was that it was completely useless. Just the thing for a man as basically impractical as himself, he said. I found his claims of being incapable of handling practical matters to be greatly exaggerated since he seemed handy enough when he needed to be.

"You found the fish," I said.

"I did, indeed. I have a little fellow in the fridge who will feed the three of us nicely. Stuffed with my wife's prize stuffing recipe and ready to be popped into the oven. You will drool when you eat it, but the secret of the stuffing will not be revealed to you in spite of your pleas. Not even the beautiful Zeolinda Madieras, for all her manifest charms, will extract it from me."

"Is that the recipe I gave Mattie last year?"

"I was afraid you'd remember that. Oh, well. Yes it is, so you know what to expect. Julienned beets and carrots on the side and white rice."

"Is that my julienned beet and carrot recipe?"

"Now that you mention it. But I got the rice recipe off of the box."

"Sounds like an excellent meal."

"It will be. Well, here's to summer and the end of another academic year."

We sipped our icy martinis.

"I take it that Jack Scarlotti and his gang got back to West stock in one piece," I said.

"Indeed. I got a bottle of very good Scotch as thanks. Young Dr. Scarlotti and his crew apparently did some good work while they were down here and Jack was settled down to devote his summer to organizing it and getting the results published. I am to get a copy of the book for my collection. I can probably get one for you too, if you want it."

"What were they doing?"

"I never asked, but I dare say it will be of great interest to some people."

"I doubt if I'm one of them, but if you get an extra copy of the book I'll take it."

"Smart thinking, J. W." John glanced out of a window. "I do believe that Zee has arrived."

She had, indeed, arrived, and naturally she looked terrific. As John waved her through the kitchen door, I met her with a chilled martini for which I got a nice-tasting kiss.

"I may have succeeded in training you, after all," she said.

"You mean the bit about the hardworking woman coming home and being met by a clean house, her man, and a martini?"

"That's it." She sat down and crossed lovely long legs. I ogled them shamelessly. She smiled and pulled her skirt up another inch. Then, surprising me, she allowed a little frown to ripple across her face and pushed the skirt down again.

What was that all about? And what was it that made a glimpse of forbidden flesh more exciting than a beach full of bikini-clad nymphets?

"Very nice, Zee," said John, "but I'll thank you to keep your clothes on. My wife is two thousand miles away, remember, and if you keep adjusting that skirt I might have a spasm."

"Don't listen to him," I said. "Adjust, adjust!"

"It's splendid to have this power," said Zee without expression in her voice. "No wonder women rule the world." Then she pushed away any frown that might have been on her face and lifted her glass. "Good to see you, John."

"And you."

"I saw that beautiful young professor and his doting students the other day. His students seemed to adore him."

"The good ones mostly do," said Skye. "He drives them hard, but they like it. The youngest associate professor at Weststock. Were he and his gang any kind of problem, J. W.?"

"I never saw them while they were here. The normal dirty linens, dishes, and rubbish were here when they left. I found an earring, three stray socks that I added to the rubbish, and that backpack I mailed to its owner. I'd call them a pretty good crew."

We ate in the kitchen.

"Say," said Zee, "this is good fish, John. I think I recognize the stuffing. Jefferson's recipe, isn't it? And these julienned beets and carrots!"

"Simple, but delicious," said John, modestly.

"Let me guess. Cook a pound and a half of carrots and a pound and a half of beets, then peel and julienne them and mix them up and heat the mixture through with some butter in a frying pan. Right?"

"Hmmmph," grunted John.

"They look good and they taste great and they're easy to fix! Terrific for a bit of color on the table at Christmas or Thanksgiving. Jeff showed me how to make this dish. Where did you learn it, John?"

"Have some rice," said John. "You'll love it. J. W. showed me how to read the recipe on the box. And have some more wine. J. W. had me bring it over from the mainland."

"What's for dessert?" asked Zee, with a laugh.

"Cognac. My own, by God!"

Over cognac and coffee John learned of Zee's August plans. He looked at me. "Seems that you'll be the only one left on the island, J. W. I'm headed for Colorado in August."

"There are worse places than this to be abandoned by your friends," I said.

"How long since you've been off the island?"

I thought about that for a while.

"Last fall," said Zee. "We went to a Red Sox game at Fenway. Remember?"

"That was it." I get off once a year or so. It's usually enough.

"They even won," said Zee. "That was an unexpected bonus. We had a good time. Beer under the stands, popcorn and peanuts, all the stuff you're supposed to do. We even met an old cop buddy of Jeff's. He was there with his wife and kids."

"Brad Tracey."

"Nicknamed Dick, naturally. He and Jeff got to talk cop talk for a while. His wife was nice. Two nice kids, too." Zee's voice changed tone when she mentioned Brad's wife and children. Zee was getting close to thirty and I wondered if she was hearing the famous biological clock ticking inside her and if that might be one of the reasons she was going off to conferences in New Hampshire. It didn't seem the time to ask her.

"If you can hold the island down until September," said John, "I'll be back to do some fishing before the fall term starts. The girls will have to be home early in the month so they can start school, but I'll have a couple of loose days."

"I thought you scholarly types never really had a day off. I thought you were always thinking and thinking."

"Hey," said John, "I have to think all winter. When summer comes, give me a break."

After supper, we went for a walk in the evening light. There was a lane leading south from John's barn. It ran along between trees on one side and a meadow of high grass on the other. A hundred yards along, John snapped his fingers.

"Oops. Gotta go back. Got to call Mattie. Don't get lost."

We watched him move back toward the house.

"I don't think he really had to call Mattie," said Zee. "I think he got a look at your face and decided we should talk."

"Could be. Should we?"

"Half of me says yes, the other half says to hell with it."

I had to smile. "Me, too."

"Well?"

"Well. Well, well. Well, so far I've asked you to marry me several dozen times and you always say not yet. Now you're going away for a month to find out what you want to do with your life. If you decide to go to medical school, you'll be gone for years and I wouldn't be surprised if you didn't come back at all. If you decide not to go to medical school, you still might not come back. I want you to do what you want to do, but I don't like the idea of being out of your life. That's it, I think. I don't want to be out of your life, but I think that's the way you're leaning. But if this is what you want, then I think you should do it. Life is too short to spend doing things you don't want to do."

"You sound bitter."

"I'm not bitter. I don't like bitter people and I won't be one. But I'll miss you and I'm afraid you'll leave the island forever. That doesn't make me bitter, it makes me unhappy. But I've been unhappy before and gotten over it, so my unhappiness shouldn't concern you . . ."

We walked through the dimming light down the sandy lane. "Look," she said. "I'm almost thirty years old. I'm not a kid. I want things I don't have. I want a normal family. I want a job that I can live with all my life. I love being a nurse, but why shouldn't I be a doctor? I love being with you, but I want children . . ."

"Marry me and you can have all the children you can handle. Or if you don't want the marriage, you can still have the children . . ."

She took my arm. "You don't even have a job, Jefferson."

"I have a lot of jobs. I fish, I look after some houses . . ."

"And you're the envy of every man who works nine to five, but . . ."

"But what? Are you telling me I should start chasing bucks? Why? I'm doing just fine. I've never missed a meal."

"But I'm not sure you're really husband material. A husband has responsibilities. A husband has to make sure his kids grow up right . . ."

"A role model?" I didn't want to be a role model. One of the reasons I'd come to the Vineyard and lived like I did was because I was tired of being responsible for other people.

"Look at you. You live in an old hunting camp on

Martha's Vineyard, you go fishing and shellfishing whenever you want, you grow a garden, you cook like a dream . . ."

"I chase after you . . ."

She squeezed my arm. "And you catch me, too. Anyway, you live this wonderful life of yours and it's right for you. But I don't know if it's right for me or for a family . . ."

"You come by every now and then."

She didn't miss a step. "You're a terrific guy and a great lover and the best friend I have, but I'm not sure you'd be as good a husband and a father."

I tried to imagine being the father of her children. It didn't seem to be a bad job. I wondered if I needed to change in order to be a father. I thought of my own father and wondered what he would think.

"And there's something else," said Zee. "It has nothing to do with you, but it's important. I'm tired of being somebody's somebody. I want to be myself. When I was little, I was my parents' daughter, then I was Paul's girlfriend, then Paul's fiancee, then Paul's wife, then Paul's ex-wife, then my Aunt Amelia's niece, and now I'm your girlfriend. It's not just that other people think of me as somebody's somebody, I even catch myself thinking of myself like that, and I don't like it. And here's something that maybe does have to do with you. I'm tired of defining myself in terms of my relationships with men. I think we women do that all the time and I don't think that you men do it at all, or at least not very much. Do you think of yourself as my boyfriend?"

"Sounds good to me."

"Do you?"

"No."

"You think of me as your girlfriend, don't you."

"When I'm feeling lucky."

"There. You see? I'm tired of that. I'm going away to think about that. All of those things. The one conference is about work and the other one is about everything else."

"I don't have any chain around your neck," I said. "I don't make you do anything you don't want to do . . ."

"You are bitter."

"I want you to be free," I said. "I want you to be free and to choose to come back so I can have you in my life. I want you to choose that out of all the other choices you may have. But I don't want you to come back and feel that you've missed your life and I don't want you to come back because you feel sorry for me. I don't like people who feel sorry for me or for themselves and if you ever start feeling that way, I probably won't hang around. If you choose not to come back, I want you to make that choice with joy, because it's what you want."

We walked on. After a while I noticed that it was dark.

"We'd better get back," I said.

We turned and walked back up the lane toward the lighted windows in John's house.

Outside of John's door, we paused. Zee looked up at me.

"Do you love me?"

"Yes."

"Will you love me if I go away in August?"

"Yes."

"Because I am going to go."

"I know."

She put her head against my chest and I put my hand in her hair and pressed her against me. I could feel my heart beating.

After a while we went inside to escape the night. John looked at us thoughtfully.

Long afterward, I wondered if, far away, someone else had been looking out at the same darkness, his soul cold, his feelings twisted, forming the plan which would, in not too great a time, lead him to stalk me through that curious moral jungle where manhunters seek their prey.

■ 4 ■

Three days after John's supper, I got word about when they were going to open the Edgartown Great Pond. This annual exercise is to insure that salt water gets into the pond so the shellfish there won't die. The opening through South Beach is dug by heavy equipment and for a while the tides sweep in and out of the pond, allowing the fresh water to escape and the ocean water to run in. After not very long, Nature closes up the opening again, but by that time the shellfish are in good shape for another year. Since I do my oystering in the Great Pond, I have a personal interest in those shellfish. Moreover, while the opening is open, it is a popular place for fishing, since both bass and bluefish are attracted by the bait that is carried by the tides in and out of the pond. For reasons which elude me, the exact time of the opening of the pond is not widely publicized, and fishermen play games trying to be among the earliest at the new opening. This year my hot tip turned out to be true, and I was there at dawn when the bass showed up.

I didn't normally fish for bass since I don't hunt for fish I can't keep, and the minimum keepable length for bass that year was 36 inches, which meant that most of the ones you'd catch you'd end up throwing back. The minimum length rule was in force because for years the bass population had been declining and efforts were being made to bring the fish back. I also didn't like to keep the bigger fish because they're mostly the females who lay the eggs.

But this year I did a bit of bass fishing, so I could tag them and let them go again. It was part of an effort to learn more about the migratory and other habits of the fish. The tagging was simple and, according to the island's resident marine biologist, painless to the fish: You ran a needle, threaded with a strip of plastic printed with the address of the Littoral Society in New Jersey, through the fish's flesh just behind the dorsal fin, knotted the plastic, and let the fish go. You recorded the size of the fish and the time and place of the tagging and sent that information to the New Jersey address. If the fish was ever caught again, the person catching it could send the plastic in along with information about the size of the fish and the time and location of the catch.

Lest I give the impression that I am a dedicated law keeper and environmental moralist, I should confess that if I catch a bass when I feel like eating one I keep it no matter what size it is. Unless someone is looking, of course.

I had tagged five bass running about two feet and weighing six pounds or so and had just recaught a particularly dumb one I'd tagged not an hour before, when I saw a blue Jeep Wagoneer coming west from Katama. I had decided that if I was doomed to recatch fish that I didn't want in the first place I would quit fishing, so my rod was racked and I was having coffee when John Skye drove up with Iowa.

Iowa got out and looked around. He was disappointed.

"Where the hell's Zee?"

"Working."

"Damned shame. Any fish here?"

"Small bass."

"Get any?"

"No keepers. Tagged some."

"Good enough."

He got his rod from the roof of John's Jeep and stepped down to the surf. Iowa would fish in a bucket if that was the only water around.

"What's Iowa doing riding around with you?" I asked John.

"His pickup is in the shop. Tore up his muffler at the jetties. He'll have his own wheels again tomorrow."

"Didn't bring his niece with him this trip."

"She's home with Jean. Kid's had a tough time, I understand."

"Somebody roughed her up. Boyfriend, I'd guess."

"How'd you know that?"

I told him about the bruises. "I figure she's here to either get over the bastard or decide to go back to him. Women have a hard time leaving these guys, sometimes." It was a truth I could never really understand.

"You hit it on the head," said John. "Guy living with her lost his job and started beating on her. She took it for a while, then got out. Came here. Iowa's a favorite uncle."

"I see her walking the bike paths. She's looking better. She going to stay?"

"I don't think she knows, yet."

"The guy know she's here?"

"I don't know."

When I was a cop in Boston, I learned a lot about women and the men who beat them up. I knew that men beat up women here on the island, too, but I wasn't a cop anymore, so I didn't have to deal with it. I had had enough of cop stuff.

"Maybe she'll be sensible enough to shake him."

"Sometimes the men come after the women who leave them."

True enough. About half the killings you read about in the Boston papers are the result of turf wars or drug wars. A lot of the others are men killing the wives and girlfriends who want to leave them or who have left them and been hunted down.

"Let's hope she's smart enough to shake him for good."

John nodded and looked for a new subject. "When I saw your truck, I thought Zee might be here. I didn't know she was working mornings."

"Maybe she isn't. I haven't seen too much of her lately."

"Oh." John dug around in his Jeep and came up with a thermos and a box of doughnuts. He pushed the open box at me. I found what looked like a blueberry-filled doughnut and took a bite. Skye squinted at me. We chewed doughnuts. He swallowed the last of his. "Maybe you should get off the island for a while. Why don't you come out to Colorado with me? Different country. Change might do you good."

"Maybe so." I remembered flying over the Rockies long ago on my way to Vietnam. The mountains had been covered with winter snow and had gleamed white in the sun.

"I'm going out there early in August," said John. "I'll be back in September. Zee'll be back by then, too." He raised an eyebrow.

"Um."

John drank coffee for a while. "Well, if you don't want to go that far, maybe you'll do me a favor and drive up to Weststock with me when I go, and then bring my Jeep back down here."

I looked at him.

"Get you off the island for a couple of days, at least," he said. "We can drive up together. I have to pick up some gear at home, then I'll fly west from Boston. I want the Jeep here when I get back so I can get a little fishing in before I go back to slaving over hot students. You can stay in the house up there in Weststock after I head to Durango, if you want. Go into Boston to see a show or two. Whatever."

Weststock was close to the New Hampshire border. Zee would be there somewhere. My ex-wife was not too far away either. She and her husband and their little kids lived north of Boston in a suburb where fewer bullets flew than had been the case in the city when I'd caught mine and she had decided that she didn't want to spend her life wondering if I was going to come home at all the next time. The two most important women in my life would both be within miles of Weststock, but neither one of them would want to see me.

Still, John's offer had appeal. I hadn't been to America for quite a while. Getting away felt like a good idea.

On the other hand, the fish still filled Vineyard's waters, my garden was flourishing, and in a few days the annual used-book fair in West Tisbury would allow me to turn in the books I'd finished reading during the past year and get another year's supply. Books, beer, fish, and fresh veggies on Martha's Vineyard made a winning combination, one which had made an islander (howbeit a transplanted one) out of me.

"I'll drive you up and bring the Jeep back," I said. "I don't know about staying over. There are still a lot of fish around . . ."

"Good. You'll be helping me out."

I left them there and drove home, where I yelled at a bunny who was looking thoughtfully through the chicken-wire fence that surrounded my garden, and went inside just as the telephone rang.

It was Manny Fonseca, the Portagee Pistoleer. Manny had for years taken great pleasure in insulting the Wampanoag Indians who inhabit Gay Head. Then, to his dismay and his wife's great amusement, he had discovered that he himself had enough Wampanoag blood in him to be an official Native American. After he had recovered from the shock, he gradually stopped telling his jokes about "professional Indians" and being "ready to pull yourself into a circle if you go to Gay Head," and "Fort Wampanoag," and in their stead began to develop some "white eye" wisecracks.

"Hail, Chief," I said. "What's going on in the pre-Columbian community?"

"Gottum new firestick," said Manny, whose idea of tribal languages was primarily acquired from the comic books all of us had read in our youth. "Got an electronic dot reticle scope, too," continued Manny. "Brand-new. I'm headed for the club to try it out. You want to come along?"

Manny's profession was as a finish woodworker, but his avocation was pistol shooting. He shot up his share of the family entertainment money at the Rod and Gun Club target range and was greatly involved in the buying and selling of guns and ammunition. If it was new and interesting and had to do with shooting, Manny bought it. He was, in fact, an excellent combat pistol shooter.

I was not into the sport. I had had a brief experience with real combat in a faraway land and had not found it sporting at all. On the other hand, I didn't have anything else to do at the moment and needed some distraction. Among other things, I might find out what an electronic dot reticle scope might be.

"I'll see you there, Cochise."

I got my earplugs out of the gun cabinet where I kept the shotguns and rifle I'd inherited from my father and the police .38 I'd carried for the Boston PD. I was still into a bit of duck and goose shooting in the winter, but my gunning seemed to be slackening off more and more as time went by. If I hadn't enjoyed eating the birds so much, I'd have given it up completely. Still, the guns in their cabinet were so much a part of the house that I'd never considered getting rid of them.

The Rod and Gun Club was within sound of my house. I could hear the guns popping there while I sat in my yard or worked in my garden, and had grown so used to them that I often did not hear them at all. With the key that came with my R and G membership, I let myself in through the locked gate to the club and waited at the new target range until Manny showed up in his shiny Ford Bronco.

He was wearing his shooting gear: a black belt with a holster on the right side and extra clips and other gear attached elsewhere. He got out a satchel and walked down to the table at the twenty-five-yard marker.

"How?" I said, holding up a hand.

"You foreigners will regret making fun of us original Americans," said Manny. "If my ancestors had had hardware like this stuff I'm carrying, instead of clubs and stone axes, you never would have made a beachhead."

"You're not original Americans," I said. "You're a bunch of Asians who came across the land bridge up in Alaska. You probably ran somebody out who was here before you were."

"Nah. We've always been here. Probably we went across the land bridge the other way and settled the whole damned world. You're probably one of my descendants. Look at this."

He opened the satchel and got out a long-barreled pistol mounted with a lumpy-looking sight that looked too big for the gun.

"Llama M-87 Competition Pistol," glowed Manny. "Got your built-in ported compensator, got your beveled rapid-load fourteen-round magazine with your rubberized base pad, got your oversized safety and your fixed barrel bushing."

"No kidding."

"Better yet, look at that scope. Thirty mm tube, coated optics, adjustable click-stop rheostat so you can adjust your red dot, lithium battery power pack, polarized filter, filter caps, glare shields, and a 3X booster. Nifty, eh?"

"The Pilgrims should be glad you guys didn't have that in 1620."

"Bet your ass. Let's put up some target and see what happens."

We walked down and hung three paper targets on the frames in front of the dirt backstop.

"What's the advantage of this fancy sight, Tonto?"

"Simple. You put the red dot on the target and that's exactly where your bullet is going to go. Especially good in dim light."

"There are those who say you shouldn't hunt in light that's so dim you can't really see."

"What do they know? Besides, now you can do it just fine. Got night sights, for that matter. See in the dark."

"Modern technology is awesome."

"I loaded both clips at home. Let's pop some caps." Manny put on his shooting glasses and stuck plugs in his ears. He slid a clip into the pistol and jacked a shell into the chamber. He locked his right arm, cupped his left hand below and around his right, and the gun boomed. I looked at the targets. There seemed to be a hole near the bull's-eye of the center one. A tiny red dot danced near the bull's-eye, then steadied. The gun boomed again. Another tiny hole near the bull's-eye. Another boom. Another hole.

Manny made a small adjustment on the sight. "Shooting right," he said in that loud way people have of speaking when they have muffled their ears. He raised the weapon in one smooth motion. The red dot bounced on the target and then steadied. The gun jumped and boomed. "Better," said Manny. He emptied the clip carefully into the target, jacked out the clip, and slid in a second one. He put the gun on safety and laid it on the table and we walked up to the target. There were fourteen bullet holes near the center. We covered them with tape. It didn't take much.

"You try it," said Manny. "Just remember that the red dot tells you where your bullet is going to go. Don't yank the trigger, just squeeze it."

I plugged my ears, put on my shooting glasses, and took up the pistol. The red dot danced all over the target. I steadied my arm and the dancing slowed. When the dot touched the bull's-eye, I squeezed off the shot. A bullet hole appeared six inches to the left. Not good, Kemo Sabe. Again the red dot touched the bull's-eye and again I fired. High. I fired again. Closer, this time. Eleven more shots. One in the bull's-eye. It took fourteen pieces of tape to cover the holes.

"Well," said Manny, "if it'd been a man, you'd have hit him most of the time."

"If it'd been an elephant, I'd have hit him every time."

"We don't shoot many elephants on Martha's Vineyard," said Manny, reloading the clips.

"There used to be mastodons or woolly mammoths or some such creatures out west before you red-skinned savages killed them all," I said.

"I think those other guys did that," said Manny. "The ones you say we ran off when we came over the land bridge. Here, try again."

We shot his new pistol for a while and then shot another one, since Manny always shot more than one pistol when on the target range.

Two trucks pulled up beside my Land Cruiser and Manny's Bronco, and guys with guns and satchels got out.

"I guess we've used up our time," said Manny. He put his guns and gear away. I put my earplugs and glasses in my pocket and got our targets. "What do you think of the scope," asked Manny, as we walked.

"I think that Crazy Horse or Sitting Bull or whoever it was that did in Custer had a bunch of them at the Little Bighorn."

"Red dot, red power," grinned Manny, raising a clenched fist.

I gave him some money for my share of the ammunition we'd shot up and went home. After lunch I went to the Eel Pond and spent an hour and a half on my hands and knees digging soft-shelled clams. When I had my bucket full, I went home and put them in a bigger bucket full of salt water, so they could spit out the sand in their systems. Tomorrow I'd freeze them. You can steam frozen clams just like fresh ones and never know the difference, and I always liked to have a batch on hand in case an irresistible clam boil urge came over me unexpectedly.

Manny thought digging clams was a nonsensical way to spend time. I liked it. He liked to shoot guns at targets. Everyone to his own madness, I say. Almost everyone, that is. Some madness can be fatal.

▪ 5 ▪

It was mid-July and hot when I discovered I had to actually go downtown into Edgartown. This is a venture I undertake in the summer for only the most serious of motivations, since the lovely, narrow streets of Edgartown are filled with tourists and jammed with cars and there is never anywhere to park.

But I was out of books and the big book fair in West Tisbury was still days away, so I had to make a run to the library to keep myself going. Normally I have at least one book to read, since I keep one in each place I expect to be. I have a bedroom book that I only read before sleeping, a bathroom book that I only read while on the throne (poetry here, since it comes in appropriately short slices), a kitchen book, two living room books, and a car book for traffic jams. However, a cruel fate had touched my life: I had finished all of these books within days of each other and was suddenly bookless.

So downtown I went.

Edgartown is so quaint and lovely, so filled with flowers and greenery, so fairylandish and make-believe, that pedestrians think that cars are just part of the scenery and the middle of the street is as much for them as for automobiles. They are surprised and even resentful when they discover some car attempting to occupy the street they are walking in while ogling the sights, and only reluctantly move to the brick sidewalks as the car inches by. Edgartown summer cops do their best to keep both drivers and pedestrians moving, and actually do a pretty good job of it by late summer. In mid-July, they are still a bit green and have a hard time untangling traffic, and need wise advice from the chief.

I found him, walking down North Water Street, Edgartown's classiest street as well as the location of its excellent library. This surprise was almost as great as the one I had experienced only moments before when a car parked right in front of the library had pulled out just in time for me to pull in. Shocking.

"You look pale," said the chief, "and I don't blame you. An actual parking place."

"Perhaps you'll take my arm and lead me to a chair before I faint. What brings you up to this part of town? Don't tell me that the weed of crime is bearing bitter fruit on North Water Street."

"The weed of crime in this case was a lady in that big house there who phoned that somebody was trying to break through the back door. It turned out it was her cat that she'd forgotten she'd put out, trying to get back in out of the heat."

"Your story has done much to make me feel more secure on these mean streets. How's the summer going?"

He wiped his brow and replaced his hat. "Be glad you've turned in your badge. We have more jerks in jail than I can ever remember having before."

In every community the size of the island's winter population, there are about twenty people who cause ninety percent of all the problems. They are the vandals, the drunks, the druggies, the car racers, the thieves, the people who rob their parents, who beat up women and children, who trash houses, who hate cops, and who never seem to change.

"If you'll give me immunity and a whole lot of money, I think I know some guys who will shoot the guys who are giving you most of your trouble," I said.

"Hell," said the chief. "If you could just move a couple of families off of the island, I could retire. How's Zee?"

"Fine, I guess. I haven't seen her for a while."

He nodded and his eyes floated down toward the four corners, where Main met Water Street. Many cars were not moving there. A summer cop in traffic trouble. The chief tugged on his hat brim and started on down the walk to do his duty.

"Protect and serve," I called after him and turned to see Geraldine Miles coming down the walk from the library.

She was wearing a wraparound skirt and short-sleeved shirt, and the bruises were no longer apparent on her arms. She was tanned and looked happy. There was a man with her, a tall, strong-looking guy about her age wearing new summer clothes: Vineyard Red shorts and a white shirt that said "Frankly scallop, I don't give a clam." He carried a canvas beach bag. His face and arms were tanned, but his legs were still white.

She looked at me, reached into her memory and came up with my name, and smiled.

"J. W. How are things on the beach?"

"You're looking well," I said.

"I am well. I'm very well. I'd like you to meet Lloyd Cramer. Lloyd, this is J. W. . . . I'm sorry, but I don't think I know your last name . . ."

"Jackson."

"J. W. is a friend of Uncle Dan."

Lloyd had a mouthful of good teeth and a strong grip. There was a tattoo of a skull on the arm attached to the hand that took mine. There was a tattoo of a knife with a wavy blade on the other arm.

"Any friend of Dan's is a friend of mine," said Lloyd in a hearty, Midwestern voice. "Pleased to meet you, sir."

Sir. I was only six or seven years older than he was.

"You're new in town," I said.

"I wrote to him and he came all the way from Iowa City just to visit me," said Geraldine in a happy voice. "Isn't that sweet?"

Lloyd shuffled his feet and put his arm around her shoulders. "After she left home to visit Dan and Jean, I realized how important she really is to me, so I just took some time off and came right here to tell her that. We've got a lot of things to talk about and we're having fun doing it. Isn't that right, honey?"

"That's right," said Geraldine, taking his hand. "We're getting everything straightened out. Isn't this weather just wonderful?"

I thought that right now Geraldine would feel that a hurricane or a blizzard was wonderful weather.

"I'll let you get on with your talking," I said.

Lloyd put out his big hand again and I took it in my big hand.

"Nice to have met you, J. W.," he said as he gave me his friendly smile.

"How long are you going to be around?" I asked Geraldine.

She looked up at Lloyd and smiled. "Oh, not too much longer, I imagine. I think maybe I'll be headed back to Iowa City soon."

Lloyd beamed down at her. "Great to hear you say that, sugar. Hey, let's hit the beach. I gotta tan up these legs before I go back home." He looked at me. "You got a really beautiful island here, J. W."

He showed me his fine teeth and she waved and they walked up North Water Street, headed, I guessed, for Lighthouse Beach. They looked like a happy pair. I hoped that it would last, but I didn't share the belief of many women that their men would reform if given one last chance.

I thought, Good luck to you, Geraldine Miles, and went into the library.

Libraries are some of my favorite places. They're filled with books and information and give you the good feeling that no matter how much you've read there's an endless amount of reading material still ahead of you, so you never have to worry about running out. It's a nice certainty in an uncertain world. I calculated the time left before the West Tisbury book sale, and got myself three books, including one about the popular inclination of conquering armies to burn books and destroy libraries.

The idea of destroying libraries was one that irked me, and it occurred to me that maybe I took the book because I was already irked that Geraldine Miles had gotten back together with Lloyd and irked even more that I hadn't gotten myself loose from my resentment that Zee was going off to New Hampshire. Reading of the destruction of the great libraries of Alexandria and Constantinople was only one more irritant in my irritated life. I apparently wanted an excuse to be out of temper. I turned this notion over in my mind and was not pleased with what it told me of myself. I went home and called the hospital and invited Zee to supper. She accepted.

She was still wearing her white uniform when she got out of her little Jeep. She inhaled as she came into the house.

"Ah, another delicious meal from the kitchen of J. W. Jackson."

"Indeed. But first this." I gave her a perfect martini and waved her back out the door. We went up onto the balcony and I put a plate of smoked bluefish pâté, Brie, and saltless crackers on the little table between our chairs.

We looked out over the garden and Sengekontacket Pond to the sound where, in the haze of the summer afternoon, sailboats were leaning with the wind as they beat for evening harbors. Along the road between the pond and the sound the cars of the beach people were pulling out and heading home.

"I was beginning to wonder whether I was ever going to get another invitation to come here," said Zee.

"It's been a while," I agreed.

"In fact, we haven't seen each other very much since May."

"True. My nose has been out of joint ever since you told me you were going away next month. I've been sulking."

"But you're over it now?"

"Over enough to want to see you a lot before you go off on your pilgrimage."

"Good. Me too. You're really over it?"

"I don't like sulkers, especially when one of them is me. I want to make up for the time I've lost. I know I'll miss you, but I'm not mad about it anymore."

"Good." She got up and came around and leaned over and kissed me. I kissed her back. She went back to her chair.

We sat and drank and ate and looked across at the boats and cars.

"I doubt if New Hampshire is as nice as this," said Zee.

"Well, you can always come home early."

"No, I'm going to do it all."

"A woman's got to do what a woman's got to do. A manly man like me understands that. It's a kind of code you have to obey."

"You're so sensitive I sometimes wonder how you survive. What's for supper?"

"A simple but elegant Scandinavian baked fish served with little boiled potatoes and fresh beans from my very own garden. Madame will find it quite satisfactory."

"Tell me more."

"Normally the chef never reveals his secrets, but I know I can trust you to be discreet. You cook a bunch of sliced onions in a skillet with butter until they're soft, then put them in a baking dish, put a pound or so of fish on top, add a couple of bouillon cubes and cover the whole thing with a couple of cups of roux. Easy and mega-delish. I like to use fish with white meat best, by the way. Today you're having cod caught up off Cedar Tree Neck. First, though, another drink."

I brought more martinis and we worked our way through the hors d'oeuvres. I felt happier than I had in a while. When the time was right, I went down and got supper going. At seven, we ate, washing everything down with a nice Graves

I'd been saving. Zee ate everything in front of her, leaned back, and patted her lips.

"Yum. You have not lost the touch, François."

"Note my modest smile. If you will place yourself on the porch, I will bring the coffee and cognac."

She did and I did and we watched the night darken around the house. She put her hand in mine.

"I've got to go home," she said.

"Sad words for one who has plied the maiden with his best booze and food."

"I have to go to work in the morning."

"You can go from here."

"I don't have a clean uniform here, J. W."

"Wear this one."

"This one needs to be washed. It has smudges from when I helped today's first moped accident up onto a table where we could patch him up. No, I've got to go."

"I want to see you a lot before you leave."

She put her arms around my neck. "Why don't you come to my place for supper tomorrow?"

"Can I bring a clean uniform with me?"

She laughed. "Yes."

The next day, early, I was on East Beach looking for bluefish that weren't there. Coming back to Wasque, I found Iowa with his head under the hood of his pickup. Two small bluefish lay at his feet.

"Glad to see you, J. W. By Gadfrey, will you look at this? Broken radiator hose! What next? First a muffler and now this. I have to get me a new truck. This one's beginning to fall to pieces. Your truck there is even older than this one. How in blazes do you keep it going?"

"Good Japanese engineering. You should stay away from American machines."

"By Gadfrey, maybe you're right."

"Actually I use the ride-it-a-day, work-on-it-a-day technique. I spend a good deal of time underneath this monster.

I'll give you a ride into town then bring you back out. Toss your fish in my box."

"Damned glad you came along. Not another soul on the beach. Thought I was going to have to radio for help."

We drove through the dunes and then along the south side of Katama Pond until we got to the pavement.

Iowa looked at his watch. "Let's go to my place first, so I can put the fish in my big cooler. Have a cup of coffee. By that time the parts place will be open."

Iowa lived out near the big airport. In the early morning, there wasn't much traffic, so we were there in pretty quick time. As we pulled into his driveway, Iowa cursed and said, "What's that son of a bitch doing here?"

There was a car with Iowa license plates in front of the house. As we stopped behind the car, I could see the front door of the house hanging open. Suddenly Iowa's wife came running out. Iowa caught her in his arms.

"What's going on, Jean?"

Her voice was high. "He's in there, Dan! He broke in the door and came right in! He went into her room! I've called the police, but . . . He's in there with her now. I think he's going to kill her!"

I didn't have to be told who "he" was. I turned Jean to me. "Does he have a gun? A knife? Anything like that?"

"What . . . ? No! I don't know! I didn't see anything, J. W. . . . I tried to stop him . . ."

Jean was small and in her sixties. Far away, I could hear sirens. I put Jean back into Iowa's arms.

"Get out to the road and make sure the cops don't go to the wrong place by mistake. Go on!"

"My shotguns are upstairs in my closet," said Iowa. "He may have gotten to them . . ."

"No," said Jean. "He went right into Geraldine's room!"

"Get to the road," I said and turned and ran to the house. I slowed at the door, listened, and went in through the splintered frame.

The grunting of a man's voice and the moans of a woman came from a room down the hall from the living room. I went down the hall and into the room. Furniture was overturned and a throw rug was wadded in a corner. Geraldine Miles lay across the bed while Lloyd Cramer knelt over her, his left hand on her throat, his right rising and falling, striking with sodden thumps against the bloody thing that had been her face. I thought I saw a bit of bone through the blood. With every blow he grunted and between grunts he cursed her with vile and unimaginative names.

He heard me and turned as I came in. His face was glowing with a kind of happiness.

"I got the bitch," he said.

I took him by a shoulder and his belt and jerked him away from the bed. He hung on to Geraldine's throat and brought her with him. I let go of his belt and hit him as hard as I could under the ear. He let her go and staggered back against a wall. I went after him and his hands came up. He was possessed by the strength of a sort of madness. He got hold of my throat with his left and hit me with his right hand, a punishing blow which I partially blocked. He was a big man and in good shape, so I jerked away and kicked him in the knee. The sound of the kneecap dislocating mixed with his cry as he felt the pain. As he reached for his knee and started his fall, I grabbed his hair with both hands, jerked his head forward and brought my knee up into his face. His nose disappeared in a spray of blood. I brought my knee up again. Then, hanging on to his hair, I drove his face into the floor. He lay there and didn't move.

Geraldine Miles lay on the floor. Her face was making little red bubbles. I put a finger on her pulse. It was faint, but still there. I heard the siren die in the yard. I turned and kicked Lloyd Cramer in the head. A moment later, the cops were in the room. There was an older cop and a young summer cop.

"You'll need a couple of ambulances," I said, and kicked Lloyd again.

"Hey!" said the summer cop. "Don't do that."

"Aw, just one more time," I said, and kicked Lloyd again. "This is the guy who did that to her," I said, pointing at Geraldine. "I'll wait for you outside."

"That'll be all right," said the older cop, looking at the figures on the floor. He looked at the summer cop, who was getting pale around the gills. "Joe, go out and put in a call for two ambulances and another car. Tell 'em it's a Domestic."

■ 6 ■

"They flew them both to Boston by helicopter," said Zee. "I was on duty when they brought them in. It was pretty bad. Her jaw and cheekbone were broken. She may have a fractured skull. I don't know whether they can save her eye. She had some broken ribs and a broken arm, and she was bleeding internally. He had a broken nose and a dislocated knee and head injuries of some kind. They both had blood coming out of their ears. I never like that."

We were having a drink at her house that evening. Normally Zee didn't talk much about her work. Like a lot of doctors and nurses, she had learned to put her work away when she went home. Unless they learn to do that, many people in the medical game would soon become dysfunctional. They are like cops in that respect. Of course, also like cops, some of them can't put aside the sights they see and the things their work obliges them to do, so you're never surprised to learn of doctors and nurses on the bottle or taking pills or other drugs. It's a professional hazard.

I had calmed down a lot since morning and no longer regretted that I'd been wearing only sandals when I'd kicked Lloyd Cramer. I had spent some time reminding myself that I had quit the Boston PD because I'd had enough of trying to save the world. But there was a perversion in me; I still doubted if I'd be sorry if I'd been wearing steel-toed boots.

"Is she going to be all right?" I asked.

"I don't know. I think he will be. As right as he ever was, anyway. Why do men do that to women?"

I thought it was for the same reason I might have beaten Lloyd Cramer to death if the cops hadn't walked in. "I think we hate the things we fear," I said. "I think we're afraid that those things will win out, that they'll ruin our worlds."

"How could she have frightened him? It doesn't make sense."

"Somebody said it's transference. We transfer our fear to someone we can hurt," I said. "Cramer's world is a bad one for him, so he beat up Geraldine because he couldn't beat up his real world, the one that scares him."

"That doesn't make any sense."

"We don't make sense when we take symbols so seriously that we'll kill for them. When we kill you because you're Catholic or because you're a different color, we're all crazy. I think we're the same way when we die for the Cause. The flag, our country, whatever. Fear makes us do it."

"It sounds to me like you're saying we're all like Cramer. I don't think I am, and I don't think you are, either."

"I think all of us have that little monster inside us. Most of us keep it caged up most of the time, but when we feel threatened, the cage door opens. I know that every time I've been angry, it's been because something frightened me. I don't get mad at things I don't see as dangerous."

"You're waxing philosophic this evening."

"I'm the guy who sent Lloyd Cramer up to you in pieces. I guess I'm just talking it out."

Zee looked at me in surprise. "You did that to him? I never heard your name mentioned."

"I got there just before the cops did. Afterward I talked to Iowa and Jean, and Jean said that Geraldine had come home and said she'd argued with Cramer and decided not to go back to Iowa with him. I think that after a while everything built up inside of him and he came after her. I stopped him, but I don't know if I was in time . . ."

She put her healer's hand on my knee. "Let's put the subject away. If I'd known you were involved, I wouldn't have brought it up. I'm sorry."

"Me, too." We sat for a while, then I said, "How are the Red Sox doing?"

"Now there's another sorry tale," said Zee. "Don't you have anything cheerful to talk about?"

I narrowed my eyes, wet my tongue, and licked my lips. "How about your primary and secondary erotic zones?"

She grinned and her hand patted my knee. "Now, now. You haven't had supper yet. I think you're probably too weak to even think about such things. I don't want you to hurt yourself. Get us more drinks while I start on the cooking and maybe we can talk about it later when you've got your strength up to a satisfactory level."

I got it up to a proper level later in the evening.

The next morning, Zee went off to work and I hung around to wash up the breakfast dishes and make the bed before heading home. As I drove through West Tisbury I stopped at the general store and got a *Globe*. On the other side of the street was the field of dancing statues. I crossed and went walking among them, looking for a new one but finding the old ones quite adequate. As usual, they cheered me up. They told me not to take myself too seriously, that life was comedy, that the universe was an ode to joy and whimsy in spite of death, in spite of pain, in spite of chaos. I heard the song of birds and saw them flashing through the trees. The wind stirred the grasses, and clouds floated across the blue sky. I willed Lloyd Cramer out of my life and felt better for it.

Too soon, as it turned out. At noon I heard the phone ringing as I was picking veggies (lettuce, radishes, a tomato, and a small zook) for a luncheon salad. It's always a toss-up whether I can get from my garden to the phone before it stops ringing. It rang again before I decided to try to get it. I put down my basket and galloped into the house. The chief was on the other end of the line.

"Just thought you'd like to know that Cramer signed himself out of the hospital this morning. He's gone and the last thing anybody heard him say was that he was going to get you and the bitch both. I've arranged for a guard to stay outside Geraldine Miles' hospital room. Do you want one too?"

"The guy's got a wrecked knee. How dangerous can he be? Besides, they're sure to pick him up before he can get here. Even Boston cops should be able to capture a man on crutches."

"Yeah, if they wanted him for anything. Right now, there are no charges against him. He could be anywhere by now."

"If he comes here, he'll have to come by plane or bus, and he'll be easy to spot and remember. Crutches and a face wrapped in bandages and all. His car's still down here, isn't it? And he can't drive it anyway, if his knee's no good. You going to call Dan and Jean Wiggins? Cramer might have a grudge against them, too."

"I did that already. They'll keep their eyes open and I'll have a car swing out that way every now and then."

"Well, you don't have to have a car swing out by my place. Thanks, anyway."

The chief rang off and I went out and got my veggies. I brought them in and washed them off and cut them up in a largish bowl. I added some salty olives and feta cheese I'd found at the A & P Deli, laced the works with some good olive oil and just a tad of vinegar, and *violà!*, an excellent Greek salad appeared. I ate it with homemade Italian bread and washed it down with a couple of bottles of Dos Equis, Mexico's best beer. International cuisine. Nothing like it.

That evening, I showered and got into my go-to-town clothes—a blue knit jersey with a little creature over the pocket and Vineyard Red shorts, both found almost new in the thrift shop, and boat shoes without socks. I know a guy at the yacht club who, on racing days, wears his captain's hat with scrambled eggs, his blue blazer and tie, his gray slacks and boat shoes, and a red sock on his left foot and a green one on his right, symbolizing port and starboard. I was not so formal because I was only going out to eat, not out to watch the races.

At seven, Zee's Jeep came down the long, sandy road to my house. She got out wearing a pale pink summer dress that perfectly set off her deep tan and long blue-black hair. She was dazzling.

"You're dazzling," I said.

"You look pretty Vineyardish yourself." Her teeth flashed between lips colored to match her dress. She came to me and put her face up and I kissed those lips, then licked my own as I looked down at her.

"We don't absolutely have to go out," I said.

"Yes, we do! I don't often get an offer to eat at the restaurant of my choice and you're not going to weasel out of taking me. So let's go to Edgartown. You can romance me later."

"Not a really bad idea. Food first and then lust. It worked like a charm last night."

"You have a long memory, Babar. It's one of the things I like about you."

We ate at the Shiretown, where I've never had a bad meal. Rack of lamb for me, salmon in a croissant-like crust for Zee, washed down with very satisfactory wine. Coffee, brandy, and a chocolate torte for desert. The bill came and I paid with cash. Zee stared, aghast.

"All that?"

" 'Farewell, paternal pension,' " I said. "But it was worth it." The J. W. Jackson criteria for judging restaurants are three: good food, reasonable price, and good service. If I get two out of three, I'm content. If I get three out of three, I'm in heaven. If I get one or less out of three, I figure I got ripped. That goes for every kind of place, from a hot dog stand to a four-star restaurant. I explained all this to Zee.

"Gee," she said, "what a sophisticated thinker you are. Tell me, have you ever actually been to a four-star restaurant?"

"I saw a picture of one once in the *Globe* food pages. Does that count?"

"Close enough for the likes of us," said Zee. "Let's go walk on the docks."

We did that, looking out at the lights of the anchored yachts and at the house lights on both sides of the harbor. Summer people were in the streets behind us, looking in shop windows and doing business at the ice cream stands and the clam shops. Zee's arm was in mine.

"It really is a beautiful place, isn't it?" said Zee.

"Yes."

"You can see why all these people come here."

"Yes."

"I'm going to miss all this."

"New Hampshire is beautiful, too."

"I know, but . . ."

"But it doesn't have an ocean? Yes it does. Down by Portsmouth."

"It doesn't have one where I'm going in the mountains."

"No, I guess not."

"I'm going to miss you, too."

"Good. The more, the better."

We walked up to North Water Street and then out to the Harborview Hotel, where we leaned on the railing beside the street and looked out toward the outer harbor. The Edgartown lighthouse flashed its endless message to the sea. There were lights on Chappaquiddick and stars and a sliver of moon in the sky. After a while, we walked back, got in the Land Cruiser, and drove to my house. The next morning Zee ran naked out to her Jeep and brought back a shiny clean white uniform.

"Smart," I said, reaching for her. "You nurses are smart."

She danced away. "Don't do that! This is my only clean uniform! Get away! I've got to go to work!" She ran around the room, snatching up pieces of her underwear. Then she stopped suddenly and put up her lips. I kissed them and slid my hands down her sleek brown body. "I really do have to go to work," she said a little breathlessly.

"I know." I held her a moment longer, then let her go and stepped away. She pushed a hand through her thick, tumbled hair, looked at me thoughtfully, sighed and smiled, and went into the bathroom to ready herself for the day.

I saw her almost every day for the rest of the month. We fished in vain from beach and boat. We fought the friendly crowds at the West Tisbury book fair and later those at the Chilmark library book sale. We brought home treasures from both. We went shellfishing and hit the Saturday morning yard sales. Then one morning she drove her little Jeep onto the early morning ferry to Woods Hole, and the world which had seemed such a good place was now, of a sudden, weary, stale, flat, and unprofitable.

For two days I fished in the fishless sea, made complex meals which were tasteless in my mouth, and tested previously untried beers which I found as flavorless as water. On the second night after Zee left, the phone rang. It was John Skye.

"Well," he said, "my bags are packed and I'm ready to go. I've got a reservation for the seven o'clock boat tomorrow morning. You still want to come up to Weststock with me?"

"I'm ready to roll," I said.

▪ 7 ▪

It takes forty-five minutes for the ferry to cross the sound between the Vineyard and Woods Hole on the mainland. By eight o'clock the next morning we were in the line of traffic emptying from the boat and headed for Falmouth. From there we went north to the Bourne Bridge over the Cape Cod Canal and finally fetched 495 North and drove toward Weststock, which lies northwest of Boston and not too far south of the New Hampshire border.

It was a foggy, warm, damp day on the island and I was glad to be elsewhere. The ride in John's nice, new blue Wagoneer was smooth as a baby's behind and the countryside rolled past us like a motion picture image. It was quite unlike the rattle and bang of travel in my rusty Land Cruiser. As we drove north, the fog and haze of the shoreline were left behind and we came out into bright sun. There was a lot of commuter traffic on the highway, but it moved along at its normal ten-miles-above-the-speed-limit pace and after a bit we were out of most of it. Green fields and trees flowed by us.

"I've got a luncheon meeting," said John. "At Weststock we like to clothe our business meetings with food whenever possible, since it seems to be true that food hath charms to soothe an academic breast, to soften deans, or bend a knotted prof. Personally, I'd probably be more cooperative after a cocktail or two, but some of my colleagues get spiteful and too honest for their own goods when they tipple, so we eat instead of drink. Probably it's for the best. The drinkers can always meet later down at the Duke of Ellington, and usually do. Anyway, the meeting will probably last for a couple of hours, so I thought you could drop me off at the college and then go on up to the house and get yourself settled in."

"Sounds okay to me."

"Of course, if you'd rather come to the college, I'm willing to pass you off as a visiting scholar. You can walk the ivied yards and ogle the women like the rest of our younger colleagues."

"No thanks. I'll go to your place and then maybe take a stroll around town. It's been a while since I was up here."

"A wise decision. This evening, I'll take you to supper at the Duke and afterward we'll go upstairs to the Higher Realm and play some poker with the chaps."

"My poker-playing skills are pretty rusty."

"You'll be in good company. Most of the gang who play are good scholars but terrible poker players. They leave their brains in their briefcases and are easy picking for guys like Lute Martingale. You'll meet Lute tonight, if you decide to play. He's a sort of permanent part-time teacher and grad student here, but actually supports himself playing poker with rich undergraduate kids who've had a floating game on campus for as far back as I can remember. As long as you don't let Lute sucker you into a big pot, you'll be okay. The rest of us are suckers."

"Sure."

"You can trust me, I'm a professor!"

Two hours after leaving Woods Hole, we turned off 495 and drove north into Weststock, a lovely little village nestled near the large mill towns along the Merrimack River but untouched by the grime and smudge of those once thriving industrial centers. Instead of great abandoned mills and rows of sagging tenement houses, Weststock's winding streets were lined with clean brick homes, white houses with flower gardens and green lawns, and small stores catering to the college community which dominated the town.

The college itself was a Georgian collection of brick and frame buildings built around yards and scattered with green playing fields. It had been established almost two hundred years before by enterprising New Englanders who thought they could produce a college at least as good as Harvard and Yale and who had been right. Weststock College was much smaller than either of its famous rivals, but bowed to neither in its claim to academic excellence, particularly in the liberal arts. It was, in fact, almost idiosyncratic in its insistence upon studies which, in John Skye's words, "taught its graduates nothing whatever which would help them earn money," but which nevertheless produced notable figures in the humanities and theoretical sciences.

It was not quite my kind of place, but it was ideal for John. I followed his directions to the college building of his choice and accepted the key to his house.

"I'll walk home after this is over," he said, getting out. "I'll see you there, probably about three or so. Stick the vodka in the freezer. Your room is the one in back, by the garage."

"Gotcha."

I drove across the campus, looking at the summer students in their shorts and sandals, books under their arms, small packs on their backs. Some walked the brick sidewalks, some sat on benches; others lay on the green lawns, books and satchels beside them. They talked, studied, lazed, and looked young and healthy. I tried to remember what it had been like to be that age.

One reason that it was hard for me was that when I *had* been that age, I'd been going to, living in, or being shipped back from Vietnam. I'd come home after a very short tour with some metal in my legs, the gift of a Vietnamese artillery man or mortar man who had lobbed a shell right next to me while I was blundering around in the dark looking for his friends. Even now small pieces of the metal occasionally worked their way out of my skin. I hadn't gone to college until I was older, and when I had gone, it had not been to so pastoral a campus as this, but to Northeastern University in

Boston, where you combine work and study as you go. My work had been as a Boston cop. It had all happened quite a while back, and none of it had happened in places as pretty as Weststock.

I turned up Main Street and drove up the hill past the town center, where youthful buyers were spending their parents' money in neat shops—clothing stores, bookstores, record stores, eating emporiums, furniture stores, and stores selling expensive objets d'art and decorations for the abode of the modern college student or academician. Weststock had long since bowed to economic reality and unabashedly directed its sales to the members of the college community.

Similarly, it had politically more or less given up the notion of town versus gown identities, although there were, of course, still a few hostile locals who felt oppressed by the college and whose youths occasionally engaged in fisticuffs with Weststock boys or, better yet, struck an even more wicked blow at Privilege by dating and mating with college girls. Lingering manifestations of this division were two bars which catered almost completely to clients in the particular camps. The Millstone was the bar of choice for townies, and the Duke of Ellington was the college pub. Some of the town's most famous fights had started when members of one group accidentally or purposefully entered the wrong bar. This had resulted in the hiring of large bouncers who now guarded the doors of the establishments.

John Skye, naturally enough, attended the Duke of Ellington, whose owner, Morey Goldthorpe, was an ex-teacher of English literature. All decent English teachers, John had explained, secretly want to own a pub. Not just a bar, but a pub in the English tradition. And not just a pub in the English tradition, but a pub in the English tradition *as it ought to be,* not as most English pubs actually are. That is to say, it should have broad beams in the ceiling, should serve drawn beer, should have a dart board, chessboards, and dominoes, and should be a place where a man or woman could have a companionable pint without risking reputation, life, or limb. Morey Goldthorpe, unlike most other dreamers of pubbish dreams, had actually quit teaching and bought a bar which he had then transformed into the Duke.

Over the mirror behind the bar was a large sign announcing that drunks and loud arguments were not allowed, and that the management reserved the right to forbid service to anyone who disliked real ale. Instead of television, the Duke of Ellington, as its name and the namesake picture on its sign suggested, offered live jazz five nights a week. The Duke's clients were not obliged to listen to the music, but those who did not received silent frowns of protest from the regulars. If you liked jazz, you could come and listen even if you were a townie. Morey could not refuse service to a jazz fan.

Upstairs were the Goldthorpe quarters and two rooms known as the Higher Realm to which only members of the college faculty and their guests were allowed admittance. This undemocratic practice was Morey Goldthorpe's bow to his past profession and was strictly enforced. Weary professors could escape from their students and others by withdrawing upstairs to a private bar, a lounge, and several oak tables at least one of which served as the site of the faculty game, an illegal poker game such as the undergraduates' famous floating game, both of which the police overlooked because no one ever complained about them or admitted that they really existed.

I drove past the Duke and, two cross-streets later, turned left onto the avenue where John's large frame house sat back behind a large lawn and flower beds. I turned into the driveway, parked, and got out my bag. It was a clean, comfortable, tree-lined street of faculty homes. In the hot summer sun, the shade of the lofty trees was welcome.

I went inside and down a hall and found my room. The house was old-fashioned and had many fireplaces. There was one in my room with an ancient gas burner disguised as a log. The kind you lit with a match after opening a valve. I hadn't seen one of those in years and didn't even know they still had them. Only an antiquarian like John Skye would have such a thing in his house.

One thing I didn't need on an August day was a fire in the fireplace. I opened a window to air the room out and had just put the vodka in the freezer when the phone rang. It was John Skye.

"I was in Weststock but my brain must have been in Colorado," said John. "I left my briefcase in the Jeep. Can you run it down here for me? There's a secretary just inside that door I went in. She'll shuttle it on to me. Fifteen minutes?"

"Fifteen it is."

"You're a good man, Charlie Brown."

I locked the door and went out to the Jeep. It was a beautiful day, so I decided to walk to the campus. I got John's briefcase and stepped along. I wondered if a passing stranger would take me for a professor. Did professors wear pink button-down shirts found in the thrift shop? Did they wear chino shorts and Teva sandals without socks?

The test would be in the town center. When I got there, nobody paid any attention to me. Was this a good sign or a bad one? I wondered if I would appear more professorial if I grew a beard. What kind? A little pointy one or a big bristly one? Maybe just a moustache.

I walked through the town center and slanted across the road to enter the college campus. There was a nondescript blue car quite a way up the street, but I had plenty of time to cross before he got there. When I was about halfway across I heard the roar of an engine behind me and a simultaneous scream from a girl on the sidewalk I was approaching.

"Look out!" she screamed, and put her hands up to her face.

I turned, saw the grill of the car filling my vision, and dived for the gutter. Something touched my foot and tumbled me, and John's briefcase went flying. Then I was on the pavement, rolling, and looking at the rear of the car as it careened on its way. I caught a glimpse of a youthful face glance back at me. The face wore dark glasses and was topped by a mass of yellow hair. Then I was rolling some more and hitting the curb.

The girl who had screamed came across the street and other people, students all, I guessed, came running.

"Are you all right?"

"I think so."

"You're bleeding!"

True. Some skin was missing from my knees, calves, elbows, and hands. A shoulder hurt. I eased slowly up into a sitting position. I moved various parts of me. Everything functioned. "I'm okay," I said.

"You're bleeding!"

"I need a couple of Band-Aids."

"The infirmary is right over there," said a young man. "Should you try to walk?"

I got up. The young man and a young woman put their hands out as though to catch me should I fall. "I think I'm fine," I said. "Did that guy stop?"

There were confused replies.

"I thought it was a woman!"

"No, it was a guy with a weird wig. Or maybe hair down to here."

"I never saw his face, but the son of a bitch kept going! We should call the cops! What an asshole!"

"You'll get no argument from me," I said. "Would any of you recognize him if you saw him again?"

"I'd recognize that wig!"

"It wasn't a wig, it was a woman!"

"No, it wasn't!"

"How about the car?" I asked. "The license plate?"

There were shakings of heads and angry noises.

"Here, sir. I think this is yours." A boy handed me a Teva.

The car had knocked it off my foot and he had found it down the street. I put it back on.

"Here. It didn't even open." The girl who had screamed handed me John Skye's briefcase. She looked pale.

"You saved my life," I said. "Thanks."

"Oh, I was so scared!"

"You should go to the infirmary, sir," said the young man who had pointed it out. "You should let them check you out and get some bandages on those abrasions. You're bleeding all over your clothes."

True on all counts. I looked at the girl who had screamed. "What's your name?"

"Amy Jax."

"You're a student here?"

"Yes."

"Amy, you've already saved my life, but I want you to do me another favor." I pointed to the building John Skye had entered. "I want you to take this briefcase through that door and give it to the secretary you'll find there. Tell her it's for Professor Skye." I gave her the briefcase. "One more thing," I said. "Lean forward."

She leaned and I kissed her forehead. "Thanks again, Amy Jax."

She actually blushed. Hands clapped approvingly around us. Amy went away with the briefcase and I allowed myself to be conducted to the infirmary by one of the young men who insisted on calling me "sir." Zee would have said I looked like another moped accident and she would have been right.

After I was bandaged up, I did the right thing. I went to the police station and reported the incident. The guy behind the desk wrote everything down and said they'd certainly look into the matter. I suspected that he was a townie who probably wasn't too sorry that an obviously academic type like me had gotten bunged up a bit. On the other hand, maybe he was an old Weststock grad who probably wasn't too sorry that an obvious townie like me had gotten bunged up a bit. In either case, I was more work for a department that probably already had enough to keep it busy.

I smiled at him and limped out.

8

When I left the police station, I barely had time to get home and change my clothes before John was scheduled to some strolling in. I put on socks and slacks and a long-sleeved shirt to cover various bandages and got myself a drink, which I downed while walking around John's fine old house. I was getting a little stiff in the joints and hurting in small ways I hadn't noticed earlier. My hands were sore and I was also feeling a bit ethereal and shaken, the way you sometimes do after the danger is over. America was as risky a place as I remembered it being.

I got another drink and went into John's nice big library. Thousands of books, comfortable chairs with good reading lights, a worn oriental rug, a big, battered desk with a brand-new computer on it signifying that John was entering the twentieth century just as it was ending. I opened a book about Mencken and immediately read that human existence is always irrational and often painful. Very Menckenish, but I didn't need to be told that because I'd just experienced the proof. I put the book back and tried a little John Gay. Gay, I learned, had written his own epitaph: "Life is a jest, and all things show it. I thought so once, and now I know it."

Cute. A footnote informed me that Gay's monument was in Westminster Abbey and that the *Dictionary of National Biography* considered the words on it flippant. Irreverent to the last, eh, John? I read some more.

A bit later, the phone rang. It was John Skye again.

"Hope you weren't wondering where I've been. Damned meeting went on for hours. Just as well, because if we'd cut it short, we'd all have had to continue it tomorrow. This way, we're done today! I don't think I'll bother to come home right now. I could use a drink. Why don't you meet me down at the Duke?"

"Why not? See you there."

I went out into the summer afternoon and walked downtown. The air seemed clean and good. I was very careful crossing streets. By the time I got to the Duke, I'd walked some of the stiffness out of my knees and hips. I knew that it would come back during the night, but I also knew that sooner or later it would go away for good.

It was about five o'clock. John was standing at the bar with a glass of dark beer in his hand. A tall, thin man was talking with him while nursing a glass of whiskey. He was one of those people who might be in his twenties or his forties. When I came up to them, the man looked at me with a gambler's deadpan eyes.

John smiled. "Lute, meet J. W. Jackson. J. W., meet Luther Martingale. Morey, a pint of bitter for Mr. Jackson!"

I shook Martingale's hand. It was smooth and strong. I wondered if he sanded his fingertips. Martingale placed a smile on his face. When he did, it made him look almost innocent.

"I've heard about you," I said. "I've been advised not to get in any big pots with you."

"My enemies are everywhere," said Martingale. "Don't listen to them."

"Part of that is true," said John. "He does have enemies everywhere. Mostly people who still think the poker money he won from them is rightfully theirs. Some folks just can't get it through their heads that once they toss their money into the pot, it's not theirs any longer."

"If it weren't for the lambs, the lions would starve," said Martingale.

My beer arrived. Martingale lifted his glass. I got a whiff of its contents. Scotch. "To the lambs," he said.

We drank.

People were beginning to fill the place.

"If we eat before the crowd gets here, we might even find a table," said John.

"Another round first," said Martingale. "On me."

"What the devil did you do to your hands?" asked John, noticing my missing skin for the first time.

"A funny thing happened to me on the way to your office," I said, and told them about my near miss on the street.

"Good God!" said John. "You really are all right?"

"Lost a little skin, is all."

He shook his head. "Mattie says that'll happen to me someday if I don't pay more attention to traffic when I walk to the office or back home. She claims that I am a classic absentminded professor and that someday after a truck runs over me, my last words will be 'Who was the Green Knight, really?' I think you deserve another drink, my boy. Morey! Another round!"

We drank to my survival. I was beginning to feel better. As the sign behind the bar said, Malt does more than Milton can, to justify God's ways to man.

Graduate students talking of things academic and otherwise continued to come into the bar. The noise level gradually rose. John lifted a hand to someone across the room. I turned and saw Dr. Jack Scarlotti sitting at a table with the attractive young woman I'd seen with his group on Martha's Vineyard. Waitresses and waiters began to move among the tables. A second bartender appeared. We finished our round and found a table in a corner.

"Popular place," I said.

"It's the beer," said John. "Imported from Jolly Olde. Damned fine."

"Indeed."

"Good food, too. Pub fare. Simple but filling."

"And better than you get in most pubs in England," said Martingale, surprising me since for some reason I'd never imagined him being in England. "You might go to Britain for the beer, but you'd never go there for the food."

We ate chicken pies with fine crisp crusts, tossed salads with a nice house dressing, and bread that tasted homemade. Not bad. John and I washed ours down with beer. Martingale drank white German wine. He saw me looking at the bottle and smiled. "You don't go to Britain for the wine, either."

He was hard to dislike, but hard to like, too. There was an elusive quality about him. He looked at John.

"You hear about Bernadette Orwell?"

John shook his head. "What about her?" He shoveled in a bite of salad.

"OD'd. Fatal. Just about the time you left for the Vineyard."

John stopped chewing and looked at Martingale. Then he swallowed and put his napkin to his lips. "No. I knew she was a little flaky, but I didn't think she was that strung out. Too damned bad. Very bright girl. She was in one of my classes year before last. I liked her."

Martingale nodded. "Rumor is that somebody dropped her. Hard. Unrequited love. Very sad, they say."

John frowned at him. "Are you telling me that Bernie Orwell OD'd because somebody left her?"

Martingale lifted his wineglass. "No. I'm just passing on gossip. I like gossip."

John dropped his eyes and stared at the table. "Well, damn," he said after a moment. "I like gossip, too. Sorry to get this piece, though."

I thought of Bernie Orwell's white powder and pills, and of her joy in Jonathan, who was beautiful and brilliant, and able to make her tremble at the very thought of his touch.

"I believe I just saw a couple of the lambs going upstairs," said Martingale. "Shall we join them in a small game of chance?"

John finished his beer. "Yes. I was having a good day until a minute ago and I'd like to get back into it."

We went upstairs to the Higher Realm. Three men and a

woman were already seated at a table. There were poker chips in front of them and a few in the middle of the table. Five card stud seemed to be the game. I was feeling the drinks I'd had.

"Dealer's choice, nickel ante, two-bit limit," said John. "You don't have to lose much, but you can drop a few bucks if you want to. Let's sit in." We sat and John waved an arm around the table. "J. W., here are some of the great minds of the Western world. First names only, so you don't get confused. Tom, Mike, Dick, and Mary. This is J. W. Jackson, just up from the Vineyard and ready to have his features plucked."

A waiter arrived, took orders, and went away. A bit later he came back with drinks. I stuck with the excellent bitter drawn from the cellar. I noticed that Lute Martingale shared one habit with me. We both folded early and often. Once I caught him looking at me as I tossed them in. A little smile played on his face.

My father had taught me a few simple rules for poker. Don't stay with less than openers, don't stay if you're beaten on the board, lose now and then when it's cheap so people will think you're a bluffer, drive people out if you've got a so-so hand that can be beaten by a lucky draw, suck them in and then stick it to them when you've got the cards, but act surprised when you win. The math of poker is easy, he'd said, but the real players go beyond the math and play the players. In games played when I was in the service, I never lost a lot in any game and made money overall. Some other people made much more and a lot of other people lost much more. On balance, I didn't consider myself a real player.

When the jazz started downstairs, I was still holding my own, but finding it harder, thanks to several additional pints of beer. Martingale, John, and Mary had made some money and the other three were losing. I found myself yawning and then almost losing money in dumb ways. I pushed back my chair and stood up.

"Folks, I'm just a sleepy country boy and you city slickers are taking me for every dime. Stay right there, John. I expect you to win back my money for me. I'll see you in the morning."

"You okay?" asked John. "You seem to be listing."

"There are worse things than listing," I said, straightening.

John looked at his cards. "Well, I must admit that these beauties make me want to stay a bit longer. We usually break up about eleven, so I'll be home then. You can find your way in the dark?"

"Eyes like a cat," I said. I made my farewells and walked carefully down into the music. A drummer was working his way through a *Caravan* solo. It took him almost ten minutes. After the other players got back into the song and wound it up to justifiable applause, I headed home. When I crossed the street I was quite wary, but no blue cars came at me out of the dark.

The warm night air cleared some of the cobwebs from my brain, but after I let myself into the house and got to my room, I was suddenly weary again. Beer fatigue. I took two aspirin, the Jackson wisdom for helping to ward off a hangover, got out of my clothes, turned out the light, and hit the sack. I think I must have gone to sleep instantly.

I had strange dreams. I was sick. Someone was shouting in a tongue I could not understand. Great wailing noises and roaring sounds beat into my ears. Then there were slapping sounds. Slippity-slap, slippity-slap, slippity-slap. I didn't like any of it. Then someone started to whack my face. I tried to get my hands up to stop the blows. Slippity-slap! Slippity-slap! Slap! Slap! Slap!

"Stop that!" I said. "You stop that slapping! I didn't do anything to you!"

But the slapper didn't stop and the roaring didn't go away, so I tried to turn my head and get away, but I couldn't, so I tried to hit the slapper. "Get away from me!" I said.

Then the roar became words. "Wake up! Wake up! That's

it, my boy! That's it!" I got my eyes open just as a hand lightly slapped my cheek. John Skye's face floated out in front of me. "That's it," he said. "Can you see me, J. W.?"

I nodded. His floating face smiled and became more three-dimensional. Then I saw that it was attached to his body, as was the hand that presumably had just slapped me.

"You're okay," said John. "Just lie there and breathe deeply."

I lay there and breathed deeply. I didn't feel well, at all. After a while I noticed that I was lying outside, looking up at stars in a black sky. I turned my head and looked around. I was on John's front lawn. There were firemen coming out of the house. John was sitting on his heels, looking at me. The lights from his front room windows touched his face.

"How are you feeling?"

"Better."

"I never should have let you come home alone. You were drunker than I thought."

"How did I get out here? I thought I went to bed." I looked down at my body. It was covered with a light blanket. I lifted the blanket. It was me, all right. I don't wear nightclothes. "I really must have been drunk," I said. "Are you telling me that I stripped and went to sleep right here?"

"No, no. You made it to bed all right. But when you were kicking off your sandals, you kicked one clear across the room and hit the valve on the fireplace. The whole house smelled of gas when I got home. It was coming out from under your door. I got in there and closed the valve and dragged you out here. Then I went in and opened up your window and every other window in the house and came out here with you. I figured the whole place might go up any second."

I looked at the house. My mind was pretty fuzzy. "Still there," I said.

He nodded. "Yeah. All aired out now, too. No damage done, after all." He stood up and went to talk to a fireman.

The fireman looked at me, shook his head, and walked to the street where other firemen waited by a fire truck with a red, swirling light. They got in the truck, turned off the light, and drove away. People in other houses stood on porches and looked at us. John waved to them and came back to me. "I told them you were fine," he said. "Are you?"

I sat up. My head ached. "I owe you one," I said. "Glad your game didn't last any longer."

John smiled grimly. "I see now why they keep you chained up on that island. You're a danger to yourself up here in the real world. I'm not going to let you wander around alone after this."

"It's not been my best day," I said. I wrapped the sheet around me and put up my hand. John pulled me to my feet and we walked into the house and down the hall to my room. The window was open, and warm night air was blowing in.

"I suppose I should get rid of that antique fireplace," said John. One of my sandals was lying by the valve. "I don't think you could hit that valve again if you tried," he said. "And why you didn't have the window open on a warm night like this beats me. It only shows you the power of booze, I suppose. Maybe God is giving you a message about your drinking habits."

It wasn't the first time I'd had too much to drink, but it was the first time I couldn't remember what I'd done. I couldn't believe it.

"The window was open," I said. "And my sandals were right there by the bed."

John smiled. He went over to the fireplace and got the sandal and put it with its mate beside the bed. "Now they are," he said. "Get some sleep. I think you need it."

It was good advice, I thought. I looked at my watch. It was well past midnight. A new day. The previous one had been hard on me. I was glad it was gone.

The next morning I got up feeling not too bad. I went to the window and leaned out, breathing in the cool, clean air.

In the soft soil of the flower garden below the window were the prints of shoes. At the time I thought they belonged to some fireman who had been checking things out the night before. I was wrong.

9

I was stiff and thickheaded, and my scratches and abrasions were sore. But I was alive, so things could have been worse. The aroma of breakfast floated down the hall from the kitchen and I followed my nose to juice, coffee, toast, sausages, and eggs. Your classic high-cholesterol American breakfast. I wolfed it down and after another couple of cups of coffee felt better.

"Some fireman squashed a few of your flowers," I said.

"Hey," said John, "I'm out of this state this afternoon on the two-thirty plane. By the time I get back, a lot of my flowers will probably be in that great greenhouse in the sky." He squinted at me. "You have any plans after you drop me off at Logan? You sticking around up here for a while, or heading right back for the Vineyard?"

"I thought I might drive up to New Hampshire, but I've changed my mind."

"Zee?"

"Yeah. She didn't go up there to be with me. I guess I'll head back for the island. With stops at various stores on the way, of course, to load up on stuff at mainland prices."

"But of course. Tell you what. I haven't exactly lied about it, mind you, but I've dropped a few hints that I'm going back down there myself. This Colorado trip is a little secret of mine. I don't want any phone calls from the college telling me I have to be back early because of some crisis or other. If they call the Vineyard, they'll get no answer." He shoved a paper across to me. "Here's my mother's address and telephone number. If you really have to get in touch with me, you can do it there. Pick up my

Vineyard mail, if you will, and forward anything that looks important."

"Your secret is safe with me. And I'll keep an eye on your place and your car."

We washed the breakfast dishes, made the beds, and closed the windows. John gave me the rest of the eggs, juice, bacon, and bread. Then we put our gear in the Wagoneer and I drove us over to 95 South and on into Logan International.

We shook hands and John got out with his bag and headed inside the terminal. I drove to Boston through the tunnel and found the hospital where Geraldine Miles was being treated. I went in only to be told that Geraldine was in the operating room having some part of her put back together again. I left a note, then got onto the Expressway South, and headed for the Cape.

By the time I got to Woods Hole and found a place in the standby line to the Vineyard, John's Wagoneer was bulging with booze, food, and other goodies I'd purchased on the way. I'd saved myself a pretty penny. A man might be able to make a living by contracting with Vineyarders to go to the mainland in a van every now and then and buy them stuff that was overpriced on the island. What island stuff wasn't overpriced, after all? He could charge a pretty good fee and the islanders would still get their stuff cheaper than they could buy it on the Vineyard. I ran this old idea through my head for a while and discarded it. I didn't like shopping that much. Besides, somebody was probably already doing it. Enough people had thought about it, certainly. People were always trying to figure out ways to live cheaply on the Vineyard, and there weren't many new ideas left.

I got on the last boat. Last car on, last car off. Perfect timing. I drove to my place through the night and unloaded my treasures, stuffing the freezer and filling shelves. I thawed some of last winter's scallops and got some rice going. Then I chopped some veggies, including plenty of onions (since onions improve any dish except dessert), and some green peppers, stir-fried the veggies and scallops, and poured the mixture over a plate of rice. A bit of soy sauce and . . . Delish! I found a bottle of Rhine wine in the fridge and had a few glasses while I ate my late night supper. Some lingering scent of Zee was in the air and the house felt lonely, but I'd been lonely before. I went to bed and read until I got so sleepy that my eyes hurt. Then I went to sleep.

In the morning I discovered a dilemma: I wanted to leave John's Wagoneer at his house, but I didn't have a ride home. I thought of Manny Fonseca, who always went home for lunch. I phoned him at his shop.

"Hey, Red Cloud, how about swinging by John Skye's place at noon and giving me a ride home?"

"Us noble Native Americans are always willing to lend a hand to strangers in our land even though it gets us nothing but trouble. I'll be by about twelve-fifteen."

"May your tribe increase."

It was almost eighty degrees, hot by Vineyard standards, and the wind hadn't come up, so it was sticky. I weeded the garden for a while, before it got even hotter, then stripped and lay in the morning sun with the first beer of the day, perfecting my tan. If a low-flying plane filled with beautiful women flew over, would it circle before going on? Would anyone parachute out? The plane didn't show up.

At eleven-thirty I climbed into shorts, sandals, and a tee shirt that said Ban Mopeds on Martha's Vineyard, and drove the Wagoneer to John's farm. I parked the Jeep on the east side of the house, away from the prevailing southwesterlies, and checked things out. Barn and corrals were okay, so I walked around the house. The windows were locked and nobody had tried to get in the doors. I unlocked the front door and walked through the house. Everything was fine. I went back outside. The foundation of John's house was made of large granite slabs. The outside door to the basement was one you got to by opening wooden doors that slanted against the foundation and going down some steps made of smaller granite slabs to the basement door. I opened the outer doors and started down the steps, thinking that Manny Fonseca would be arriving at any time.

I noticed an odd red dot on the door beside me as I stepped down. It seemed to move toward me and my heart jumped and I dived down the steps.

Wood exploded over my head. I dug out my set of John's keys and frantically tried to find the one for the basement door. I tried a wrong one, then the right one, and was inside in the darkness slamming the door behind me. My heart was thumping and I was gasping. I quieted myself down, groped for the stairwell, found it, and ran upstairs. I listened. No sounds in the house. I ran silently to John's bedroom, unlocked his closet, and got out his 12 gauge Savage. Shells were on a top shelf. I stuffed the magazine full and went to a window. I stood to one side and looked out. Nothing outside. I listened. Nothing inside. I went to the library and looked outside. Nothing. I moved from room to room, looking and listening. Nothing. The outside door to the basement was under a window in the dining room. I looked out and saw that a corner had been blown off the door. I looked beyond the lawn and into the trees. Someone had been there waiting for me with a weapon with a laser scope. If I hadn't been thinking of Manny Fonseca, I wouldn't have recognized the dot of red on the door. I felt light-headed and leaned against the wall.

No time to be scared. I looked out at the trees. Maple and oak and pine, with undergrowth that made good cover for someone who knew how to use it. I looked for what seemed a long time and saw nothing. Then I heard a car coming down the driveway.

Manny Fonseca was driving right into trouble he knew nothing about. If the shootist was just potting whomever he saw, Manny might be next. On the other hand, maybe he was only after me. If I went outside to warn Manny, I'd be a target again. Maybe if I stayed put, I could get a shot at the guy before the guy got a shot at Manny. On the other hand, maybe I couldn't.

There was no right thing to do, but Manny was an innocent party. I glanced at the trees and saw nothing. I ran to the front door and threw it open and ran to meet Manny's Bronco as it came into the yard. As I ran, I waited for the bullets to come through my ribs.

▪ 10 ▪

No bullets came. Manny saw the shotgun in my hand and was quick on the uptake. He slammed on the brakes and threw open the passenger door as I came up. I was inside while he was still moving.

"Get us out of here, Crazy Horse!"

Manny spun the Bronco, sending grass and sand flying, and we roared back up the driveway between the trees. I looked for red dots, listened for bullets coming through breaking glass or thumping through steel. I stared ahead and on either side and through the back window, but saw nothing. I heard nothing but the scream of the Bronco's engine. Then we were on the pavement and Manny spun the wheel and sent us racing toward Edgartown.

Parked under the trees on the side of the road was a blue two-door sedan. No one was in it. I caught a glimpse of the license plate. New York. I got the last three digits.

As we passed it, I looked back and saw no rifleman leaping from the trees, no movement around the car, nothing. I looked some more. Still nothing.

"Okay, Hiawatha, slow down. The bad guys are gone. Was that car there when you went in?"

"Yeah, it was there. What the hell was going on back there, J. W.?"

I told him what had happened. I was shaking.

"Damn! We'd better get the cops!"

"An excellent suggestion."

We drove to the almost new Edgartown police station beside the fire station. The chief was downtown looking after his summer cops, but after a radio call for him went out, he was in his office in five minutes. I told him my tale. I could hear a little tremble in my voice. He looked at my bandages.

"You okay? You look a little banged up."

I had been thinking. "I got these scratches up at Weststock. There may be a tie-in."

"You can tell me about it later. Right now we'll get some men up to John's place and see if we can nail this guy." He sent cars out to the farm and called the communications center. He put out a description of the blue car and asked that its driver be held for questioning. He was very efficient.

"I'm going out to John's place," he said, getting up and grabbing his hat. "You come along, J. W., so you can show me what happened. You may as well bring that shotgun so you can put it back where it belongs."

"How about me?" wailed Manny, who constantly complained that he never got to do anything really interesting. All the wars had been fought without him, and the wild West had long been tame before he'd been born, let alone before he had discovered that he was an official Wampanoag.

"He probably saved my neck," I said to the chief. "When the guy heard Manny coming, he must have taken off."

"Okay," said the chief, heading for his car. "Come on. Now what about that tie-in between this and Weststock?"

As we drove, I told him about the hit-and-run accident. "A blue car something like the one outside John Skye's driveway. I don't know if it was the same one because I didn't get much of a look at it in Weststock."

"So that's where you lost that skin. You file a report with the Weststock police?"

"I'm deeply hurt. I used to be a cop. Remember?"

"You act like a damned civilian."

"I am a damned civilian."

"I'll give them a call when we get back to the station. Maybe they know about the guy or the car . . ."

"This is probably just paranoia," I said, "but there is one other thing." I told him about the incident with the gas fireplace. As I talked, I began to calm down. Anger began to replace fear.

"You admit you were drunk," said the chief. He put on the siren.

"I've been drunker. I walked home, got undressed, and went to sleep. I didn't close the windows and I didn't kick my sandal into the fireplace and I sure didn't stand in John Skye's flower bed."

"Or so you say."

"You bet so I say."

"When we get to the house, stay in the car. We'll check the place out and then you can come in."

"The guy's long gone, Chief."

"Stay in the car."

We came to John Skye's driveway. The blue car was gone. We drove down the driveway and found two more police cars ahead of us at the house. Cops were walking around looking at things. Two of them were looking at the outer cellar door. The chief got out, talked to his men, and went into the house. After a while, he came out again and beckoned. Manny and I got out of the car and joined him and the other cops.

"Show us what happened," said the chief.

I told them what I'd done while I'd been waiting for Manny and then took them to the cellar door and showed where I'd seen the red dot. I told them how I'd been thinking of Manny and recognized the dot and ducked, and how the wood blew up behind me. When I finished with the rest of it, the chief turned and surveyed the woods behind us. He looked at a middle-aged cop. "Morgan, you and Soames check out those woods. Any other deer hunters here? Okay, you two go, too. See what you can find."

A State Police car came down the driveway and a corporal got out and came over. The chief filled him in. The corporal went over to the door and looked at the splintered corner.

"One explosive round? A burst? How many shots did you hear, Jackson?"

"I don't know," I said. "More than one, I think. Maybe just one. I wasn't counting. I know I heard the first one."

The corporal grunted and looked back at the trees where the Edgartown men were starting their search. "Came from back there, all right." He turned back and looked at the door and the granite foundation slabs. "Slugs should be about here." He walked to the foundation and knelt and peered at the stone for a while. "Yep, here's where they hit. Not much left. Looks like about 9mm. A pistol, maybe? Quite a long shot for a pistol."

"A pistol is easier to hide than a long gun," said the chief.

The corporal grunted assent. "There's a million different guns in this country. Some of the pistols you can buy have barrels ten, twelve inches long. Shoot straight at considerable distance. You know the difference between the sound of a pistol and a rifle, Jackson?"

I was feeling dumb and getting tired of it. "Somedays, maybe. Not today. I saw the red dot and ducked. All I wanted to do was get inside the house before the guy with the gun came up and tried again while I was down that cellarway. I didn't try to figure out what kind of a gun he was using."

"Why do you think it was a guy?"

"Because I do. Maybe it was a girl. Usually it's guys who shoot."

"You got a girlfriend?"

"Yeah."

"She mad at you?"

"She's up in New Hampshire. You can ask her yourself."

"Maybe her hubby's the one who's mad at you."

I put my face closer to his. "She doesn't have a hubby."

He was beginning to enjoy himself. "Her boyfriend, then."

"Take it easy," said the chief. "I know the woman. You're barking up the wrong tree."

"Yeah? Well, maybe so, maybe not. Somebody's sure as hell mad at this guy." The corporal looked at me. "Unless, of course, you just made this up."

"You're sharp," I said. "I had everybody fooled but you."

"How'd you get yourself all banged up?"

"Protecting a state trooper from a mad Brownie scout. He was trying to give her candy outside her schoolyard and she caught on to him. Guy looked a lot like you, in fact. I made her give his gun back to him."

"You did, eh?" He bunched his shoulders. His face was red.

"Yeah."

"Hold it," said the chief, stepping between us. "Hold it right there. J. W., you take that shotgun inside and put it back where it belongs. Corporal, let's have a look back in the trees."

The corporal and I exchanged glares. I felt suddenly childish and turned away and went into the house. I unloaded the Savage and returned it and the shells to their proper places. From an upstairs window I watched the policemen move in and out among the trees and undergrowth.

There was a telephone beside John's bed. I looked at it, then sat down and phoned the fire department in Weststock. When the phone was answered, I gave my name and said, "The night before last you sent at least one truck to a house belonging to Dr. John Skye on Academy Row. Problem with a gas fireplace. I want to talk to the fireman in charge of the operation. I'm the guy who may have caused the problem."

"Hold on. You want to talk to Scotty." I heard hollow-sounding voices speaking. A minute later a new voice came on the phone.

"Scott Wenham."

"J. W. Jackson. I'm the one John Skye hauled out of his guest room night before last. You guys came then and made sure everything was okay. I have one question. Did you or any of your men have occasion to go outside of the room where the fireplace is located? Did any of you stand outside of a window and maybe look in as part of your work?"

"No sir. Our work was all done in the house. Nobody went around back."

"You're sure."

"I'm sure. Dr. Skye had shut the valve and opened the windows and doors before we got there. We just made sure there were no leaks or fumes left. How are you feeling today?"

"Fine," I lied. "Just fine. Thanks for your help."

I rang off and thought about things. As the man said, "Once is happenstance, twice is coincidence, three times is enemy action."

I went downstairs and outside. The police were gathered around a clump of bushes. I found a space in the circle. In the center of the circle, grass was flattened where someone might have been lying down.

"If you lie down there," said the chief, glancing up at me, "you get a clear view of the house, but they can't see you. Back there in the woods we got some footprints coming in and going out. About a size nine shoe. Maybe a boot. We'll take casts. Guy came from a car parked out there and he went back to it. He came slow and went back fast. Figure it was the blue car you and Manny saw."

The corporal opened a beefy hand. In it was a plastic bag holding three shells. "Found these," he said. "You own a 9mm weapon?"

"No."

"Maybe you borrowed one."

"Maybe I borrowed a set of size nine feet at the same time."

The corporal looked down at my twelves. "Well," he said, "if it wasn't you, it must have been somebody else. You got any enemies?"

"Just two," I said. "You and maybe a guy named Lloyd Cramer."

"Who's this Cramer?"

"He's a guy with a sore knee and a busted face."

"Cramer's the guy who beat up Dan Wiggins' niece," said the chief. "J. W.'s the guy who, ah, held Cramer until the authorities could get there."

"Oh, yeah?" said the corporal. "I think I heard that story." He almost smiled. "Maybe I just changed my mind about you, Jackson."

"To know me is to love me," I said.

"I don't know you that fucking well. This look like Cramer's work to you?"

"The chief says this shooter hurried back to his car. I don't think Cramer could manage that. In fact, I don't think Cramer can bend his leg enough to drive a car."

"Maybe he hired somebody to do the job."

"Maybe. But could you find yourself a hired gun if you were a stranger on Martha's Vineyard? Cramer's from Iowa, for God's sake."

"Maybe he hired him in Boston," said the chief. "After all, Cramer got out of the hospital several days back. He had time to make some contacts."

"Same problem," I said. "Cramer may be a turd, but he's no professional criminal. I doubt if he knows any of the Boston pistoleers. If you were Cramer, could you find a shootist to come down here and pop me off?"

"I doubt it," said the chief.

"I could," said the corporal.

"That wouldn't surprise me," I said. "But if this guy wanted to shoot me, why didn't he do it at my place? That makes more sense. If I was going to kill me, I'd scout my place when I was gone, maybe stand behind a tree until I got back and pot me at my leisure. I wouldn't have come sneaking through the woods to do it here."

"Spread out, boys," said the chief to his men. "See if you can find anything else."

"There's something else," I said to the chief, and I told him about my telephone call to the Weststock fire station.

The corporal frowned at us. "What are you two talking about?"

I told him my Weststock story.

"You mean you think this guy tried for you twice up there before he tried for you down here?"

"Somebody stomped John Skye's flowers right under the window to his guest room. It wasn't a fireman and it wasn't me."

"So you think it was this same guy. He came in through the window, saw you drunk in bed, and decided to let the gas fireplace do the job? Put your shoe over by the valve, left, and shut the window behind him. All without waking you up."

"Maybe. It almost worked."

"This guy must really want to kill you."

I'd been wondering about that. "I don't think so," I said. "I think he wants to kill John Skye."

11

The chief looked at me quickly. Then, just as quickly, he raised a brow. "You could be right. It makes sense out of some of this."

The corporal nodded. "Yeah. Could be. The guy's got it in for Skye, but doesn't know what he looks like. That's kind of odd, but it wouldn't be the first time a guy tried to hit somebody he'd never met. Guy finds out Skye's coming up to Weststock for a meeting and waits for him. Sees you pull up in Skye's car and go into Skye's house. Thinks you're Skye."

"Yeah. Then he sees me walk down toward the college carrying a briefcase and decides to get me right there in the street. If it works, it's just an accident. But it doesn't work, so he tries again that night. Seems to me like he must have been inside Skye's house sometime before I got there."

"Yeah," said the chief. "He could have scouted the place out while John was down here and his family was out west. That would explain how he knew about that fireplace. Thing that saved you was that he didn't expect anyone else to come home later that night."

"Maybe he was one of the people watching the firemen save the house," said the corporal. "Anyway, yesterday morning he knows he didn't get you, so he follows you down here."

"I made a lot of stops on the way," I said, "and he must have seen a lot of me here and there. But he decided to wait until we got on the island. Probably figured to get me last night while I was asleep. But when I got the last place on the last boat last night, he had to wait until this morning to come over."

The corporal grunted. "Guy knew or found out where Skye lives here on the island. Why didn't he just drive down and wait for you to show up?"

"Because he thought I was already here and would recognize his car?"

"Yeah. Maybe. So instead, he parks on the road and walks through the woods and makes himself cozy in the brush and waits for his shot. What does that tell you?"

"That he's not a city slicker," said the chief. "And that he got here after J. W. did, not before. Otherwise, he'd have shot a lot earlier."

"Yeah. Guy knows how to move in the woods. Came here and made his nest without Jackson hearing or seeing him."

"I was probably inside the house. If I'd been outside, maybe I'd have seen him."

"Maybe," said the corporal. "And if you did, he'd probably have seen you too and shot you on the spot. Sounds to me like maybe he spotted Skye's Jeep on the highway and followed you to the driveway and walked in after you. We got too many 'maybes.' We'd better call Weststock and have them take casts of the prints in the flower bed, if they're still there, and check the house for signs of B and E. If those casts match the ones we'll get here, we'll know we're doing more than guessing. I think we'd better get after that car pretty hard."

"I'll see how that's going," said the chief, moving away toward his car.

"Guy hasn't had time to get off the island," said the corporal. "We have a good chance of getting him, if he hasn't just abandoned the car."

"Which is what I'd do," I said.

He nodded. "Me too. But maybe somebody will see him do it and we'll get a description of him. One good thing: without a car, he'll be on foot. Less mobile."

"If you find his car, maybe it will tell you who he is," said Manny.

"Everybody's a cop," said the corporal. "I know that I wouldn't try a hit and run in my own car. Stolen, probably. We'll contact New York and see if they can help us out. You watch your ass, Jackson. This guy is still out there and he still thinks you're Skye."

He walked away. I looked at Manny. "Exciting times on Martha's Vineyard. You'd better call Helen and tell her where you've been. She'll think you fell into a band saw or something."

"Damn! You're right!" He headed for the house.

An hour later, I was back at the station. Manny had gone reluctantly back to work. The wheels of island justice were turning, and there were a lot of them. It is one of the absurdities of Martha's Vineyard that on an island with a permanent population of ten thousand, there are at least ten different police agencies: six town police forces, the Sheriff's Department, the State Police, the Registry of Motor Vehicles, the Environmental Police, and probably one or two I don't know about. All of these were looking for the blue car and its driver, who was presumed armed and dangerous.

"What a summer" said the chief, sucking on a cold pipe and reaching for a tape recorder. "Now, what do you remember about the guy driving the car in Weststock?"

"Not much. Youngish face, maybe thirty. I have a hard time telling how old people are these days, what with everybody trying to look younger than they are." I reached into my memory, but found very little. "A white guy. Tanned skin. Yellow hair. Shades. That's about it. The kids who saw the incident couldn't agree about much. I got the impression from what they said that the yellow hair might be a wig. Shades and a wig make a fast, easy disguise."

"You get the names of any of those people?"

"Just one. Amy Jax."

"And you think this blue car might have been that one, too."

"I think so. I couldn't swear to it."

"Okay. I'll have somebody drive you home. You think you'll be okay there? If not, I'll have an officer hang around with you for a while."

"I'll be fine. If the guy thinks I'm Skye, there's no reason he'll come looking for me at my place."

"Yeah. Now you may know John Skye better than I do, so tell me, why would somebody want to kill him?"

"I have no idea at all."

"He never mentioned anything that might give us a lead? A woman? Gambling? An argument with a neighbor?"

"Not a thing. With Mattie and the girls he's got all the women he wants or can handle. He plays a nickel-ante poker game where he couldn't win or lose much if he tried. I've never heard anyone say a bad word about him."

"A mad student he might have flunked? Some colleague who lost a committee vote somewhere along the line and blames John?"

"I don't know, but I doubt it. John's not the type to strike fire in people. He's a mild guy."

"Save me from mild guys," grumbled the chief, sucking his pipe.

I thought of Bernadette Orwell's journal entry. In the beginning, John Skye was a wonderful, wonderful person. By the following fall, Jonathan was beautiful and brilliant and she trembled at the very thought of his touch. That didn't sound too mild.

"You going to try to contact John and tell him what's going on?"

"No," he said. "Not yet. So far, we're just guessing. Besides, we may nab this guy before he gets off the island. If we do, we'll know what's really going on. You're right when you say that a guy after Skye probably wouldn't come looking for you at your place. But what if the guy really is looking for you?"

"The only guy who might be looking for me is Lloyd Cramer, and Lloyd's not going to be in shape to do me much damage for a while. I can look after myself, so don't plan on having one of your summer kids watching over me. If it turns out that I do need to protect myself, I don't want to have to worry about protecting your guy, too."

"Famous last words," said the chief. "I'm going to have people keep an eye out for Cramer anyway. If he comes onto the island I want to know about it, and I'll let you know."

A young cop drove me home. She was very careful about her driving and very serious when she asked me if I was sure I didn't want her to stick around. She had a pistol at her belt which meant that she had taken the training and passed the tests which allowed her to carry the weapon. I thanked her and said no and she drove carefully away.

No assassin was waiting inside my house or in my shed or in my woods. I unlocked the gun case where I keep my shotguns and the rifle my father used for deer hunting in Maine. From a drawer at the bottom of the case I got out the old .38 I'd carried when everybody else in the Boston PD was opting for .357 Magnums. I'd bought the pistol cheap from a young cop who was moving up in firepower. I fired the weapon only once while on duty and it had done its job even though it was a mere .38. Like most cops, the kid who bought the Magnum never had occasion to draw his weapon. I hoped he never would.

I loaded up the revolver and went out and put it under the seat of the Land Cruiser so I'd have it in case I met the guy in the blue car while I was on the road. It struck me as a melodramatic act, but then again, people didn't try to kill me very often and I felt rather melodramatic.

I needed to think, so I got my rake and basket and headed for the quahogging grounds. Quahogs are hardshell clams which you can eat in a lot of excellent ways: as littlenecks on the half shell (with just a touch of lemon or seafood sauce), as clams casino (broiled with a bit of garlic butter and bacon), as stuffed quahogs (Euell Gibbons' recipe is the best—next to my own, of course), or in chowder. There's not much bad about quahogging. Preparing them is pleasant work, eating them is joy, and raking them is a time for leisurely thought.

I was after chowder makings, so I drove down to Katama, turned east over the sand, and drove all the way to Pocha Pond, on the southeast corner of Chappaquiddick, where, for reasons known only to the Great Quahog in the sky, there were no little quahogs but only big ones. How the big ones got big without being little first is a cosmic mystery whose answer I do not expect to discover until I reach that Beautiful Clam Flat with Sands of Gold.

I saw no man in a two-wheel-drive blue car trying to follow me in my four-wheel-drive Land Cruiser. Even if he had somehow prevented me from noticing him, he would have been in sand up to his hubs as soon as he left the pavement, so I felt secure.

I put on my shellfishing hat, the one with a picture of a helicopter on the front and my shellfishing license pinned to the side, and waded out into Pocha, rake in hand, basket-in-inner-tube in tow. It was an hour before low tide, so I could get a long way out, where the big ones grew. When I got there, I began to rake. I rake in circles, pivoting until I've covered the ground all around me, and then moving a few yards away and doing it over again. In an hour I can usually get a basketful and during that same hour I can think without interruption and perfect my tan. Not bad.

I ran various things through my head. None of them made sense to me. One problem was that I couldn't see John Skye as the type somebody would try so systematically to kill. On the other hand, I'd never thought of him as wonderful or beautiful, either. But then, how much do we really know about even our close friends? How much do they really know about us? We all have private, even secret, selves which we do not share. We all have dark parts of our lives, little shames, if nothing else, which we keep to ourselves. All of us, perhaps, have given offense, some of which we may not even be aware. All of us, perhaps, have committed at least petty crimes. Dostoyevsky was not the only one to note that there is little difference between prisoners and prosecutors. Perhaps some act of Skye had provoked these assaults on his life. Perhaps I had nearly died because of Skye.

Of course, the hunter could be after me. I wondered whom I might have so offended. Cramer? Or an agent of Cramer? Who else?

A few things were fairly clear. The hunter was systematic about his work, not merely a killer on impulse, as are so many murderers who, once the moment of rage has passed, are as confused by their acts as anyone else. Skye's nemesis, or mine, as the case might be, wanted his victim dead, was willing to stay at the job, was good in the woods, and possessed the sort of weaponry most people, including most killers, don't have.

What did he do for a living? How was it that he could spend so much time hunting his victim? Most people have jobs that would prevent them from going off for a week or two to kill somebody. If they did leave, they'd be missed. Or fired. This guy apparently had both time and money.

Was he a car thief? Most people wouldn't know how to steal a car unless the keys were left in the lock. All of us have heard about jump-starting or wiring ignitions, but how many people actually know how to do it?

Not many.

If he wasn't a car thief, where did he get the blue car? Where would I get one, if I wanted one to use in a hit and run?

When my basket was full of quahogs, my brain was still pretty empty. I drove back to Edgartown and went to the police station. The chief and the corporal were there.

"Well," said the chief, "I see you're still alive, at least. Any new ideas?"

"Only two old ones," I said. "Cramer is not the guy. It's somebody after Skye, all right."

▪ 12 ▪

The corporal had a cigar in his mouth. It was unlit, but he had a match in his hand. He looked at me over the flame. "How do you figure?"

"The same way you two do. If Cramer was after me or had hired a hit man, I wouldn't have been attacked up in Weststock, because Cramer or his man wouldn't have known I was there. I didn't know I was going myself until the night before. Ergo, it was somebody after Skye."

The corporal lit his cigar. "Keen thinking," he said.

"I was really dumb before I met you," I said. "But you're so smart that it oozes out of your pores and guys like me get smart just by being near you."

The corporal blew a stream of smoke in my direction. "We called Iowa City, Iowa. They called back. Cramer is back home. His mommy is taking care of him."

"We called Weststock, too," said the chief. "They don't have anything on the hit and run, but they'll see if they can get a cast of the footprints in Skye's flower bed and get back to us."

"You'll be famous soon," said the corporal. "The *Gazette* has already called us."

"How'd they find out about this?"

The corporal feigned innocence. "Keep a shooting quiet? When you got local cops with local friends? You got to be kidding."

The local cops crack caused the chief to bite down hard on his pipe stem. "I doubt if any of my people tipped them off, Dom."

"Somebody did."

"Yeah."

"What did you tell the reporter?" I asked.

"That shots had been reported, that nobody had been hurt, that the police are investigating. The usual. Of course, they'll be back, looking for the details."

"If they get them all, the shootist can read all about how he almost killed the wrong guy. Then he can start looking for the right guy."

"We thought of that all by ourselves," said the corporal. "Maybe you called them. Get the guy off of your ass and onto Skye's."

"You read me like a book, Dom. I figured that once he knew about me, he'd leave the island. Then you'd be off the case and some real policemen could get on it and maybe we'd have a chance of solving it."

Dom inhaled his cigar and seemed to grow larger. His face got a little red, as it tended to do when he was annoyed.

"You're a real convivial couple," said the chief. "You want to call each other names, you do it somewhere else, not in my office! I've got work to do."

"What was the reporter's name?" I asked.

The chief looked at his notes. "Patterson. New guy. Don't know him."

"Neither do I."

The phone rang. The chief picked it up and said, "Yeah." After a while, he said, "Did he, now?" Then, "What was his name?" He listened for a while longer and then said, "I guess it doesn't make any difference now. Don't worry about it, but don't talk about it anymore, either."

He hung up and looked at the corporal and me. "That was Manny Fonseca. Seems like Patterson called him at his shop and got the details he didn't get from us. So much for official reticence."

"I never knew you used big words like 'reticence,' " I said. "I'm impressed. Why don't you call the *Gazette*? See if they've got a new reporter named Patterson."

The chief frowned, dialed, spoke, hung up, and stuck his pipe back in his mouth. "You're right," he said. "No Patterson. Damn."

"Nervy," said the corporal. "Guy wants to know what people know, calls the cops, gets nowhere, calls Fonseca, gets everything. How'd he know to phone Fonseca?"

"He saw the Bronco pick me up and take me out of there," I said. "Manny's logo and phone number are painted on the doors."

"That's probably it." The corporal looked at me. "Well, your pants can stay dry now. This guy knows that he made a mistake, so he won't be bothering you anymore. Chief, we'd better . . ."

He was interrupted by a young policemen at the door to the office. The corporal glared, but the young cop wasn't looking at him. "Chief, they found the car. Up in Vineyard Haven, parked right on Main Street. New York plates. They're running a check on them right now."

"Good. Let me know when the report comes in."

"How'd he ever find a parking place on Main Street in Vineyard Haven?" I wondered. "I can never find a parking place on Main Street."

"You can go now," said the corporal to me. "We don't need you anymore."

"I never needed you at all," I said. "By the way, cigars are bad for your health. Cancer of the mouth and throat. Give it some thought, if you can. See you, Chief."

The corporal was between me and the door. I walked up to him. Our eyes were on a level. He didn't move.

"Excuse me," I said. We stared at one another. Then he stepped back half a pace, I stepped around him, the chief muttered, "Jesus Christ, you two!" and I went out the door.

I felt curiously alive yet empty. The shootist would no longer be after me. I hadn't realized how tense I had been. The air seemed charged with energy and the street in front of the station was mysterious and lovely. I got into the Land

Cruiser and drove home. The highways and then my long driveway seemed endless.

The shootist would no longer be after me, but he would still be after John Skye. I was relieved, yet simultaneously appalled. How would Blondie now go about his hunter's quest? Would he stay on the island in hopes that John would return? That would be a dangerous course of action, but a resourceful man—and Blondie seemed very resourceful—might pull it off if he had money enough to pay Vineyard rents. Or would he go to Weststock and wait there, knowing that John would have to come back to his classes in September? One more young man in a college town would not be noticed. Just another grad student arriving early to get a good choice of quarters.

Both of those plans required a lot of money and a lot of time. Few people had both at their disposal. Even schoolteachers usually had summer jobs. So, would Blondie try to find out where John was now and go find him there? Not much chance of that, since John had not told the college where he was really going. As far as I knew, I was the only one who had John's address. Would Blondie just go home, wherever that was? Go back to his job, whatever it might be, then come back to New England in the fall to complete his work?

Why not?

I went back to the schoolteacher idea. If Blondie was a schoolteacher, it could explain why he had so much free time. Maybe he was a schoolteacher who didn't have to work summers. Not all teachers had to. Academia. Maybe the chief was right to wonder about some disgruntled student or colleague of Skye's. Skye's world was filled with people who didn't work in the summer. Suppose John Skye's enemy was from Weststock. That made sense, since most of the people John met and therefore might anger were in Weststock, and scholars were famous for their feuds.

But how many of these academic adversaries performed

assassinations? Scholars probably committed as many killings in hot blood as did any other group, but Blondie's efforts were those of an icier sort. I remembered the line "Revenge is a dish Italians prefer to eat cold." Blondie might not be Italian, but he was a cool customer.

I drove into my yard, parked, and got my .38 out from under the seat. I was glad not to need it anymore.

Something moved in the corner of my vision. I spun away behind the Land Cruiser and lifted the pistol. A man was running with uneven strides from my house toward my shed. I raised the pistol and shouted a shout I'd not shouted in years: "Stop! Police!"

The man ran on. He carried something in his left hand. I raised the pistol barrel and fired into the air. "Stop! Police!"

He ran behind my shed, where I fillet my fish and keep my smoker.

I ran around the house and looked from the far corner toward the shed. There was no cover between the house and the shed. Damn. I ran toward the shed, looking everywhere at once, pistol thrust forward. I got to the shed door, ducked low, whipped a look around back, jerked back, looked again, and saw the figure running through the trees, moving very fast with his odd, loping gait. I ran out and shouted again, then aimed well over the man's head and let go another shot. He spun around and raised his left hand. I saw flame dance from the object he held, and I dived for the ground and heard the smack of bullets hitting the shed behind me.

Jesus Christ! An automatic weapon! And me with a .38! I burrowed into the oak leaves and tried to be very small. I heard another burst of sound from the gun and tried to get deeper into the dirt. After a while I realized I was listening to silence.

I picked my face up out of the leaves and looked where the man had been. He was gone. I rolled over and looked at the side of the shed behind me. High across the wall was a row of bullet holes. I got up and went to the wall and put my arm up. The holes were too small for my finger to fit into them. On the other hand, they looked plenty big enough.

The cops might nail him on the road. I ran to the house and got to the phone. Dead. I wasn't surprised. I ran outside to the Land Cruiser and stopped short. The left front tire was in shreds. I sighted between the house and the shed, and, sure enough, found myself looking right at the spot where the gunman had turned and fired. His second burst had been aimed at the tire.

I went back inside to the phone. My address book was beside it, open to the S's. I put the .38 back in the gun case and went outside again. I got out the jack and lug wrench and mounted my spare tire. It wasn't the world's best tire, but it beat the hell out of the one it replaced. It was three miles to the police station. To avoid some of the A & P traffic jam, I ducked right at Al's Package Store and took the back route, thus saving at least thirty seconds of travel time. I arrived at the station for the third time that day, and inside found the chief and the corporal still at work. I told my tale.

"I see why you quit the Boston PD," said the corporal. "You yell 'stop,' and he doesn't stop; you fire warning shots and he shoots real shots."

"Real shots, but not at me. He stitched my shed at least eight feet up. All he wanted to do was stop me, and his plan worked like a charm. Then he blasted my truck so he'd have time to make it away without worrying about me following him or getting to a phone to call in you intrepid minions of the law. He could have hit me as easily as he hit the tire, but he didn't."

"A nice guy."

"I wouldn't go that far, but at least we know he doesn't like to shoot anybody he doesn't have to shoot."

"Except your friend John Skye."

"Yeah. And now he has John's Colorado address."

"How'd the guy know you had it?" asked the corporal.

"He talked to Manny Fonseca," said the chief, stuffing tobacco into the bowl of his briar. "Yeah, that's how he knew. Manny must have told him who you were and why you were out there at John's house. Guy figured since you take care of John's place, you'd know where he was, and Manny told him where you lived. Guy probably told Manny he wanted to interview you. Something like that."

"Guy moves fast," said the corporal. "Leaves the car in Vineyard Haven, makes a couple of phone calls, gets himself some new transportation, car, maybe even a moped, parks it, and walks into your place. This guy likes to walk in the woods. Snips the phone wires, gets Skye's address, and takes off just as you pull in. He cut it pretty thin, didn't he? What if you'd come in sooner, before he had a chance to find the address book? Would he have taken you out because he had no other choice? What did the guy look like?"

"He looked about average. Vineyard summer clothes. Jeans and pullover shirt. Light jacket, like golfers wear. Everything blue. Left-handed, I think. Yellow hair. Maybe that wig, again. Shades. About thirty. Runs with an odd stride, a limp. When I first saw that, I thought it was Cramer, but it wasn't."

"Cramer's in Iowa City."

"I know that. I'm just telling you what went through my mind. I knew it wasn't Cramer as soon as I thought it. It was the limp that made me think it. Smaller guy than Cramer. He had some sort of automatic weapon. Looked like it was twelve, fifteen inches long. About .30 caliber, from the looks of the holes in my shed."

"Weapon fits," said the corporal. "Explains why you couldn't count the shots out at Skye's place. A short burst."

The chief was already sending out the description. Our man was armed and should be presumed dangerous. The corporal looked at his watch. "Maybe we'll be lucky."

"Maybe the moon is made of green cheese," I said.

He looked at me. "A Dr. David Rubinski from Newark rented the blue car on the afternoon of the twenty-ninth.

Charged it on his Visa card. We talked to his wife. The real Dr. Rubinski thinks he lost his wallet at his health club on the morning of the twenty-ninth. Driver's license, credit cards, money, everything."

"Ah. And did you talk to the real Dr. Rubinski?"

"We did. At his office. Turns out he did all the right things. Called his credit card companies, his bank, everybody. But by that time our guy had rented his car and headed north."

"You talked to the car rental agency?"

"How do you think we learned all this? They rented it to a Dr. Rubinski, all right, and their Dr. Rubinski had a beard just like the Dr. Rubinski in the driver's license photo."

"Only the real Dr. Rubinski was back in New Jersey at the time. Who was at Rubinski's health club that morning?"

"We're checking that out. Which is to say that the New Jersey guys are checking it out for us. Rubinski works out early, about six every morning, before going on his rounds at the hospital. Maybe we got a break, since not too many people are usually at the club at that time. Maybe one of them was a guy with a limp. We'll see."

The chief lit his pipe. "I think we'd better get in touch with John Skye and let him know about all this."

I handed him the address and telephone number John had left with me.

"Hummph," grunted the chief. "Durango, Colorado, eh? An RFD box number on a country road. That doesn't tell us much." He dialed a 1, a 303, and a seven-digit number. He waited. Then he held the phone away from his ear and we could hear it ringing. He let it ring some more, then put it down. "Nobody home."

"It's his mother's ranch," I said. "He grew up out there. Maybe they're all out on the south forty, or something."

The corporal looked at me. "The south forty?"

"I'll try the Sheriff's Department," said the chief. "No, I won't. I don't know the county. I'll try the Durango police."

He talked to the Durango police, told them his story, got the Sheriff's Department number and called them, and told the story again. Then he listened for a while and scribbled on his notepad and hung up. He looked up at us. "Lots of Skyes out there. I got a number for one of them." He dialed, waited, and then spoke, introducing himself and asking how to get in touch with John Skye. He listened, said, "Thank you. Have him call me when he comes back," and hung up. Again, he looked up at us. "John Skye's gone camping with his family. Up in the mountains. Someplace called the Hermosa range, where his daddy used to run cattle in the summertime. Going to do some trout fishing and hiking. The twins are going to ride every day. Won't be back for a couple of weeks."

"Somebody may be waiting for him when he comes back to the home corral," said the corporal.

My very thought.

"I'll send the Sheriff's Department and the Durango police and the Colorado State Police the information we have," said the chief. "Maybe they can get somebody up to Skye's camp or cabin or whatever and let him know what's going on."

"Then what?" I asked. "Who'll they be watching for? A guy with a beard, a blond wig, shades, and a machine gun, who runs with a limp, wears blue Martha's Vineyard vacation clothes, and goes by the name of David Rubinski?"

"Yeah," said the chief, irritated. "Something like that. By then, though, we may know more about the guy."

"You got any better ideas?" asked the corporal.

"Yeah," I said, "I do. I'm going out there myself. At least I know more or less what Blondie looks like."

"Blondie?" The corporal arched a brow.

"You better stay here, J. W.," said the chief.

"Good advice," said the corporal. "As a cop you ain't too effective."

"I'm not a cop anymore," I said. "I'm just a young man going west, like old John Soule advised."

"You ain't so young. And I thought that was Horace Greeley that said that."

"Another example that life isn't fair. Horace got the credit, but he was quoting John. Anyway, I'm taking their advice."

"Maybe that's a good idea," said the corporal. "Maybe if you get out of state, we can have some peace and quiet around here."

The chief sighed. "I'll write you a letter," he said. "You can show it to the cops out there. It won't be official and they can ignore it if they want to, but maybe it'll get you some cooperation you might need."

"Meanwhile," said the corporal, "I guess we'll all go have a look at the scene of the latest crime. You're using up a lot of taxpayers' money, Jackson. Are you worth it?"

"You're just not used to earning your salary," I said. "Real cops do this sort of thing all the time."

"Okay, okay," said the chief. "Enough of that. Jesus, what a day."

▪ 13 ▪

Sometimes your mouth is right here, but your brain is miles away. Why had I announced I was going to Colorado? Maybe I should have changed my mind. I drove home and after somebody from some police department or other sprinkled powder around and lifted a lot of prints, including, certainly, mine and Zee's, I rewired my telephone while various police officers walked through the woods, took photos and measurements, and otherwise investigated. When they left, I used the phone, in vain, to try to call John Skye. Still nobody home. Where was his mother, now that I needed her? Out on the range with the deer and the antelope?

I waited for a call from the police telling me that Blondie was in custody. No call came. Instead, some more police arrived and went into the woods to make a cast of footprints Blondie had left behind.

I waited all afternoon, then, just before five, phoned a travel agent and made airline reservations, discovering what everyone who ever tried to fly from Boston to Durango no doubt already knew: that it costs almost as much, and is twice as hard, to fly from Denver to Durango as it does to fly from Boston to Denver. Getting to Durango was apparently like getting to the Vineyard. You can fly to Boston from anywhere in the world, but you can go crazy trying to get the last hundred miles to the island. My trusty travel agent finally got me a cheaper route via Albuquerque. I drank two martinis before supper.

By the next morning, as I was packing, I had thought a lot about why I'd decided to go west. I was bored and worried and resentful because Zee was in New Hampshire deciding what to do with the rest of her life and maybe deciding to lead one without me in it; I was deeply angry with Blondie, who, after all, had tried to kill me three times, and then had broken into my house and shot in my direction after he knew I was the wrong guy; mostly I wanted to stop Blondie before he actually killed John Skye or anyone else. I didn't like to admit this last motive, because I'd been trying hard not to get involved with problems I didn't have to get involved in. But here I was.

I decided I had plenty of reasons to go to Colorado, even though some of them might not stand too much inquiry. Hemingway once said something like moral is what you feel good about afterward, and immoral is what you feel bad about. I didn't feel good about going to Colorado, but I would have felt worse not going.

The phone rang. It was the Edgartown police. I felt excitement; maybe Blondie was in jail. He wasn't, but the cops did have some news. Yesterday Dr. David Rubinski, beardless this time because his wife had made him shave it off, had rented a car in Vineyard Haven, paying in cash, but leaving his Visa card with the dealer to assure him of his trustworthiness. The car had not been returned as scheduled, and the cops had found it in the parking lot in Oak Bluffs where the *Vineyard Queen* docks before and after its run to Falmouth. The bogus Rubinski was presumably now on the mainland.

I asked if they'd heard anything more from Newark about who he might really be. They hadn't. I phoned for a taxi. It was the first taxi I had ever ridden in on Martha's Vineyard. The driver took me to the Martha's Vineyard airport and frowned at my tip.

"You drive too fast," I said, and went to check in for my flight to Boston.

In Boston, I had almost two hours before my Albuquerque flight, so I took another taxi to the hospital and went in to see Geraldine Miles. I hate hospitals. They're unhealthy places. Probably more people die there than anywhere else.

There was no cop outside of her door, so apparently the Boston PD had gotten the word that Lloyd Cramer was back in Iowa and that Geraldine was no longer in any danger from him. Presumably, Geraldine had gotten the same word. I walked into the room.

Geraldine looked out at me through bandages wrapped around her face. Her lips were swollen and I could see stitches in them. One of her arms was in a cast. She wore a lacy gown, not one of those backless things they give you in the hospital, so I knew that Aunt Jean Wiggins had been to see her and had made her get prettied up. There were flowers beside her bed. I sat down. Her eyes rolled to follow me.

"How's it going, kid?"

She held up her good hand and formed a little O with her thumb and forefinger.

"You don't have to talk," I said. "I just came by to see how you're doing and give you the gossip." I told her that the bluefish were pretty much gone, but that there were still plenty of shellfish and that I'd take her out and show her my capturing secrets when she got back to the island. I told her I was going out to Colorado for a while, but I imagined I'd be back on the island about the same time she was. I told her about the weather and complained about the Red Sox annual August slump, and told her the joke about the Portuguese doctor and the guy who cut off his finger. That got a little choking, muffled noise that might have been a laugh. Then I put out my hand and she put hers on it and we sat there as I babbled on. After a while, it was time for me to go.

"You're going to be okay," I said. "You're a gutsy girl. I'll see you when I get back. You'll be on the island by then."

She formed the O again and moved her fingers in a slow wave.

In the hall I met a nurse coming in. "How is she?" I asked.

"Are you family?"

"I'm her brother."

"Well, she's not brain-damaged, but it will be a long time before she's over this."

"Plastic surgery?"

"Oh, yes. But you should talk to the doctor."

"Thanks. When will she be able to leave the hospital?"

"You'll have to speak to the doctor."

"I will." I turned away. Behind me, the nurse spat out a word. I turned back. "I beg your pardon?"

The nurse looked at me with hot, tired eyes. "I said, 'Bastard.' Damn the bastard that did this and all like him!" She drew a breath, eased it out, and went into the room. I heard her voice, now gentle, say, "Hi, sweetheart."

I taxied back to Logan and later, only half an hour behind schedule, not bad for modern times, was in the air looking down at Boston as my plane banked and climbed toward the west. Airplanes do not bother me, because there are walls between me and what's Way Down There. I actually enjoy the view.

Due, perhaps, to my life on an island only twenty miles long, I was impressed by the sheer size of the United States. We flew for hours over mountains, farmlands, rivers, and lakes. I changed planes in St. Louis, home of the Cardinals who, fortunately for the Red Sox, were in the other league. I did not see the famous arch.

We flew on, over lands less green, then lands that were brown and gold, then lands that were very brown, then over mountains, then over real desert, then down into Albuquerque, where I stepped out into August heat. I tried to imagine having come all that way by covered wagon or on foot. Ye gods!

Albuquerque was, I knew, an ancient town, where people had lived long before the gentlemen of Seville had come north from Mexico to search for the seven cities of gold. I did not, however, have time to explore it; instead, I caught Mesa Airlines north to Durango.

Mesa Airlines consisted, in my case, of one of those

cigar-shaped airplanes which is so cozy that you'd better be on good terms with both the pilots and your fellow passengers. Still, it flew us north toward the rising Rockies as well as any plane might. We passed over desert, then mesa country, and almost to the high mountains themselves before the plane descended over a final mesa and landed with barely a thump. If truth be told, I actually like little airplanes better than the big ones, because I believe the little ones can fly, but I don't believe the big ones can. Look at a 747 someday, and you'll know what I mean. A thing like that will never, ever, get off the ground! Too big. Too heavy. No way!

There was a car rental place at the La Plata County airport, and I took advantage of it to rent the cheapest car they had. I had no idea where I was or where I hoped to go, but the country out there was so big that I knew I'd need a car to get there, wherever it was.

I was faintly aware of my breathing. No wonder. I was at 7,000 feet, and the mountains all around me went up from there, especially the ones to the north. I asked the way to County Road 302. Nobody at Mesa Airlines knew where it was. One of a number of men wearing wide-brimmed hats and cowboy boots said, "Damned government's put numbers on all the damned roads and now nobody Goddamn knows where to find anybody! Who you looking for, son?"

"I'm looking for a ranch owned by some people named Skye," I said. I gave him the box number.

"Hell, son," he said, "there's Skyes all over the place. A big bunch of 'em live out there on the Florida Mesa. You get yourself a phone book and start calling Skyes and you'll soon find your man." He pointed west. "Florida Mesa's right there, just the other side of the river. Highway to Durango goes right over it. Ya can't miss it." He put a large Western hand on my shoulder, smiled, and went outside and climbed into a pickup and drove away. He'd pronounced Florida in the Spanish way, with the accent on the second syllable. I wondered why they didn't do that in Florida.

His advice seemed sensible. I found a phone and called John Skye's mother's number. The phone rang and rang. Nobody home. I had the telephone number for the Skye the chief had talked to from Edgartown, so I tried that one. A woman's voice, touched by a faint twang, said, "Hello?"

"Mrs. Wilma Skye?"

"Yes?"

"I'm J. W. Jackson. I'm a friend of John Skye, back in Massachusetts, and I'm trying to find his mother's place, but I don't know where it is. Can you help me out?"

"Oh, John's up on the Hermosa someplace. That nice wife of his and the kids are up there too. Won't be back for a couple of weeks. From Massachusetts, eh? Got a call from some policeman back there. You're a long way from home."

"Yes, I am. I understand that his mother still lives out on the ranch. I'd like to see her, but when I phoned just now, nobody answered. I thought she might be outside someplace. Can you tell me how to get there?"

"Well, I don't know if Aunt Vivian's there. Since John was going up into the mountains, she was planning to drive up to Glacier National Park, the last I heard. Ever since she got that little green Mazda, she's been batting around all over the place."

"Can you tell me how to get to her place? It's on County Road 302, but I don't know where that is."

"I suppose giving numbers to all these roads makes sense to somebody back in Washington, but it hasn't done much for the local folks, so far. Where are you?"

"Out here at the airport. Just flew in."

"Oh. Well, welcome to the San Juan Basin. First time out this way?"

"Yes."

"Sure hope you'll have time to see some of this country. We figure this is about the prettiest territory there is."

"Sure looks that way. How do I get to Vivian Skye's place from here?"

"Lots of things to do: fishing, the little train to Silverton, Mesa Verde, riding, sight-seeing, river rafting, skiing in the winter, you name it."

"Sounds good. Now, just where am I with respect to County Road 302?"

She told me and I finally got off the line. I wondered if I was going to be friendlied to death before I got out of Colorado.

There was a map in my car and on it, with the help of Wilma Skye's directions, I found County Road 302. I drove out to the highway and turned west, dropping down into a valley where the Florida River flowed over a stony bottom. The sides of the valley were rocky and covered with the sort of tough vegetation that grows in dry, desert country. I climbed the other side of the valley and found myself on a green mesa covered with farms and ranches. To the north, the blue mountains rose into the sky and ahead of me other high peaks climbed out of blue foothills. To the west, south, and east a ring of lower mountains, blue-gray and dry, fled away toward the desert country I'd flown over on my way in. It was sagebrush country, and there were cedar and piñon trees growing where there were no fields. The soil was a red clay and there were rotating irrigation devices spraying water over the fields. Fairly prosperous-looking farmhouses sat beside sometimes shakier-looking barns, sheds, and corrals. Occasionally, the barns and outbuildings looked better than the houses. The sky was bright blue, but there were thunderheads hanging over the mountains to the north.

I found County Road 302 and followed it until I found a mailbox with the right number on it. I turned in and parked in front of a large, old, well-maintained farmhouse surrounded by elm trees, a green lawn, and flower beds. Behind the house I could see a gnarled orchard. Across the road were a barn and outbuildings. Beyond them was a pond and beyond that, beside a thick grove of blue-green piñon and cedar trees, in a field of alfalfa stubble, a half-dozen horses grazed.

Barbed-wire fences lined the road and divided the land

into fields. High grass marking irrigation ditches wound around the contours of the fields. I saw a few cattle in a far corner pasture and checked my directions. Yes, by God, it was the south forty! There really was a south forty!

I didn't see a green Mazda. I went to the house and knocked at the front door. Nobody home. I walked around to the orchard, then on around the house. Nobody. I peeked in through a window and saw a comfortable, old-fashioned room with furniture that had been there a long time.

I went around to the front door again and tried the knob. The door opened. So there were still people like me who didn't lock their doors. I was pleased. I shut the door and walked across the road to the barn and outbuildings. Nobody.

I crossed the road again and went into the house. There was a phone on the wall of the kitchen. I called Wilma Skye and told her where I was.

"Nobody home," I said. "No Mazda. Can you tell me how to get to the Hermosa range?"

"I sure can. We all used to run our cattle up there, before the cattle business got so bad we couldn't afford it anymore. But that's big country up there, and I don't rightly know where Cousin John is camped. Might be he's down on Clear Creek, though I doubt it. Might be there on the flats where the old Turnip Patch Cabin used to be. Might be up on Little Elk. Or he might be up at the top of the Hermosa Cliffs, up near where the old Arnold Cabin used to be. We all used to crawl around the cliffs when we were kids. Danged near scared our parents half to death when they caught us. If I was to guess, I'd guess he's up there someplace, up toward the top of Dutch Creek. Around the Bath Tub, maybe. Good graze for the horses up there, good water, sun comes up early and goes down late, not too far from some good fishing. You get yourself a horse and somebody who knows the land, and I imagine you can find John's camp in a couple of days. Not that many places to look, if you know where you're looking."

"Where is this place?"

"Why, you just drive up the valley north of Durango and a few miles along you'll cross Hermosa Creek. You can drive up the creek for a ways, and you'll go through a drift fence. That's the lower drift fence for the range. Then you can go on up past the old sawmill for a half mile or so. But from there on, it's all trail. The Hermosa range is mostly on your right. All those little creeks come down out of it and run into the Hermosa. Range runs all the way up to the other side of Big Elk. A lot of square miles and some rough country until you get up to the meadows at the head of Dutch. The cliffs mark the east end of the range. You're going to like them! A thousand feet high, rising right out of the Animas Valley. You jump off one of them, you might starve to death before you hit the ground!" Wilma had a healthy-sounding laugh, I thought.

"So you think I'll need a horse and a guide."

"Heck, there are hikers and mountain bikers and dirt bike people who get way up there, too. And you can get yourself a Forest Service map, and try to find John's camp by yourself, if you want. But unless you know the area, you might walk around there for a week and never find squat, if you know what I mean."

"I don't have a week to spare. Where can I find a horse and a guide?"

"Where can you find a . . . ? Just a second." I heard her distant voice. "Billy? Billy Jo, come here."

Billy Jo apparently came. I heard an exchange of voices. Then Wilma Skye came back on the line. "Tell you what," she said. "I think we can take care of you right here. We've got horses and a horse trailer and Billy Jo, who knows that range better than I do. That is, if you don't mind being guided around by a genuine college graduate who doesn't have a steady job yet."

A voice protested in the background.

"I don't mind," I said. "I don't have a steady job myself. How do I get to your place?"

She told me. I went west to 550, then north, then east again at the top of the big hill. "If you go down the big hill, you've gone too far," Wilma had said. I spotted the big hill just in time and took the road to the right. A couple of miles farther along I came to a gate topped with steer horns and the name Flying Shirt-tail Ranch. There was no missing that name, and I pulled in and stopped in front of another large farmhouse. A tall, handsome, rawboned woman came out of the house as I climbed out of my little car. She put out a hard hand.

"You'd be J. W. Jackson. I'm Wilma. Mack's in town getting some part or other for that danged tractor. Pouring good money after bad, if you ask me. He should be home anytime." A dazzling girl in jeans, cowboy boots, and a checkered shirt came out into the sunlight. Her hair was dark and fell in two braids down over her shoulders. Wilma grinned and waved her forward. "Come here, sweetheart. Mr. Jackson, this is my youngest, Billy Jo. Billy Jo, this is Mr. Jackson. Mr. Jackson's come all the way from Massachusetts. He's a friend of Cousin John."

Something tingled between me and Billy Jo. She came forward and I saw that she wasn't a girl, she was a woman.

My hat, the forest green one with the Martha's Vineyard Surfcasters Association logo on the front, which I had carefully selected for the trip from my collection of hats with other things printed on the front, was already in my hand.

"I'm the one without a steady job," she said, putting out her hand. A little smile played across her lips. Her hand was firm and lightly callused.

"My friends call me J. W.," I said. "I'm a stranger in a strange land, and I need somebody to lead me to John Skye. I gather that you can do the job."

"I can find John Skye for you, if that's what you want. When do you want to go up there?" Her eyes were dark, like her mother's, and she had the same fine bone structure in her face.

"I want to see him as soon as possible."

"That'll be tomorrow, then. Too late today. I've got to bring in the horses from the north pasture." She looked up at me. "Must be important."

I put a smile on my face. "Life or death," I said.

▪ 14 ▪

Billy Jo had wise eyes, for one so young. "Can you ride a horse? If you can't, you can either walk in, which will be tough on you because of the altitude—it's nearly ten thousand feet at the top of the cliffs—or you can give me a message to take up to John."

"I imagine I can stay on a tame horse for a while."

Her quick smile flickered across her face. "All right. Where are you staying?"

"I don't know. I just got here."

"It seems like there are a thousand motels in Durango. Find one and call me and tell me where you are, and I'll meet you there in the morning. Say, nine o'clock?"

"Nine o'clock is fine." I pulled my eyes away from her and looked at her mother. "You and John close?"

Wilma looked at me thoughtfully, then nodded. "Yes. We're kinfolk. We're friends, too."

I thought of how policemen always start looking at the kinfolk when they encounter a crime of violence and don't know who did it.

"All right," I said. "There's a man from back east who wants to meet John, but it's not in John's best interests to meet him now. The guy may come around here pretty soon looking for John. If he does, I advise you not to tell him where John is. Instead, I think you should phone the Sheriff's Department and tell them that the man is here. They should know what you're talking about. If they don't, have them call the Chief of Police in Edgartown, Massachusetts. I need to see John right away so he can decide what he wants to do." I looked at Billy Jo. "The story's too long to put in a letter. I need to talk to John."

The women looked at me.

"Of course, you could be the guy from back east that John shouldn't meet," said Wilma. "Billy Jo here might be taking you right to him."

"I can't prove I'm not."

"What's this fellow's name?"

"I don't know. He's about thirty, Caucasian, about average size, has something wrong with one leg that makes him run with a limp but may not be noticeable when he's walking. He's left-handed, and he may have blond hair, or a blond wig. That's all I know."

"No." Wilma shook her head. "That's not all you know."

"You're right. He may be dangerous. Not to you, though."

"To John."

I shrugged. "Maybe."

"Why?"

"I don't know."

A pickup truck turned in at the gate and pulled alongside my little car. A big man got out. He was wearing the regional uniform of cowboy boots, jeans, and Western shirt. His broad-brimmed hat was stained around the sweatband. He looked cheerful and curious. When he got near, he put out a large, leather-like hand.

"Howdy. I'm Mack Skye. You ain't the guy that's been trying to sell me a new tractor, I hope, 'cause if you are, you're out of luck. I just got the part I need to keep the old Case running a while longer."

"I'm not that guy," I said. "I'm trying to talk your daughter into taking me up to find John Skye's camp." I gave him my name.

"Mr. Jackson's from back east," said Wilma, without too much expression one way or the other. "Says he's a friend of John's."

"Martha's Vineyard Surfcasters Association," read Mack Skye, squinting at the hat that was now back on my head. "That's that island where John's got a summer place. He's been trying to get us back there for years to try ocean fishing, but I'm happy with the trout we've got right here."

"We never go anywhere," said Billy Jo. "I'm a college graduate, for goodness' sake, and I've never been east of the Mississippi. And I wouldn't have gotten that far if we didn't have kin to visit in Kansas."

"Kansas!" exclaimed Mack Skye. "One trip to Kansas is enough! Nothing to see. Flatter than a punctured Texan! No mountains! Telephone poles walking in a straight line from horizon to horizon. Hell, honey, we don't have to go anywhere; we got the best of everything right here."

"Now, Mackenzie," warned Wilma, "you just stop that kind of talk. There's a world on the other side of these mountains and your daughter is going to have a look at it."

"Well, I imagine she will, but I hate to think about it. Tell me I'm right, J. W., I'm outnumbered by all these women."

"A whole lot of men can be outnumbered by just one woman," I said. "I'm staying out of this argument."

"Smart. I can just see this sweet child back east at one of them resorts, wearing one of them crotch-flossing bathing suits by the pool, and gettin' all foofed up when the sun goes down, and God knows what all . . ."

"I'm old enough to know what I'm doing, Daddy."

He wiped his broad brow. "I know you probably are, honey, but you're the last chick in the nest, and I hate to see you go. Man, it's hotter than a sheep. You like a brew, J. W.?"

"I've got to find somebody to take me up to John Skye's camp," I said. I looked at Billy Jo. "I'm not sure your daughter still wants the job."

Billy Jo opened her mouth, but her mother spoke first.

"Oh, I guess she'll take it," said Wilma. She looked at me. "If you were the man you've been talking about, you wouldn't have told us about him unless you were crazy, and you don't look crazy to me." She turned to her husband. "Mack, you take J. W. around back to the table under the big elm. J. W., you tell Mack what you've been telling us. Come with me, Billy Jo. We'll lay out some cheese and crackers and beer for all four of us. No reason why the women should work while the men loaf."

Mackenzie Skye and I walked around the house and sat in the shade of a tall elm. Once out of the sun, we were cool. I commented on it.

Skye smiled. "Air's so thin up here that your sunny side can be hot and your shadow side cold. It can be below freezing in the morning and hotter than a two-dollar pistol by noon. What is it that Wilma thinks you should be telling me?"

I told him what I'd told her. About then, the back screen door of the house swung open and Wilma and Billy Jo came out carrying a platter of cheese, crackers, and sliced ham, and four cans of Coors, made with pure Rocky Mountain spring water. Not a great beer, but not a bad beer, either. There is no bad beer.

The Coors was just what I needed. The dry Colorado air was already sucking the moisture from my skin.

"You ain't told us much," said Mack Skye.

"He's told us enough, I reckon," said Wilma. "John's business may not be any of ours."

"John's kin," said Mack. "If he's got troubles he doesn't deserve, maybe we should know more about 'em."

"I don't know about his troubles," I said. "But I do have reason to believe that this guy doesn't have John's best interests at heart."

"Why do you think that?" asked Billy Jo.

I got some cheese and ham and put it on a cracker, took a bite and chewed, then washed the crumbs down with a slug of Coors. The Skyes munched along with me as they waited for me to decide whether to answer Billy Jo. I finished off the cracker and got myself another one. Then I told them of the incidents in Weststock and on the island. While I talked, I looked at the huge landscape to the north of the house. The green fields on the mesa flowed north to a line of willows a mile or so away. An irrigation ditch, I guessed. Miles beyond was a ridge of blue foothills topped with a jagged rimrock. Beyond that, blue-green mountains climbed into the air and beyond them, far to the north, peaks like fangs thrust toward a high bank of thunderheads. John Skye was up there somewhere. Tomorrow, with Billy Jo's help, I'd go find him.

I became conscious of a silence at the table and realized that I had stopped talking.

Mack Skye tipped up his beer and drained it. "That's a pretty good story," he said. He looked at Billy Jo. "Well, honey, I agree with your mom. You should take this man up to find John tomorrow. J. W., we'll keep an eye on Vivian's place."

Wilma nodded. "I'll get on the phone and let the other Skyes out here know about this fellow. We've got to figure he'll phone one or another of them looking for information about John. I'll tell them to call the sheriff if this guy contacts them, and to get his name if he gives it, even though it'll probably be a fake."

"And I'll go bring in the horses right now," said Billy Jo. She looked at me with her dark eyes. "Has John got a wild side we don't know about?"

I'd wondered about that myself. "Not so far as I know. Do you know anything about him that I don't?"

"John Skye doesn't have an enemy in the world," said Wilma firmly.

"He's got one at least," said Mack. He looked at me. "Our boys are both grown up and gone, so we got room for you to put up for the night, if you'd like. Be more than welcome."

I thanked him, but declined the offer and asked him how to get to Durango. The three of them walked me out to my car. I pointed a finger at Billy Jo. "You make sure you get a nice, gentle horse."

"Sure." She grinned. "Trust me."

"Give him Mable," said her mother.

"I thought maybe I'd give him Big Red," said Billy Jo.

"No," said her father. "Don't give him Big Red."

"No," I said. "Don't give me Big Red. Give me Mable."

"I'll make sure you have a rope to tie yourself on," said Billy Jo.

"Good." I felt myself smiling at her, and thought of Ulysses. A rope had kept him from responding to the call of the sirens. Maybe it would do the same for me.

I drove back to 550 and headed down the big hill. At the bottom I took a sharp left and drove up a wide, dry valley to Durango, crossing the Animas River not once but twice before getting into town, and crossing it once again before I found a motel I could afford. As I'd crossed it the second time, a river raft full of life-jacketed passengers and crew, everyone looking happy and excited, had swept under the bridge and downriver.

Durango was a fair-sized town, with a Victorian air about parts of it. It lay in the valley, and foothills and the beginnings of mountains climbed away from it on both sides. Narrow-gauge train tracks led through the town and followed the river north, up the Animas Valley, between rising mountainsides. Steps of white and red stone lined the valley above town, and beyond them blue mountains climbed into the sky.

I'd seen signs of abandoned coal mines south of town, and knew there was farming and ranching on the Florida Mesa, at least, but it was clear that Durango, like Martha's Vineyard, lived off its tourists.

My first impression of Main Street was that it consisted entirely of saloons and shops selling souvenirs and Western arts and crafts. Once I crossed the river, heading north, the choice seemed to be between fast food places and motels. I found a room in one of the latter, went to the nearest liquor store (it wasn't far), bought myself a cooler, ice, and—when in Rome—two sixes of Coors, and went back to my room. It was hot and there seemed to be dust in the air, although I couldn't see it. I sucked up a Coors and opened another one and called the Edgartown police station. I was two hours ahead of Edgartown time, so I thought I might just catch the chief before he went home.

I didn't. He'd already gone home. I called him there. His wife answered and I told her who I was. A moment later, the chief's voice said, "Yeah?"

"It's me." I told him about my day.

"So you're going to see John Skye tomorrow?"

"Yeah."

"I'd pay some money to watch you try to ride a horse up a mountain."

"Hey, you don't have to be born out here to be a cowboy, you know. Hell, Billy the Kid was born in New York and Bill and Ben Thompson were born in England, for God's sake. Maybe I have a natural talent for riding horses."

"Billy the Kid was just a punk who went west, and I never heard of those other two guys. I do have a name that might mean something, though: Gordon Berkeley Orwell. Ring any bells?"

"No."

"Old New Jersey money. Men mostly career military officers. This guy is the latest in the line. Family belongs to the same health club as our Dr. David Rubinski. Orwell was there the morning Rubinski says he lost his wallet. Thing is, this guy picked up a leg wound somewhere down in Central America or some such place. Some sort of a botched job. Limps sometimes. What leg did that guy at your place favor?"

"The right."

"That's the one. What hand you say he shot with?"

"The left."

"This guy's a southpaw. He's about Rubinski's size, but a

lot more physical. Special Forces type. Runs, limp or no limp, works out, stays fit. Sounds like a man we'd like to talk to."

"Sure does."

"Trouble is, Orwell's up north somewhere in the Maine woods. Camping and white-water canoeing. Went in the day Rubinski's wallet went missing, and nobody knows how to get in touch with him."

"That's too bad. Anyone see him go in?"

"Yeah, he left his Jeep at some outfitting place up in the Allagash. The Orwells have done business with them before. People there saw him go off with his canoe."

"No word of him since? The family's not worried?"

"Apparently he's done this sort of thing before. Outdoorsman, like the rest of the Orwell men. His mother expects him out anytime. She's not worried."

I ran that through my head. "If he went in that day, maybe he came out someplace else, got back into his rented car, and drove to Weststock."

"Yeah. Dom Agganis and me had the same thought. If we find him, we'll ask him about that."

"And if I find John Skye, I'll ask him about Gordon Berkeley Orwell."

"If you don't fall off that horse and break your neck, let me know what you find out. I'll try to get a picture of this Orwell guy. We'll send that and what we know about him to the police out there. If you go by the Durango police station in your travels, you might pop in and have a look at his face. See if it looks familiar."

I rang off, then phoned Wilma Skye and told her where I was.

The next morning at nine o'clock, a pickup truck towing a horse trailer stopped in front of the motel, and I got in. Billy Jo, wearing her very own cowgirl hat, smiled at me as I got in, checked the rearview mirror, and pulled out. She gestured at a paper bag on the seat beside us.

"Colon cloggers, in case you missed breakfast."

I peeked into the bag. Fresh doughnuts, a thermos bottle, and two tin cups.

"I was up with the sun, almost," I said. "Ate down the block. Sausage and eggs, hash browns, toast, juice, coffee."

"The old bloat breakfast, eh? Well then, you're probably not interested in these cloggers and coffee."

"Oh, I don't know," I said. "I think I might choke one or two down."

She grinned. "Me too. You pour."

I did and we munched our way up the Animas Valley.

▪ 15 ▪

Between rising mountains, the valley was narrow, green, and fertile. The river wound through it and the railroad tracks paralleled the highway. A black engine sending puffs of dark smoke into the air chugged along, towing a string of yellow cars filled with people. It looked like something out of the last century.

"The *Little Flier*," said Billy Jo. "Goes up to Silverton and back through the canyon. A lot of fun, and in places pretty spectacular even by local standards. Tourists love it. You should take the trip before you go home. The best way is to ride the train up to Silverton, then have somebody meet you up there in a car and bring you back down by the highway. That way, you get two good looks at the country."

"It's worth looking at," I conceded. I'd never seen such mountains. Their lower slopes were covered by oak brush and pines. Farther up the slopes, quaking aspen grew, mixed with more pine and spruce. Great rimrocks broke the slopes into steps, and red sandstone escarpments climbed up from the valley floor. Along the edges of the valley, houses, old and new, could be seen.

"Old ranch houses and new places built by folks who've retired or who just love the country," said Billy Jo. "Lots of Texas and California money. Otherwise, this hunk of country is what you might call economically deprived. It used to live off of mining and ranching, but now it lives off of tourists."

"Let me guess," I said. "Wages are low, unions are rare, prices are high, houses are expensive, and work that really pays anything is hard to find."

She nodded. "You've got it. How did you guess?"

"Places that live off of tourists are all likc that. I live on an island that's like that. College kids who want to vacation come in the summer and take what jobs there are, and then leave in time to go back to school . . ."

"Right again."

We crossed a small, clear river running from the mouth of a narrow valley off to the left. A promontory topped by red cliffs split this valley from the Animas Valley.

"Hermosa Creek," said Billy Jo. "We could go up there and ride in from the end of the road, but we're not going to. We're going around to the foot of the Hermosa Cliffs and taking the Goulding Trail up to the top. I think John will be up there somewhere. He likes the meadows and the cliffs more than he likes being down in the canyons."

We left the flat green valley floor behind us and drove into wilder, rockier country. Farms gave way to pasturelands scattered between granite cliffs and forests of pine, spruce, aspen, and oak brush. Rivulets of clear water flowed in and out of marshes and between rocks. To our left, quite suddenly, a row of gigantic cliffs broken only by a few narrow rimrocked cuts rose into the sky. The farther we drove, the higher they got. Ahead of us, huge ragged mountains touched the clouds with their peaks.

"Engineer Mountain," said Billy Jo, nodding toward it. "Spud Mountain yonder. Those are the Needles off there. Lots of peaks around here over fourteen thousand feet. We won't be going quite that high today."

She slowed and turned off the highway. We rattled along a dirt road between pines and oak brush, pulled off it, and stopped.

"Here we are," said Billy Jo, setting the hand brake.

I got out and looked up. The cliffs seemed to hang over me. I could see hawks wheeling in the air way up there. It was a long way to the top.

"Would it make any difference," I asked, "if I told you I

have a mild sort of acrophobia? When I stand on cliffs, I'm always sure they're going to choose that very moment to crumble. When I lean on balcony railings, I'm sure they're going to break right then. When I'm on the edge of something high, I always feel like the wind is going to blow me over."

"A fine time to tell me," said Billy Jo, putting shapely hands on her shapely hips. "If you want to see John, you have to go up there. Or you can stay here and I'll go up alone. I can tell John what you told us. What do you want to do?"

"We manly men actually know no fear," I said. "We just claim to so lesser mortals won't feel so jealous."

"It's worked with me," said Billy Jo. "I'm not a bit jealous. Shall I unload the horses or not?"

I eyed the horses. It had been a long time since I'd been on a horse. "These guys don't bite, do they? Which one is Big Red?"

"Neither one." Billy Jo laughed. "And they aren't guys, they're mares. Maude here is for you. We use her for a packhorse, usually. Not too smart, but not a mean bone in her. I'll ride Matilda. Maude's her mother, but Matilda's got some Thoroughbred in her from her sire. Good spirit. They're both good in the mountains. Shall we get them unloaded, or do you want to go home?"

She was about half my size and obviously not afraid of mountains or big animals. I looked at her, at the horses, and up at the cliffs. On the Vineyard, fishermen say, when speculating about future possibilities of success, "If you don't go, you won't know."

"Let's do it," I said.

"Good. I think you'll be okay."

The mares were already saddled. Billy Jo backed them out of the trailer, tightened cinches, eyed my legs and adjusted the length of my stirrups, put bridles over the halters, and lashed on saddlebags.

"Food," she said. "We'll be up there about lunchtime." She handed me a yellow slicker. "Tie this on behind your saddle. Weather changes fast up here, and we could get a shower."

Except for the clouds over Engineer Mountain and the Needles, the sky was brilliant blue. Nevertheless, I tied the slicker on. Local knowledge should never be ignored. When I finished admiring my work, I saw Billy Jo slide a rifle into a scabbard on her saddle. I must have raised an eyebrow.

"My 30-30," she said. "Just in case."

"Just in case of what?"

She waved toward the mountains across the valley. "You never know. Fellow over toward Emerald Lake swears he saw a grizzly earlier in the summer."

"What do you usually shoot?"

"Deer. Got an elk last year, too."

"I don't think it's deer or elk season."

"I don't plan on shooting any deer or anything else. But, you never know. Like they say, it's better to have a gun and not need it than to need it and not have it." She swung up onto her mare with an effortless grace. "Time to move out. Let's see you climb aboard."

Billy Jo and Manny Fonseca would probably hit it right off, I thought. They could sit around and swap quotations about the benefits of shooting irons. I looked Maude in the eye and told her to stand still while I got on. She did, and we started up the trail.

The trail zigzagged up through a break in the cliffs. Maude was a wide-backed, comfortable old mare, and did her best to make my ride an easy one. Ahead of me, Billy Jo rode easily, looking back at me now and then to make sure I was still there.

We climbed steadily, stopping now and then to let the horses blow. Maude began to sweat early and kept it up, but rolled along without complaint. Behind us, the valley began to fall away, and across it more distant mountains began to rise into view. We passed through a break in a rimrock and later climbed through another. The oak brush disappeared and we climbed through evergreens and white-barked aspen, whose trunks were marked in black lines by the initials and dates of previous travelers. The aspen leaves danced in the light breeze and sunlight shimmered on them.

A tiny stream had, over millennia, cut through the thousand feet of stone that formed the cliffs and had created the crevice through which we now climbed. It still flowed through the gorge, falling over rock faces, winding through tiny marshes, and then plunging on down the slope. We rose beside it and later crossed it as the gorge began to open into a more gentle vale.

Suddenly Maude's ears were up. Ahead, Billy Jo was pointing. Three deer, heads high, were looking at us from the trail in front of us. They flicked their white tails and bounded away out of sight.

"They don't let you get that close in deer season," said Billy Jo, with a grin.

We came to a cabin and passed it by. Billy turned in her saddle and gestured.

"Used to be a cabin here they called Flagstaff. Old cattle camp in my grandfather's day. Rotted down long ago. They call this new one Craig Cabin, after a local guy who loved to hunt up here. Could be that he and his friends used up more decks of cards and whiskey bottles than they did bullets, but they always had a fine time one way or another. The top is right ahead."

We rode through an open meadow and up a ridge and hit a trail and a log drift fence. Beyond the fence, the land fell away to the west.

"They fence across these breaks in the cliffs to keep the cattle west of here," said Billy Jo, while our horses blew. "Between the breaks, the cliffs do the job. The creeks that run down into the Hermosa start up here behind the cliffs and run off yonder." She pointed toward a distant cluster of mountain peaks. "Those are the La Platas. They're the ones just west of Durango."

There were mountains flowing away in every direction. I had never seen so far except from airplanes. We rode to the right, and passed through a gate in the drift fence. My rump and legs were getting sore in spite of Maude's easy gait. Billy Jo rode as if she and her mare were one being.

We came out into a green meadow and Billy Jo reined her mare off the trail and into the dappled shadows of a grove of aspen. She swung down, removed Matilda's bridle, and tied her to a tree. Matilda immediately began to graze.

"Lunchtime," smiled Billy Jo, digging into her saddlebags and bringing out sandwiches and a thermos. "I'm hungrier than a timber wolf with tentacles."

Maude was ready for food, and so was I. I swung down and immediately felt a number of pains in places I didn't remember hurting before. My legs did not want to hold me up. I forced them to do their job, took off Maude's bridle, and tied her so she, too, could graze.

"Nifty knot," observed Billy Jo.

"Bowline," I said. "You can put a lot of strain on it and it'll still untie easily. Sailor's kind of knot." I minced over to the log where she was sitting and eased myself down.

"I've never seen the ocean," said Billy Jo.

Lunch was meat loaf sandwiches and iced tea. I got right into mine.

"Mighty fine," I said after a while.

"You do seem to have worked up an appetite." Over her sandwich, Billy Jo was watching me with curious eyes. I realized that though I was just old enough to be her father, I didn't see her as my daughter. The air was thin and I was a bit light-headed. Billy Jo, on the other hand, didn't seem light-headed at all. "I've never been on an island, either," she said.

"I've never been on top of a mountain."

"After you left yesterday, I remembered the twins talking

about you," she said. "I got the idea from them that you were a lot older than you are."

"I'll have to talk to Jen and Jill about that when we get to their camp."

"You don't look old at all," said Billy Jo. "Tell me about your island."

I told her some things about Martha's Vineyard. "The highest point on the island is about a mile and a half lower than we are right now," I said, finally, "but that's high enough."

"Tell me about the ocean. I've only seen it in the movies."

I looked at the mountains sweeping away from us in all directions. "It's like this. It's huge and beautiful and peaceful sometimes, and wild and dangerous other times. And it doesn't care about you one way or the other. I like it and I like this." I gestured.

"That's how the desert is, too," she said. "It doesn't care, either. Men work it for its treasures, and sometimes they do okay. Other times they don't."

"See," I said. "You know more about the ocean than you thought." I gestured with my hand and it touched hers. A spark jumped. She looked at me. Her eyes were deep and dark. In the corner of my eye I saw something move in the meadow below us. I looked and saw a small wolf trotting along. Billy Jo followed my gaze.

"Coyote. They're beginning to come back. They were nearly wiped out years ago, but now they're back. Maybe he'll sing to us tonight."

Our hands were no longer touching. We watched the coyote trot out of sight. Billy Jo looked at the sun and then at me. "We'd better get going if we want to get back down to the valley before night."

She flowed to her feet and I climbed gingerly to mine. "I may not *be* old," I said, "but I damned well am a lot older than I was before I got on old Maude."

She laughed. We bridled the mares and climbed aboard

and rode on. At a place no different than any other to my eyes, Billy Jo led us off the trail and through a forest where I realized we were on a small trail. She pointed at the ground.

"Shod hoofs. A day old."

I looked and saw hoofprints for the first time. We went through a dark spruce forest and came out into another grassy clearing. The ruins of a cabin lay fallen against the far hillside. Beside it were three tents fronted by a grill mounted on stones over a fire bed. Smoke lifted lazily from the fire bed. There were saddles over a log beyond the tent and horses were tethered on the hillside. A spring had been dug out and fenced in so that cattle could not tramp it down.

Maude whinnied and a horse on the far slope lifted its head. Two lookalike heads poked out a tent. The twins, Jill and Jen. They squinted at us, then ran out and waved.

"John Skye's camp," said Billy Jo. "Right where it was supposed to be."

▪ 16 ▪

"Gosh," said Jill or Jen, "what are you doing here, J. W.? Hi, Billy Jo."

"We never would have guessed in a billion years!" said the other twin. "Hi, Billy Jo."

"Hi," said Billy Jo, hooking a nice-looking leg over her saddle horn, and smiling.

"Mom and John will really be surprised," said one twin.

"Or did they know you were coming?" asked her sister.

"No, they didn't," I said. "Now, which one of you is which?"

"I'm Jill," they both said.

"They do this to me," I said to Billy Jo.

"No, we don't," said one of the twins. "My sister does, but I never do."

"You do, too," said the other one. "I'm the one who doesn't. Mom says it's not nice to confuse J. W., so I'm very careful never to do it. Do I, J. W.?"

"I've always liked you best, Jill. Unlike your sister, you have an honest face."

"I'm Jen. I'm the one with an honest face."

"That's what I just said. Where are your folks?"

They waved toward the east. "Out there on the top of the cliffs. Probably just looking out across the valley. You want to see them? Come on! We'll take you there!"

They didn't bother with saddles or bridles, but ran out into the meadow, untied two horses, and swung aboard them bareback.

"Those two can ride like the wind," said Billy Jo approvingly as she unwound her leg from the saddle horn.

"What is it with girls and horses, anyway?"

"Freud probably thought he knew," she replied. "Control of something big and fast and powerful, maybe. Maybe having something strong between your legs and being swept away by it."

"Aren't controlling and being swept away opposites?"

"We're not talking logic here," said Billy Jo, her dark eyes looking at me from under the wide brim of her hat.

"Come on, you guys!" came the shout of a twin.

I caught myself actually running my tongue along my lips as I met Billy Jo's eyes. It made me smile. I looked at the twins riding their dancing horses in the meadow. "We'd better go," I said.

"Yes."

"Come on!" said a twin, and she and her sister galloped off.

"Let's trot along," said Billy Jo, kicking Matilda out of her walk.

We trotted. I bounced. Pain.

"Take your weight on your legs," said Billy Jo, looking back. "It would be a shame if you ruined yourself so early in life!"

I used my legs and tried to adapt myself to Maude's pace. More pain, but not as much. We trotted along after the twins, who in time came galloping back to see where we were and finally trotted along ahead of us.

We passed over rolling green meadows and through patches of forest and back into meadowlands. A rounded grassy hillside rose gently in front of us. On top of it I could see two horses tied to a lonesome tree.

"Come on, J. W., gallop!"

The twins and Billy Jo kicked their heels and their mounts broke into gallops. Maude, not to be outdone or left behind, broke into one of her own. I grabbed the saddle horn and hung on and we galloped up the slope.

At the top, suddenly, there was nothing in front of us. Instead, as though some giant knife had sliced straight down through the mountain and cut away its other half, we were at the rim of an incredible cliff that fell a thousand feet to the valley floor.

I yanked on the reins and Maude slid to a stop. I felt ethereal and barely heard the laughter of my companions as they swung to the ground. Maude danced a bit and I could feel both of us staggering toward the cliff.

Then Billy Jo was at Maude's head, patting the mare's nose, holding her halter rope, grinning at me.

"You've just had the official introduction to our favorite part of the cliffs." She laughed. "My dad brought me up here on a run, and his dad did it to him, and John's dad did it to him, and he did it to the twins. It's great. This little rise looks like every other one you've ridden over, but there's no other side!"

I dismounted in a rush and again felt my legs almost collapse. Some invisible force seemed to be drawing me over the cliffs, and I fought against it.

"Hey," said Billy Jo. "Relax. The rim's twenty feet away from you. You couldn't fall over it from here if you wanted to."

She was right, of course. There were several yards of grass between me and the empty air that marked the edge of the cliffs. I put my will against my fear and forced a bit of it away. I made my weak legs walk me toward the rim.

In front of me a stunning panorama revealed itself. Beyond the yawning valley below, the jagged Needle Mountains rose like shark's teeth into the sky. To their right, wave on wave of ragged mountains flowed into the distance. A thousand feet below my feet, the valley floor revealed a long lake and tiny dots that I recognized as houses. The highway was a narrow line along which moved smaller dots that I knew were cars. Hawks soared between me and the valley floor, riding the winds, gashing gold vermilion. It was an awesome view whose grandeur and wild beauty were so astonishing that for moments I even forgot my fright at being where I was.

Billy Jo walked to my side and looked out over the precipice at our feet. "When I think of Colorado, this is what I see in my mind. I can't imagine a more magnificent sight."

"I can't either." A soft wind was blowing at our backs and I felt it pushing me toward the rim. I felt lightheaded. The limb of a small spruce was near me. I closed a hand around it.

"Everybody's afraid of something," said Billy Jo gently. "Personally, I can't stand spiders. If I was a secret agent, and you captured me, all you'd have to do would be to put me in a room with spiderwebs and I'd tell you anything you wanted to know. Why don't you sit down?"

I sat. It was good to feel the ground under my rump. I was immediately more secure. I looked at the cliffs flowing away on either side of us and dropping out of sight into the valley. I felt giddy. I looked at the horses. They were grazing within feet of the cliff top, totally ignoring it. I reached inside myself and found some more willpower and pushed against my fear. Billy Jo sat beside me and pointed here and there.

"Electra Lake. Good fishing there. Some really big trout. The smaller lake is Haviland. That's Animas Canyon, where the train goes on its way to Silverton. Silverton's right over behind those mountains. Old mining town. You really should go up there before you go back east. Just north of here is the Purgatory ski area. They have lifts that bring you up about this high, and then you ski down again. Do you ski?"

"No."

"You probably water-ski, instead."

"No. I sail, but I don't water-ski. I don't like fast boats. I prefer sailing."

"I like all three: skiing, waterskiing, and sailing. Fast boats, too." She made a gesture that took in half the world. "Navaho Lake is just over south of Ignacio. They've got all kinds of boats over there. I've been on a sailboat there. I don't really know how to sail, but I liked it."

A twin came along the cliff top to us. "Hi. Mom and John are down on the ledge that goes to the cave. They said I could bring you there. Come on."

"The cave?" If there was a cave, it had to be in the cliffs. I didn't want to get any closer to the cliffs than I already was.

"John's cave," explained Billy Jo. "It's just down there." She pointed toward a grove of trees growing precariously at the top of the cliff. "He says he found it when he was a kid up here with his father. There's a ledge below those trees there that leads down and back this way. About three feet wide. It gets thin and bends around a corner, and then there's this cave that cuts back into the cliff. John's showed us all where it is. He's very proud of it. I think he actually crawled over to it when he was a kid."

"Great. The ledge is three feet wide and then it gets thin. Three feet is thin enough! Aren't any of you people afraid that you'll fall off?"

"We never go on the really thin part," said a twin. "John and Mom made us promise. We go on the ledge as far as the corner and look around, though. That's not dangerous!"

I looked at Billy Jo. "Not dangerous?"

She shrugged. "Well . . ."

"You can go on your hands and knees," said the twin. "I did that the first time myself, but I don't anymore."

"I'll tell you what," I said to her. "I'll go with you to where the ledge starts and have a look. But I'm pretty sure that's as far as I'm going. I don't like it up here. I mean, it's beautiful, but I'd rather have a big thick glass wall between me and out there, so I can look, but can't go over the edge!"

"Oh, you won't go over the edge, J. W.," said the twin, unsympathetically. "Come on."

I got a grip on my spruce limb and arranged my legs under me, then noticed Billy Jo's hand reaching down. I took it and she tugged and up I came. In hospitals little nurses toss big patients around like they're made of feathers, so I wasn't surprised at her strength. Our hands lingered a moment longer than required, then parted. I felt a bit breathless.

"This air is thin," I said, looking down at her.

"Come on, you guys," said the twin. "Mom and John want to see you!"

"You have to let go of that tree before we can go," said Billy Jo.

I let go of the spruce and Billy Jo put out a hand as if to catch me should I fall. I didn't fall. After a moment, she smiled, turned, and followed the impatient twin. I trailed gingerly after her, feeling the cliff sucking at me, enticing me over its edge.

We entered a tangle of spruce and aspen trees and fallen logs. The roots of some of the trees were exposed, thrusting out into the air beyond the lip of the cliff. Why the trees had chosen such a place to grow, I could not imagine. It was another of Nature's myriad mysteries.

Suddenly, the twin grinned at us and was gone.

"Careful now," said Billy Jo. She put out a hand and I took it, and she led me around the stump of a lightning-blasted spruce and over a rotting log. She stopped and pointed with her free hand. "There."

Where? I looked and saw nothing, then looked some more and saw bent grasses at what appeared to be the very edge of the cliff. I inched forward and abruptly saw the beginning of the ledge slanting down on my left. The twin appeared around a corner of rock, grinning and beckoning. "Come on, come on! Mom and John are right here!"

But I had gone far enough. I raised my free hand. "No way. You go and tell John and Mattie that I'll be waiting up here whenever they decide to return to solid ground. Be careful now." The twin made a face and disappeared. I pulled on Billy Jo's hand, and she turned into me, tipping back her head so she could look up at me from beneath her hat brim. "Lead me to the promised land," I said. "I don't know where it is, but it's at least fifty feet away from this cliff. A nice log to sit on would be nice. One looking out over the trail we followed to get here. You know what I mean?"

"Trust me," she said. She led me through the grove of trees to its far side, where we could look west over the rolling meadowlands through the dancing shade of aspen trees. "See? There's even a log for you."

I sat down. She sat beside me. I looked at her hand, which was still in mine. I took a deep breath, then another.

"Thin air." I looked at our hands again and then into her eyes. "I'm a little old to be holding your hand."

"I think it feels pretty good," said Billy Jo. "I haven't done this since my boyfriend and I split up this spring . . ."

It did feel pretty good. Billy Jo's hair and eyes were dark and Celtic, her hand was small and strong.

"Do you have a girlfriend?" she asked.

I thought of Zee. "I have a woman friend. She's not a girl."

"I'm not a girl, either."

"But you had a boyfriend."

"That's why we split up. He's still a boy. I was a girl when we met, but now I'm twenty-one, and I'm not a girl anymore. She's left you, hasn't she?"

They say there's a little bit of woman in every girl and quite a bit of boy in every man. I was considering this old saw when I heard voices behind us. "This will have to wait," I said. I pressed her hand and let it go, and got up to meet John and Mattie and the twins.

I kissed Mattie and took John's hand.

"What a nice surprise," said Mattie. "What in the world brings you out here?"

"I need the love of a good woman," I said. "So I came straight to you."

"You're a smooth-talking city slicker, J. W. So you took John's advice and came out, eh? Good! The girls will have you riding like the Lone Ranger before you go home."

"Yeah!" chorused the twins, who could imagine nothing better than riding horses every day.

I looked at John. "Show me your cliffs," I said. He looked surprised. I smiled at the women and girls. "Ladies, if you'll excuse us. This is manly business. You understand."

Mattie looked at me with curious eyes, then nodded. "Of course. When manly men get together, they must do manly things. Come along, girls. You too, Billy Jo. Let's go find some wildflowers for a bouquet for camp."

"Very womanly of you," I said.

"Don't be long."

"We won't," I said. "Come on, John." I started back toward the cliffs. After a moment, he followed me. I made my legs carry me through the grove of spruce, right to the edge of the cliff. The air tried to suck me over, but I put my back against a tree trunk and stabilized myself.

John came up to me, a thoughtful look on his face. "Why are you here, J. W.? Why did you want me away from Mattie and the girls? Something's wrong. What is it?"

I decided to get right to it. "Did you ever hear of a man named Gordon Berkeley Orwell?"

"Gordon Berkeley Orwell?" He stared at me and then at the ground, and then at me again. "No. Who's Gordon Berkeley Orwell?"

"How well did you know Bernadette Orwell?"

"She was a student of mine. Medieval Literature. Year before last. Smart girl. Pretty emotional at times. I know she was into campus activities. Student government, marches for women, gay rights, that sort of thing. The idealistic type. This Gordon Orwell a relative of hers?"

"You were never anything more than just her teacher?"

His face was suddenly expressionless. He cocked his head slightly to one side. "What do you mean?"

"Were you her lover? Were you her confidant? Were you her special friend? Anything like that?"

He studied me. "This isn't like you," he said. "I've never known you to ask people such questions."

"I'm asking them now."

"My private life is none of your business."

"I know."

He looked at me through professorial eyes. "You talk to me and then I may talk to you."

"All right." I told him about the shootings on Martha's Vineyard and about Gordon Berkeley Orwell. "I think Gordon Orwell is after your ass," I said finally. "All I can think of is that it has something to do with Bernadette Orwell. Maybe he's mad at you because of her."

All of the blandness had disappeared from his face. "You mean that he tried to kill you, because he thought you were me? Good God!"

"That's why I need to know if there was anything between you and Bernadette. I need to know why he's after you. You need to know that even more than I do."

He looked at me, then turned and stared out over the valley. Then he shrugged his shoulders and looked at me again.

"Bernie Orwell was one of my better students. From the first time she started attending my class, though, it seemed like she wanted something more from me. You wouldn't know, because you've never been a teacher, but now and then every teacher has had a student who has what we used to call a crush. I don't know what the current slang word would be. It's always awkward for the teacher at the time, and it's generally embarrassing for the student after the crush runs its course. Anyway, Bernie liked to stay after class and walk with me to my office. She began to make appointments with me, and then would come by without them. At first I thought she was just an eager student.

"Then I learned that her father had died that summer, and I guessed that I was a substitute. A father-lover figure, if you will. She was at a fragile time in her life. You know: emotional, quick to change mood. I felt sympathy for her, but I figured that before very long she'd see that I wasn't what she thought I was. That's usually how these crushes work out. But it wasn't until the end of the term that she stopped coming around. I figured she'd probably found somebody else, maybe somebody more her age. I didn't see much of her after she finished that one class, though we were friendly enough when we happened to meet. If Gordon Orwell thinks I was romantically involved with Bernadette, he's dead wrong."

"He may be wrong," I said. "But you're the one who may be dead."

▪ 17 ▪

John looked out over the gigantic cliffs, frowning. I looked too, and felt a wave of nausea and weakness. I forced myself to keep looking.

"I don't care about your private life one way or another," I said. "I hope you understand that."

"Yes," he said. "I understand."

"I wanted to ask you when Mattie wasn't around . . ."

"You don't have to explain. You thought that if Bernadette and I did have something going, you didn't want Mattie to hear about it from you."

"Something like that."

"Is this Gordon Orwell related to Bernadette?"

"I don't know. They both live in New Jersey. It would be a funny coincidence if they weren't related. I expect to find out more when I talk with the local cops. The chief, back in Edgartown, is checking Orwell out and sending what he knows on to them."

John was looking out into the vast space that hung between us and the mountains across the valley, but he wasn't seeing it: he was blind to all but his thoughts.

"The chief thinks Orwell may be coming out here. Is that it?"

"That's a possibility. Orwell got your mailing address from my desk. I found your mother's ranch by using the phone. Orwell could do the same."

"But I'm not there."

"I found out where you are."

"You think Orwell can do that, too? Find me up here?"

"I don't know."

An ironic little smile flitted across his face. "If I stay up here, he may come; if I go to the ranch, he may be waiting; if I go back to Weststock or the Vineyard, he can find me at his leisure. I think I have a problem."

"Maybe not. A lot of cops are aware of him. Maybe they'll find him."

"And what if they do? What charge can they bring against him?"

A good question. "Using a stolen credit card to rent a car?"

"How long will that keep him in jail?"

"Not long, if at all."

He turned away from the cliff. "We have to tell all of this to Mattie. She and I don't keep things from each other."

The wind pushed me toward the cliffs as I stood away from the tree I'd been leaning on. I thought of *The Book of Five Rings* and the wisdom that advised warriors to hold themselves already dead so fear of death would leave them. But the wind still pushed at me and my belly felt awash with acid and I had to force my legs to carry me after John, away from the cliff and into the trees where the ground beneath me felt more solid.

The women and the twins were leading the horses down from the edge of the cliff and across a meadow as we emerged from the trees. They carried wildflowers.

"Are you through with the manly stuff?" asked Jill or Jen.

"There's not enough time in one life to do all the manly stuff that needs doing," I said. "But we got some of it done."

"Good. Let's race back to camp!"

Billy Jo laughed. "I don't think that J. W. is up to a race back to camp!"

"Sure he is! Sure you are, J. W.! Come on! We'll give you a head start!"

"Forget it, Jill," I said. "Race with your sister, if you have to race with somebody."

"I'm Jen," she said.

"No, you're not," said Mattie. "You're just giving poor J. W. a hard time. You and Jen go on ahead, if you want to, but J. W. probably wants a very slow trip back to camp."

"Very slow," I agreed.

"Gee whiz," said Jill. "Well, okay. Come on, Jen!"

The two of them swung up onto their horses and were away at the gallop.

"Youth," sighed Mattie, looking after them. "I hope they don't break their necks!"

"We have to talk," said John.

"I thought as much," said Mattie.

John looked at Billy Jo.

"She knows about most of it," I said.

"Tell the whole thing then," said John.

I repeated what I'd told John. When I was through, Mattie asked the key question.

"What are we going to do?"

"I think that you and the girls should go to your mother's house for a while," said John.

"Forget that idea," said Mattie firmly. "We're a family. We do things together."

"Just until we get this misunderstanding straightened out."

"No." Mattie looked at me. "It is a mistake, isn't it? Isn't that what you said? Well, if it's a mistake, and this Orwell knows it, then he'll stop this, won't he?"

"I don't know," I said. "He apparently doesn't think it's a mistake." I looked at John. "You're sure you never heard of this guy?"

John's face looked like an honest one. Of course the same can be said for the face of any good con man. "Not that I remember," he said. "But I'm not the world's champion name rememberer."

"He's good at names before 1500 A.D.," said Mattie. "It's the ones since then that he forgets. What if we can get ahold of this Orwell and tell him he's after the wrong man? Can't we do that somehow? Can't the police get him and hold him at least long enough to tell him he's after the wrong man?" She put her hand in John's.

"If they get their hands on him, they can try to tell him that. It can't hurt."

"If we're going to get to the truck and trailer before dark, we've got to get started," said Billy Jo, glancing at the afternoon sun.

"Look," I said to John and Mattie. "Even though I knew you were up here somewhere, I'd have been a long time finding you if Billy Jo hadn't brought me to your camp. This guy's in the same boat. Why don't you all just stay up here for a few more days, and give me a chance to find out what's going on. I'll talk to the local cops and phone east, and then I'll come back up here and you can decide what to do."

They looked at one another. There was an appearance of innocence about them that I thought might be misleading. Some unspoken agreement was reached and they turned back to me and nodded.

"All right," said Mattie. "We'll stay here for a while longer."

"I'll be back in two or three days. Maybe sooner." I put a smile on my face. "I may come back with good news."

"Do you think so?"

"Sure," I said.

"We'd better get back to camp," said John. "And you two had better head on down the trail while you still have some light."

Billy Jo had been working on her saddle and now ducked under her mare's neck and handed her scabbarded 30-30 to John.

"Here. Just in case."

He looked down at the rifle in his hands. "Just in case of what?"

"You never know. The magazine is full, but the firing chamber isn't, so you'll have to jack a shell in before you shoot. You know how to use one of these things?"

Mattie frowned skeptically at the rifle, but said nothing. John slid the rifle partway out of the saddle scabbard, looked at it, and slid it back in. "My father had one of these when I was a kid. Model 94 Winchester. I think I can still remember how it works."

Billy Jo grinned. "Good. I never met a Skye who didn't know about rifles, but I wasn't sure an East Coast English professor would remember such things."

"I wasn't always an English professor," said John, with a crooked smile. He lifted the rifle. "Thanks."

Billy Jo nodded and mounted her mare. "We'd better be moving, J. W."

I climbed up on Maude and we rode down through the meadows and woods to the camp, where the twins had long since been waiting. Their parents dismounted.

"Hey," said a twin, "I thought you were going to stay, J. W."

"Not tonight. No sleeping bag . . ."

"We've got extra blankets."

"No change of clothes . . ."

"You can borrow some of John's!"

"No beer!"

"Oh, so that's it! We should have known. Are you coming back?"

"In a couple of days."

"Well, bring your sleeping bag and clothes and a packhorse loaded with booze, so you can stay awhile! We want to teach you how to ride!"

Oh, wretched thought. "Thanks," I said. Behind them, I saw John carry the rifle into his tent. Then I followed Billy Jo out of camp.

Going down the Goulding Trail was worse than going up.

My legs were rubbery and sorer than ever when we finally reached the pickup and trailer, parked now in the long shadow of the cliffs. I got off Maude and almost fell down, but managed to lead her into the trailer and tie her halter rope to the front rack. Then I crawled into the cab and admired Billy Jo as she smoothly turned us around and headed us down to the highway. There, she turned right, and we started for Durango. I looked up out of my window at the darkened cliffs and the bright sky that topped them. I liked them better from down here.

"Beautiful day for a ride," said Billy Jo. "You'll be stiff tomorrow, but you'll survive. Riding takes muscles you don't use doing other things."

I gave an experimental moan and she smiled.

"I know a fake groan when I hear one. You have a couple of shots of red-eye and a good night's sleep and you'll feel a lot better."

"Have one with me," I said. "I'll treat. The bar of your choice."

She thought awhile. "Okay. But just one. I've got to get these horses home. Let me see . . . I've got it. Just the place for a man who likes his barley hops. A joint that makes its own beer!"

I brightened. "Sounds just right!"

We drove down into the Animas Valley. Long shadows reached across the valley floor from the west, but the eastern cliffs were ablaze with sunset light. In Durango Billy Jo parked the pickup and trailer west of the railroad tracks and gimpy me walked with her up to Main Street. There, right beside Radio Shack, was Carvers bakery, cafe, and—yes!—brewery! We took a booth, declined the waitress's offer of food, and ordered two Animas City Amber Ales. They arrived and we touched mugs.

"Cheers. And thanks."

I drank. Delish! Durango found increased favor in my eyes.

"What are you going to do about this man Orwell?" asked Billy Jo.

"I don't know if I can do anything, but now, at least, John knows what's going on. I'll talk to some cops. You know, a town with its own brewery can't be a really bad town."

"Then you'll love this one. It's got two."

"No!"

"Yes. Down toward the end of Main, Father Murphy serves his own brews."

"Well, when we're done here, we can go there."

"Sorry. The horses. Remember? Next time."

"I owe you more than a beer," I said. "I owe you dinner, at least. I'd like to take you someplace. Maybe some good Mexican food. We don't get much of that on the island."

She smiled. "You get Mexican food and I'll have seafood."

"Can we do that in one restaurant?"

"Maybe we'll have to go out twice."

"Maybe we will."

"Why don't we start tomorrow night? You can talk to your people during the daylight."

"All right. Shall I pick you up?"

"I'll pick you up, since I'm the one who knows where we'll be going. Seven?"

"Seven it is."

She finished her beer and flowed up onto her feet. It seemed a shame to leave before trying the Purgatory Pilsner or the Iron Horse Stout, but she had the wheels, so I floundered up in turn.

Back at the motel, I was very conscious of her body next to mine.

"I'll see you tomorrow night, then," she said. "If I can help you out before then, give me a call. You have my number."

I got out and she drove away. I thought of her sleek body and dark eyes, and her dark hair sweeping down from her broad-brimmed hat.

I went inside and went to the phone on the bedside table. The chief, in Edgartown, would be at home. I figured he'd had time to finish supper so I put through a call.

"I thought it might be you." He sighed. "I've had a nice day. I knew it couldn't last."

▪ 18 ▪

"I'm doing your wife a favor by calling you," I said. "Everybody knows you can't talk and smoke at the same time, so she'll thank me for temporarily saving your house from another fumigation from your pipe."

"Annie likes my pipe," he said, probably truthfully. They had been married for over thirty years and he'd been puffing his briar all that time and probably longer. I had once smoked a pipe myself, and still missed it.

I told him that I'd found John Skye and that tomorrow I was going to see the local cops.

"They'll have the latest information by then," he said. "You can have it now."

"Early this morning Gordon Berkeley Orwell came out of the Maine woods, made sure he was seen by several people at the outfitting station, got into his Jeep, and drove off. We figure he had time after he left the island to ride up near there by bus, get out someplace not too far from where he was supposed to be hiking, walk into the hills, and come back out again where people could see him. On the other hand, maybe he really was up there in the woods all along, and we've had our eye on the wrong guy."

"Do you think you've had your eye on the wrong guy?"

"No."

"Did Gordon Berkeley Orwell have a sister named Bernadette?"

"Yeah. A student up there at Weststock College. Died this summer. Drugs. Weststock, that's where this Orwell guy, if it was him, tried to hit Skye the first time. Drugs, Skye, Orwell's sister. If there's a tie-in, that seems to be it. How'd you know about Bernadette Orwell?"

"I met her last spring when a bunch of Weststock students stayed at John's place doing some sort of sociology study. Skye says she was a student of his a year ago, but that he's barely seen her since."

"Does Skye do drugs?"

"He does booze."

"Did he ever do other drugs?"

"Is there anybody under sixty who hasn't at least tried grass?"

"I don't know. Some, probably. Do you believe him about not seeing the girl since the class she took?"

I'd been running that through my head. "Yeah, I think I do. Of course, I'm also the guy who predicted the Sox would go all the way last year. Where's Orwell now?"

"He went home. Back to New Jersey. He's had a bad couple of years. His father died summer before last, and his sister OD'd this summer. His mother's the only one left. Orwell was stationed down south of the border somewhere. Central America or maybe farther south. Adviser to some army or government or other, or maybe he was something more than that. Home on extended leave."

"Career man?"

"Captain. Assigned to some kind of special outfit. Too young for Nam, but he's been a few other places as near as I can tell. The Pentagon is being pretty cagey about just what it is he does."

"How'd he get the limp?"

"In the line of duty, we're told."

"How?"

"We're not told."

"Where is he now?"

"How should I know? He was home earlier today."

"Can you give me his home phone number?"

"No. Police business."

"Weststock College will have Bernadette's home address and phone. I can get it from them. It'll just take longer."

"Wait." He put me on hold. After a while, he came back.

"I had to call the station on the car radio." He gave me the number. "What are you up to?"

"I want to find out if Orwell's still there. If he is, I want to talk to him. If he's the guy who's after John Skye, I want to know it. If he isn't, I want to know that, so I can tell John to watch out for somebody else."

"His mother is at their home. She's lost a husband and a daughter, so don't be too tough."

"I'm not tough."

I hung up and called the New Jersey number he'd given me. A thin female voice answered.

"Hi," I said, putting a bit of aped Colorado twang into my voice. "This is J. W. Jackson. I heard ol' Gordy is back stateside and I thought I'd give him a call and talk some old times. Is this Miz Orwell?"

"Yes. You're a friend of my son, Mr. . . ."

"Jackson. J. W. Jackson. Pleasure to talk to you, ma'am. Yes, ma'am, Gordy and me have been a couple of places together. You know. Sure hope he's there. Like to talk to him while he's up here."

"I'm sure he'd like to see you too, Mr. Jackson, but I'm afraid Gordon isn't here right now. He's gone out to Jackson, Wyoming, to do some hiking in the Grand Tetons. You just missed him."

"Durn! Wyoming, eh? He leave you an address or any such thing, Miz Orwell? Sure like to say hello . . ."

"I'm afraid he didn't. Where are you now, Mr. Jackson? Perhaps you'd like to come by for some tea. It's always a pleasure to meet my son's friends . . ."

"Ma'am I'm in a phone booth in Atlanta, so I'm afraid I can't accept your invitation. Sure do thank you for it, though. Gordy just now headed out, eh?"

"Yes. He flew west just this afternoon. He'd been up in

Maine, you know. Why, I barely saw him before he was off again. Oh, dear. He'll be so disappointed to miss your call. Perhaps he can contact you later . . ."

Then I did a cruel thing. I said, "That'd be terrific. Say, how's that sweet sister of his doin'? I tell you, old Gordy sure dotes on that girl."

There was a silence. Then the thin voice spoke. "Oh, I'm so sorry. Of course you couldn't know. Bernadette died earlier this summer. It was . . . very sudden . . ."

I made myself go on. "Oh, damn! Pardon, ma'am. I sure am sorry to hear that. That's about as bad a thing as can happen to you. Yes, I sure am sorry. How are you and Gordy doin'?"

"It will take us time, Mr. Jackson. Right now everything is . . . You must have heard how Gordon hates those Eastern colleges. Just like his father in that respect . . . Then to have this happen . . . It's been a difficult time for us. First the colonel and now Bernadette . . . To be straightforward, it's almost driven Gordon mad. I'm half mad myself at times . . . But I must ask your pardon. These are family matters . . . Still, I do wish Gordon had a friend to talk to . . ."

"Yes, ma'am. Gordon can find me if he wants me. Just tell him J. W. Jackson called. Well, I got to go. Nice talking to you, ma'am. Awfully sorry about your daughter. You have a nice day, now."

"Yes. A nice day. Thank you."

I hung up and opened another beer. I felt like lead. Was it worth it to hurt a mother to learn only that her son was almost mad with grief? I didn't know. What I did know was that Gordon Berkeley Orwell could be showing up anytime now. I wondered if I should go out to the airport and just sit there. Sooner or later, he should step off some plane, if he was coming. Then I thought some more. I was wrong. He could fly to some other town and then drive to Durango. I thought of his mother's voice. It was the voice of a woman who hadn't had many nice days lately.

I finished my beer, got into my car, and drove downtown.

Durango was alive with automobiles, brightly lit stores, bars, and restaurants. I found a parking place and walked along Main Street. There were souvenir shops with Japanese-made Indian headbands, bows with rubber-tipped arrows, rubber-tipped lances, all apparently furnished by the same oriental wholesaler who provided the goods displayed at the Indian shops at Gay Head. There were stores with windows heavy with silver and turquoise necklaces, rings, and watch bands. There were stores with windows full of cowboy hats, boots, and belts. There were lots of restaurants and bars.

I went into the Diamond Belle Saloon and found myself in a re-created Gay Nineties bar, complete with mustachioed bartender and barmaids in tiny dresses and net stockings. I wondered if the barmaids felt exploited. The bar was noisy. Under a balcony at the back of the room was a sign I appreciated: Work is the curse of the drinking classes. True. There was a rail at the foot of the bar. I put my Teva on it and ordered a Sam Adams. No luck. I ordered a Bass Ale and did better. The Bass was smooth and good.

Half of the men in the bar were wearing cowboy hats, and the other half were wearing baseball caps. I wondered if I should buy myself a Stetson. Maybe some boots, too. Then I thought again. Where would I wear cowboy clothes on Martha's Vineyard? I listened to the noise. Western accents and tourist accents. People seemed pretty happy. I had another Bass and felt it. The altitude, maybe.

I went out and down the street to the train station. No trains this time of night. I turned and walked back up Main Street. I came to Father Murphy's Pub. I went in and discovered that Father Murphy served not one but two locally brewed beers! I drank a glass of each while I devoured a sandwich. Durango seemed to be an excellent town. Two breweries. Who'd have thunk it?

I thought some more about buying cowboy clothes. Nah. Then I thought awhile about Gordon Berkeley Orwell. After a while I went to find my car. It took a while, but I managed it, and then managed to find my motel, too. On the way I saw a lot of churches. I wondered if there were more bars, churches, or motels in Durango. I thought it would be a close contest. I wondered what Zee was doing, and then remembered Billy Jo Skye's hand in mine. I took two aspirin and went to bed.

In the morning I had a bloat breakfast at the diner and went downtown to find the police station, which turned out to be on Second Avenue across Tenth Street from the county courthouse. Arrest 'em, jail 'em, try 'em, hang 'em. All in one city block. Western justice. I was impressed. I parked and went into the station.

Police stations are a lot alike. This one was newer than others I'd seen, but otherwise pretty familiar-looking. I gave my name to the cop at the front desk and asked for the chief. The desk cop raised an eyebrow and I handed him the letter the chief in Edgartown had written for me. He read it, looked at me, then handed the letter back and gestured toward a door. "Back there, Mr. Jackson."

I went through the door and found myself across a desk from the chief. I gave him my letter, which he read and handed back.

"Sit down," he said. I sat. "Well, Mr. Jackson, what can I do for you?"

"You've heard about this man Orwell."

"Yes. So far, of course, there are no real charges against him."

I told him about my experience in Weststock and on the Vineyard. "I talked to his mother last night," I concluded. "She said Gordon Orwell flew west yesterday afternoon. To go hiking in the Grand Tetons."

"Maybe that's what he's doing."

"Maybe." I told him what I'd been doing for the past two days. He listened patiently. I said, "If Orwell really is after John Skye, he may be showing up here pretty soon."

"We'll keep our eyes open, but you have to remember that we have thousands of tourists coming in here all summer long. We might miss him. Easy enough to do. We don't know what he looks like."

Neither did I. "The chief is trying to get a picture of him. He said he'd wire it to you." I got up. "Maybe I'll talk with the sheriff, too."

"Good idea." He put out his hand and I took it. "Don't be rash, Mr. Jackson. Remember that you don't really know whether this man Orwell has actually done anything."

"Somebody really did something."

"Yes, but let the police handle it. Thanks for coming by. Stay in touch. If you learn anything more, let us know."

I went across the street to the courthouse and told my story to a deputy sheriff. He also shook my hand, thanked me, and told me to leave the matter in the hands of the professionals.

I found a phone booth and called Billy Jo Skye's house. Her mother answered. She said she was glad I'd called.

"A man phoned this morning, wondering if I knew how he could get in touch with John Skye. Said he was a friend of his."

"Did he give his name?"

"Yes. He said his name was J. W. Jackson. I did what you said. I called the Sheriff's Department and told them about it."

The deputy I'd talked to hadn't mentioned it to me. Maybe he didn't know about it. Or maybe he just didn't think it was any of my business. Some cops are like that.

▪ 19 ▪

"Funny man," I said to Wilma Skye.

"Of course, if John and his family hadn't recognized you, there was no way we'd know this guy wasn't you," she observed. "Or, for that matter, that you were who you said you were."

True. "What did you tell him?"

"I told him to call back this afternoon. That maybe I'd know then. Then I phoned your motel, but you were out. Then I got a call from Alison, that's Mack's brother's wife, and she said she'd gotten a call, too. J. W. Jackson looking for John Skye. She called the Sheriff's Department, too."

"What did she tell the guy who said he was me?"

"Told him she didn't know where John was. Fellow asked her how he could find the farm. She told him because she couldn't figure out how not to. Figured he'd find it anyway. They've got these maps with all the road numbers marked on them, you know. You can get them in town."

"No damage done."

"What should I tell him when he calls back?"

A good question. I didn't know a good answer. "I'll call you back," I said.

I went back to the Sheriff's Department. The deputy was gone. I told another deputy my story and my thoughts and what Wilma Skye had just told me.

The deputy raised a restraining hand and glanced at a page of scribbles in front of him. "Wilma Skye says that a guy calling himself J. W. Jackson phoned and said he was looking for John Skye. Later Alison Skye told us the guy talked to her, too."

"Right. And Wilma told the guy to call back this afternoon."

"Right. But the guy really wasn't J. W. Jackson, because you're J. W. Jackson, and you think the guy might really be . . ." He looked down at the scribbles, "Gordon Orwell. Is that right?"

"Right."

"Is this going to make more sense to somebody else than it does to me? I sure hope so."

I hoped so too. I went back out to the phone and rang Wilma Skye. "When this guy calls back," I said, "tell him that someone will meet him at Vivian Skye's place with a map so he can show him exactly where John is. I'll be the someone."

"That doesn't sound like the world's best idea."

"I'll have the edge. I'll expect him, but he won't expect me."

"Didn't you say this guy took a couple of shots at you?"

"Yeah, but he didn't really mean it the second time."

There was a silence at the far end of the line. Then Wilma asked, "You have a gun?"

"No."

"You swing by here on your way. Matter of fact, come for lunch. I understand that you and my little girl have a date tonight, by the way."

"There are no secrets between a daughter and her mother."

"I wouldn't be so sure about that. Come out about noon. Mack will be home thereabouts. Might want some words with you."

"About me and Billy Jo?" Good grief!

"No. Well, maybe. I had in mind this idea you have about meeting this Orwell fella. I think we might talk a bit before you go off to confront the lion."

"See you at noon then." I knew where the power was. If I didn't show up, she wouldn't give Orwell my message.

I found a window and looked at myself in the reflection. Martha's Vineyard Surfcasters' cap, thrift shop shorts, Teva sandals, and a shirt that said Al's Package Store. No weirder than the threads a lot of tourists were wearing on the street, but not very native Durangoish. I'd been wearing almost the same clothes when Orwell had shot at me on the island, and if I showed up like this at the ranch, he might recognize me and either shoot or take off before I could get close to him.

I went into one of the stores with cowboy clothes in the window and bought myself a wide-brimmed straw hat with a wire around the brim so you could bend it into any shape you liked. I also got a Denver Broncos tee shirt. Then I drove back to the motel and spent some time punching and bending my new hat and rubbing it in the dirt to make it look old. I soaked the shirt in the sink, wrung it out and tied it in a knot, and put it in a sunny window. By the time I had changed into jeans and my old army boots and it was time to leave for the Skyes' place, the hot, dry air had done its job. The tee shirt looked wrinkled and used. I put it on and drove back to the sheriff's office. I thought I looked quite local.

The first deputy was back. He and the second deputy were together. The first deputy looked at my get-up and shook his head. "Maybe we ought to throw you in jail before somebody else does. If we don't have any laws against vagrants, I think we can make one up pretty fast. We just got some news that might interest you. Come in here."

I followed him into a room and he handed me two sheets of paper.

"Faxed about an hour ago," said the deputy.

One was a picture of a man in army uniform looking intently at the camera. His hair was trim and his gaze was level. There was a slight scar on his left cheek.

"Gordon Berkeley Orwell," said the deputy. "Taken about three years ago, apparently. Now we know what he looks like, at least. I figure we'll tell the guy to come to the ranch, then put a couple of men out there in the ranch house and wait for him to show up. Ask him a couple of questions and maybe get to the bottom of this."

My first thought was that the deputies were horning in on my plan. My second was that it made sense for them to do it. My third was the first one all over again, and my fourth was the second again. I put my foot on my fifth, and told them what I'd planned to do myself.

The first deputy frowned. "Okay, but now you just stay out of it and leave things to us."

The second piece of paper said that Captain Gordon Berkeley Orwell had a private gun collection and was said to favor a Beretta 125 nine-millimeter parabellum Italian machine gun with a blowback action offering a choice of burst or single shots out of a thirty-two-round magazine. With the butt folded, the Beretta was 16.46 inches long. Corporal Dominic Agganis of the Massachusetts State Police was of the opinion that the Beretta had been fired at one J. W. Jackson on Martha's Vineyard.

"What do you think?" asked the deputy.

"The right size gun and the right caliber. Could be. Tell your men to be careful. This guy is a tough cookie and pretty slick."

"We're not too bad ourselves," said the deputy.

"I'm going out to Mack Skye's place," I said. "When the guy phones in, we'll tell him to go to the ranch. Then I'll call you."

"Call us at Vivian Skye's ranch," said the deputy, "because that's where we'll be. Jake and I will go out there right now, so we'll be able to check the place out before Orwell shows up."

"The front door of the house is unlocked," I said, "and you can put your car in the barn so it'll be out of sight. I mean it about being careful."

"Mr. Orwell is the one who needs to be careful," said the deputy.

I drove, via a liquor store, out to the Florida Mesa. I wished I had a pickup. Then I'd look perfect.

Billy Jo raised both eyebrows.

"I want you to feel I'm just like the guys you grew up with," I said.

"I'm not interested in the guys I grew up with. I'm interested in some other kinds of guys." She gave a crooked smile. "You do look the part, I must admit."

"Mine was a great loss to the stage."

"Come on around back. Mom and Dad are already into the iced tea." She nodded. "If you add a shot of whiskey to that, you'll have a seven-course meal."

I lifted the six-pack of Coors. "I'll be glad to share."

We walked around the house. The wind was gentle in the trees and the lawn was thick and green. It was cool in the shade. Mack and Wilma Skye were at the table covered with food. Mack got up and put out his large hand, which I took.

"Hey, you must have really made an impression on my little girl. Went to town this morning and got herself some new diggers for the big date."

Billy Jo blushed. "I did not! I needed them anyway."

Diggers? What were diggers? "What are diggers?" I asked.

Billy Jo gritted her teeth. "Underwear, if you must know. But I didn't get them for our date! Daddy, how could you say such a thing!?"

"Well, sweetheart, I . . ."

Wilma clicked her tongue. "Never mind, Mackenzie. Your jokes aren't always as funny as you think they are. Sit down, J. W. You too, Billy Jo. You know better than to take your daddy seriously when he's only trying to be funny. Try some of those muffins, J. W. And there's some roast beef there, or some ham if you'd rather have that. That cheese is good, too. Don't just sit there, Billy Jo, put some food on your plate. You're getting too skinny. It's not healthy."

"I'm just fine. And I'm not skinny."

"What do you think, J. W.?" asked her father. "Is she about to blow away, or not?"

"She looks fine to me." I reached for the roast beef.

"Thank you," said Billy Jo. "Now that that's settled. I think I will have something to eat." She started stacking her plate. A twenty-one-year-old woman can eat a lot, I discovered.

After a while, Mack popped one of my beers and took a long slug. "Well, son, what's this about you going over to Vivian's to meet with this fella who says he's you? Doesn't sound too smart to me."

"As it turns out," I said, "I don't have to go through with the master plan. The Law is going to attend to it." I told them about my talk with the deputies.

Wilma and Mack looked at each other. Billy Jo looked at me. "I'm glad," she said, and reached her hand toward mine.

Just then I heard the ringing of the phone in the house. Billy Jo's hand stopped. We all looked toward the sound. Wilma rose and waved the rest of us down. "I talked to him before, I'll talk to him now." She looked down at me. "I'll tell him to go to the ranch. That someone will meet him there in an hour . . . Who? . . ."

"Your nephew," I said.

"My nephew." She nodded. The phone rang. She trotted toward the house.

"The world's getting mighty strange," said Mack. With one hand, he squeezed his beer can flat. I opened another can.

Wilma went into the house and the phone stopped ringing. After a while she came out again.

"Done," she said. "I gave him the message, then called the deputies at the house, but nobody answered. They must be outside. I'll try again in a few minutes."

"How'd he seem?" I asked.

"Soft voice. Cheerful."

"I guess now we wait."

"Well, I'm going to wait up in the north quarter section," said Mack. "Still got half a field to plow. I'll see you all later.

Wilma, you stick close to the house. Billy Jo, you might show J. W. around a bit."

He went off.

"Finish your beer," said Billy Jo, easing back in her chair. "Nothing's going to happen for an hour."

Once you got out of the shade, it was a thirsty day. I took the remains of my six-pack with me and we finished it while Billy Jo led me down to the corrals and through the barn and outbuildings. It was a well-maintained place. There were horses in a pasture behind the barn and there was a pond beyond them and a grove of piñon and cedar trees beyond that.

"All sagebrush once," said Billy Jo, sweeping her hand across a panorama of green fields. "My grandfather ran cattle here, but now we mostly farm and only keep enough beef for our own table."

We circled back to the house.

"Pit stop," said Billy Jo.

"You can't buy beer," I said, quoting the ancient wisdom. "You can only rent it."

Wilma was coming out of the house as we went in. She was carrying a basket, wearing cotton gloves, and headed for the garden.

"Those deputies must be hunkered down in the chicken coops or somewhere. Called them half a dozen times, but never got hold of them. Damnation, people should stick to their plans. Too late to call them again. I'm going to do some weeding." She went past us and I looked after her. I didn't like what I'd heard her say.

Billy Jo was first in line for the bathroom, and thus it was that when the phone rang I was the only one there to answer it. I did.

A gentle, ironic voice asked for Mrs. Skye.

"She's outside. Can I take a message?"

"Who's this?"

"Just a friend. Who's this?" I thought I knew.

"Another friend. Yes, you can give her a message. Tell her

that her nephew never showed up and the two guys that came instead didn't know a thing about where John Skye is. Tell her I'm really disappointed with her."

"Orwell, is that you?"

There was a silence. Then, "Who's this?"

"J. W. Jackson. Don't hang up. You're after the wrong man. Call me at . . ."

The phone clicked in my ear.

Billy Jo came out of the bathroom and saw me with the phone in my hand. She also must have seen something in my face.

"What happened? What's the matter?"

"I think there's trouble at Vivian's place. Do you have another gun in the house? I prefer a rifle or shotgun."

She nodded.

"Get it, please. And some shells."

She went away without a word and I phoned the Sheriff's Department and told them to get some people out to Vivian Skye's ranch. As I hung up, Billy Jo came back with both a deer rifle and a shotgun. I took the shotgun and punched shells into the magazine. "I'm going to Vivian Skye's house. Stay here by the phone."

"No. I'm coming with you. I can shoot."

A rifle had better range than the shotgun. "All right. Let's go." We went out and got into my car. I saw Wilma coming out of the garden as we drove out. She dropped her basket and started running toward us, but I didn't stop.

▪ 20 ▪

There was a low ridge west of Vivian Skye's place. A large irrigation ditch ran along it, and there were willows and cottonwood trees growing there. When I got there, I stopped the car and looked at the farmhouse and then at the corrals and outbuildings on the other side of the road. The gates on either end of the corrals were open. No one was in sight. Beside me, Billy Jo punched shells into the magazine of the 30-06 she held, muzzle down, between her legs.

"When we get there," I said, "I'm going to stop the car on the road and leave the engine running. I want you to stay by the car with the rifle and cover me while I go into the house. If you see somebody laying for me, shoot him. If I get inside and you hear shooting, but don't see me come out afterward, I want you to get away. You understand?"

"Yes."

"And watch your back. Maybe Orwell isn't in the house at all. He might be on the other side of the road in the outbuildings."

"Yes."

There were beads of sweat above her upper lip, and her eyes were bright.

I drove up to the gate to the driveway and stopped and looked at the house, then at the outbuildings. No movement. I felt as I'd felt when I'd gone out on patrol in Vietnam. Hollow, fatalistic, jumpy, frightened. I got out of the car, pumped a shell into the firing chamber of the shotgun, and ran toward the house, trying to see everywhere at once.

Nothing moved.

I slanted toward the front door, stood to one side of it, and pushed it open. I heard muffled sounds from somewhere inside. If I'd had a grenade, I could have tossed it in and then ducked in after the explosion; but I didn't have a grenade. I listened some more, flattened against the wall of the house. I heard the sound again. A voice somewhere deep inside the house. I heard nothing in the room beyond the door. I took a deep breath and ducked through the door, shotgun level.

An empty room. Doorways leading out of it. I went silently to the first one. An empty kitchen with a door leading outside and another into a hall. I went to the hall. The muffled voice seemed louder.

It took me ten minutes to go through the ground floor and second floor of the house.

Nobody.

The only place left was the basement. I stood to one side and pushed open the door to the basement stairs. The muffled voice was suddenly silent. There was a light switch on the wall beside the stairs. I reached across with the barrel of the shotgun and flicked it on. Light flared up from below.

I waited, listening. I didn't want to go down the stairs. I popped my head out and tried to see down there. No good. I went down the stairs fast, shotgun thrust in front of me, waiting for the bullets. I saw a wall and spun, putting my back to it, swinging the shotgun across the room as I looked for Orwell and his Beretta machine gun.

The two deputy sheriffs I had talked to were staring at me with white faces and wide eyes. Their hands were cuffed to water pipes. Their pistol holsters were empty. One had a bloody head.

"If he's here, say so quick!" My voice sounded flat and small.

"No. No, he's gone! We're mighty glad to see you!" The deputy I'd first spoken to nodded toward a table across the room. "Our guns and the keys to the cuffs are over there."

I got the keys and gave them to the deputies and went upstairs and outside. Billy Jo stood behind the car, looking at me over the sights of her 30-06. I walked out to her and told her about the deputies. "Now we'll do the outbuildings," I said. "Cover me again. You're good at it."

She looked over my shoulder. "Wait a minute. Here comes some help."

The deputies came up. They looked happier than they had looked in the basement. I told them I was going to search the outbuildings.

The first deputy looked at Billy Jo. "You better stay out of this, miss."

"Nobody's taken her gun away from her," I said. "You two ever in the service?" They both nodded. "Okay, let's sweep these outbuildings. Billy Jo'll cover our asses."

With three men, the job was faster. In the barn we found the deputies' truck parked right where they'd left it, but we didn't find Orwell. We went back to the road.

I heard sirens to the west, and soon two Sheriff's Department cars and a State Police car topped the hill to the west and came toward us, lights flashing. The deputies looked embarrassed.

"I'll listen in while you explain to everybody what happened," I said, as Billy Jo and I unloaded our weapons and put them back into my car.

Soon we were surrounded by more policemen than had probably ever been in one spot on the Florida Mesa. One was the sheriff of La Plata County. He did not look pleased.

"The guy was here when we got here," explained the first deputy. "We put the truck in the barn and went up to the house and he was waiting for us. Must have been watching us all the time. Covered us when we came through the door. Jake tried for him and got his head broke. Took our guns and cuffed us to the pipes in the basement. Asked us why we were there. I told him we'd gotten an anonymous tip. He didn't push it. Then he went upstairs and made a telephone call and came down again."

"Asked us who'd given us the tip," said Jake, as a colleague tended to his bloody head. "Ted said we didn't know. Seemed to just be making talk to pass the time. Got nervous when the phone rang, but we never told him it must be for us. Scary bastard. Asked where John Skye was, but didn't act like he really expected us to know. Finally he said somebody would be along by and by. Told us to be sure to keep working in the country where we'd be safe. Then he left. That's all there is to tell. Guy's dangerous."

"More than can be said for you two," growled the sheriff. "What'd this fella look like?"

Jake looked at his partner. "Average-sized guy. Levi's, denim shirt, blue baseball cap, army boots. Hairy, hippie-looking guy. Brown hair, stringy, down to his shoulders almost. Big moustache, beard. Tanned, blue eyes, wire glasses. Favored one leg a little. That about it, Ted?"

"Left-handed," said Ted. Jake nodded.

The sheriff grunted. "Sounds like a makeup artist. Grant, put that description out."

Grant, who was young and clean-cut and staring at Billy Jo, jerked to attention and went to a radio.

The sheriff looked around. "You obviously didn't see his car when you came in. How do you figure he got here and then got away?"

"If I was going to do it," said Billy Jo, "I'd have parked my car in the woods behind the barn. He had the same idea. Look for yourself. The corral gates are still open and there are fresh car tracks under and on top of the ones the deputies' truck made when they put it in the barn."

All of the policemen looked at her, then all of them looked at the gates and tracks.

"Young lady," said the sheriff, "if you ever want a job, come and see me. All right, a couple of you men follow those tracks down into the woods and see if you can find anything useful. I doubt if there'll be much there. We got anything to make a cast of these tire prints? I didn't think so. Well, trooper, let's have a look at the house. Maybe this guy left his name and address and telephone number behind. We need a couple of clues like that to make up for my deputies' police work."

Ted and Jake looked unhappy.

I drove Billy Jo home. Orwell was apparently a man who was good at disguises. A blond grad student, a bearded doctor, a hippie with long hair and wire glasses. Who would he be next?

Wilma met us with a frown, and we told her what had happened. She looked at the ground and then at me. There was fire in her eye.

"Billy Jo's a grown-up woman, so I've got no say about what she does with herself, but I don't take kindly to you putting her in harm's way like that."

"Yes, ma'am."

"Mom, I made him take me," said Billy Jo.

Wilma sighed. "Yes, I imagine you did." Then she swept us both with hard, worried eyes. "I still don't like it."

"It's okay, Mom."

"Spilt milk," said Wilma. "Well, put those guns away where they belong before your father gets back to the house. No use to get him worked up for no good reason." She turned away.

"Mrs. Skye," I said. "I need some help."

She stopped, her back still turned. Then, slowly, she faced me and stood silent.

"I need to talk to Orwell. When I told the police about his phone call, I made a mistake. I should have met him myself. If I'd done that, I could have talked to him. I might have been able to convince him that he's after the wrong person . . ."

"And you might have gotten yourself handled worse than he handled the deputies," said Billy Jo fiercely. "They didn't know where John was, but you do. He might have made you tell him."

"Maybe." I looked at Wilma. "I need to talk to him."

"So?"

"So if he contacts you, will you tell him where I am, and give him my telephone number? Will you do that, at least, and tell him I want to talk to him?" I had a thought. "Tell him that he owes me that much, at least, since he almost killed me three times."

"He won't call."

"If he does . . ."

She frowned at me, then said, "Hmmph. All right. Billy Jo, you'd best get those guns back where they belong." She turned away.

Billy Jo flashed me a look. "I'll see you tonight," she said.

I blinked, then remembered. "Yes. Tonight."

I drove to my motel and got ready for the date I'd almost forgotten. My cowboy clothes were all pretty grungy, so I wore clean jeans, an almost-as-good-as-new thrift shop polo shirt with a little animal over the pocket, and my Tevas. Casual, but not too far from tourist chic. When Billy Jo knocked on my door, I was ready to go.

Billy Jo was also ready to go. A crisp blouse, a dark skirt that fell below her knees, low-heeled shoes, and a ribbon holding her long dark hair. She wore golden earrings and a bracelet in the shape of a snake on her wrist. Her perfume was elusive and tantalizing. Her bronzed skin glowed. I felt underdressed.

"Where are we going?"

"Francisco's."

"Mexican food?"

"You bet."

"Seafood?"

"You got it."

We drove downtown and parked and walked into the restaurant. When we got to our booth, Billy Jo said, "I'll have a cocktail."

"What will it be?"

"You order it. I'll drink it."

The waiter looked at me. I looked back.

"Tell your bartender to rinse two glasses with dry vermouth and then put a double shot of Stoli and two olives in each glass. I want the Stoli ice-cold."

"Yes sir."

"Sounds just right," said Billy Jo.

"Do I get to order your meal, too?"

"No, I'll take care of that. You can tend to the wine, though."

The drinks came. We touched glasses and drank. Smooth as new ice.

"You're a gutsy girl," I said. "I'm glad you were out there today."

Her face was young and her eyes were shining. "I liked it. I never had a feeling like it before. Standing there with the rifle, wondering what was going to happen. It was a rush."

It hadn't been a rush for me.

"You did well," I said, but I wasn't happy about her feelings.

"I've read about soldiers being afraid and excited all at the same time," she said. "Now I know what they mean."

"I'm just glad he'd pulled out."

"What do you think happened out there? I mean, nobody expected him to be there first, did they?"

"I think he went there early for the same reason the deputies did: to scout the place and get the drop, if need be, on whoever came out to meet him. He's an old pro, and an old pro always gets the edge if he can."

"Why did he call Mom after he'd already locked up the deputies? He must have known they were trying to set a trap. Why did he still wait for somebody to show up and tell him where John is? That doesn't make any sense."

"He didn't know whether the deputies were there instead of the messenger or whether they were there for some other reason. They told him that they'd gotten an anonymous tip, remember. Maybe he figured the messenger was still going to come. When he'd called your mother, she told him that her nephew was going to be there. It was only when the nephew didn't show up that Orwell knew it had been a trap. He must have been pretty annoyed. The interesting thing to me is that he didn't take it out on the deputies. He could have killed them both, but he didn't."

"Why didn't he?"

"I don't know. He could have killed me at my house, but he didn't. Maybe he just wants to kill John Skye. A professional killer doesn't like to kill people for no reason."

She was leaning back in her chair, looking at me with her bright, dark eyes. "I never met anybody like you. Somebody who knows about these things, somebody who gets involved in these things."

There is a C and W song that says ladies love outlaws.

"I don't know about these things and I don't get involved in these things," I said, thinking that it was time to deflect such talk. "I'm just here because I don't want John to get killed."

"I watched you out at Vivian's ranch. How you moved, what you did. I don't know anybody who knows what you know." She touched her tongue to her upper lip.

"All you saw was a guy who was in the army once. Anybody who ever had any service experience knows how to do what I did. The two deputies knew."

"But you told them what to do." She leaned forward on her elbows. "You've been shot at, haven't you?"

I have a bullet lodged near my spine. Put there one night by a frightened would-be thief I'd trapped in an alley when I was on the Boston PD. Sometimes I wonder what will happen if it moves a little bit.

I said, "I have some shrapnel in my legs from a Viet Cong artillery round. Or maybe it was a mortar round. Anyway, the guys who fired it didn't even know I was there. We never saw each other. War isn't very romantic."

"Have you ever shot at somebody?"

I had shot at the woman in the alley six times as she had

been trying to shoot me some more. After all of the shots, my partner had been afraid to come into the alley because he thought the person I'd been chasing might be waiting for him. Finally he'd come on in anyway and found first the dead woman and then me, lying in my own blood in a pile of trash. I considered him a very brave man.

I put a smile on my face. "Thousands. I shoot at one or two before breakfast every day." I beckoned to a waiter. "Let's eat."

She ordered lobster, I ordered chicken enchiladas. There was a Freixenet Cordon Negro Brut on the wine list, so I ordered that to wash things down. Spanish champagne with enchiladas? Why not?

When the waiter went away, she put her hand on my arm. "You're dangerous," she said. "I like the way I feel with you."

She had youth's fascination with Eros and Thanatos. A heady and dangerous mixture whose glamour had probably once lured me as it now lured her. She was a very beautiful young woman, and I liked the feeling of her hand on my arm and the way she looked at me. I understood why some men can't stop trying to be attractive to such women.

Just then a voice said, "Mr. Jackson? Miss Skye? I hope I'm not interrupting."

▪ 21 ▪

I looked up and saw the normal Western uniform of boots, jeans, and checkered shirt, topped by a clean-cut face that was vaguely familiar. I ran it through my memory and came up with the young deputy sheriff who had been eyeing Billy Jo out at the ranch before being sent off to make a radio call. I felt Billy Jo's hand slip off my arm.

"Sir, ma'am. Sure don't mean to intrude, but I'd like to speak to you, sir."

"No problem," I said, "Grant, isn't it?"

"Yes sir. Grant Taylor."

"Grant Taylor," said Billy Jo.

"Yes ma'am," said Grant Taylor, with a smile.

"You were out on the mesa this afternoon."

"Yes ma'am."

"This is Billy Jo Skye," I said.

"Yes sir. I know who she is. How do you do, ma'am?"

"Hello."

"Yes ma'am. Hello. You're looking mighty pretty tonight, if I may say so, ma'am."

"Thank you. Aren't you a little young to be calling me ma'am? You don't look any older than I am myself."

"I'm two years older, ma'am . . ."

"How do you know that?"

"Because I know your big brother, ma'am. We were in school together up at Boulder and he told me all about you."

She sat up straighter. "Why haven't I met you before this, then? Josh must have brought a dozen of his pals home for one holiday or other."

He ducked his head, "Well, ma'am, I was usually working on holidays, trying to stretch the money I got for being in the army after I got out of high school. Shucks, I wish now I had come down home with him!" He grinned a boyish grin. She smiled.

"You're from someplace else, then?"

"Yes ma'am. Up Gunnison way. Came down here to go to work for the sheriff. I was military police in the service, and studied criminology in college, and I like the work."

"That where they taught you to call women 'ma'am'?"

"No ma'am. I think my daddy taught me that. He said if it was the right way to address the Queen of England, it was probably good enough for most other women, too. I hope you don't mind."

The smile was still on her face. She put out her hand. "I don't mind, but my name is Billy Jo."

He stared at the hand for the blink of an eye, then shook it with his own. "Grant."

"Grant." She sat back.

"Billy Jo." He straightened.

My eyes had been moving back and forth between them. I touched his arm. "You wanted to say something to me?"

"Oh. Oh, yes sir. Sure do." He flicked his eyes at Billy Jo, then back at me. "It's about this Orwell fellow. You want to step up to the bar for a minute . . . ?"

"No. Sit down. Billy Jo knows as much as I do. You can talk to her, too."

Billy Jo nodded approvingly, slid over, and tucked her long skirt under her thigh. Grant Taylor slid in beside her, bumped against her, got red, and slid back a few inches.

"Sorry, ma'am," he said. She smiled at him.

"Well?" I asked.

"What? Oh. Yes sir." He put his elbows on the table, got his face straight, and dropped his voice. "We've been in touch with people back east, as you know, and some new information has come in. We were going to try to get in touch with you tomorrow, but when I noticed you in here, I thought I'd just get it done now. This Orwell fellow is scheduled to go back on duty in ten days. That means that he'll be out of our hair before too much longer."

"Unless he goes AWOL."

"Yes sir. But apparently he's a career officer in a family of career officers, so I doubt if he'll go AWOL. You never know, of course."

Of course. "Anything else?"

"Well, Jake and Ted have been working with our artist and the photos we have of Orwell, trying to figure if he was the guy who ambushed them. You know, adding a moustache and beard and long hair to the photo, that sort of thing . . ."

"And they think that it could be, but they can't be sure, right?"

"Right, sir. The sheriff and the Durango and State police all have Orwell's picture, so we think we might pick him up. If we do . . ."

If you do, I thought, you don't have anything to hold him on unless Jake and Ted can identify him, which they probably can't.

"If you get him," I said, "I want a chance to convince him that he's after the wrong guy."

He nodded. "If we get him, you'll get your chance," he said.

Our waiter appeared, bearing a tray of steaming dishes. Grant Taylor slid out of the booth, smiled at Billy Jo, shook my hand, and moved away toward a table of young people his age, all of whom seemed to be looking at Billy Jo and me. I turned back to her as the waiter put down our food and drink.

"I think this merits our undivided attention," I said, as I inhaled the aromas floating into my nostrils.

"You sound like you have functioning taste buds. Dare I hope that you're not just another man who'd eat a bale of hay if somebody poured some whiskey on it?"

"I'm not a logger, lover." I tried the wine and found it cold and otherwise satisfactory. "When you live alone, it's easy to get in the habit of just tossing together whatever's easiest to cook. I make a point of not doing that. I like good food and I feed myself as well as I can. Right now I plan to tear into these enchiladas, and I advise you to do the same with that lobster."

"Yes sir!"

She did, and I did.

After a while she drank some wine. "So you live alone."

I thought of the times Zee had been in my house with me. Then I thought of the times she hadn't been, and wondered if she would come back to the island after her conferences in New Hampshire.

"Most of the time," I said.

"Not all of the time?"

"Sometimes a friend stays with me."

"A friend." She popped some lobster into her mouth.

"Yes." I mopped up the last of my enchiladas. I was still hungry. There must be some appetite stimulant in thin air. We had ice cream for dessert, then came coffee and cognac and the bill. I presented my plastic.

Billy Jo looked across at me. She had a comfortable, not-yet-sated expression on her face like the one I thought must be on my own. "Now what do you have in mind?"

"I've been thinking of several possibilities," I said. "First I thought you and I might go back to my place."

"Ah." Her eyes were dark beneath half-lowered lids.

"But then I remembered that I have to go up through the cliffs and see John Skye tomorrow, and tell him what's going on. So I'm going to ask you to do something else instead. I'd like you to take me up there again in the morning. That means . . ."

She rolled her eyes. "I know what that means. That means you want me to go home so I can get up early and get the horses and gear and the trailer and the truck and meet you here . . . when?"

"Actually, I want you to go home so I can get up early. Nine?"

"Nine. You . . . ! All right, all right!" She slid out of the booth. "I'm sure you need to get right at your beauty sleep, so let's go."

As we walked by the table where Grant Taylor sat, he stood up and smiled. "Good night," he said.

Billy Jo glanced first at me and then at him. "Good night, Grant," she said. He got a friendlier look than she gave me.

At my motel, she sat stiffly behind the steering wheel as I got out.

"I appreciate your help, Billy Jo."

"My pleasure. Good night." She spun gravel pulling out. I had to smile, but another part of me hated to see her go, and I wondered if I was a fool to send her away.

There was a message waiting for me at the desk. A Mr. Malone had called. He'd call again later.

I drove to a liquor store and bought ice and a six of Coors. Back in my room, I was halfway through the first Coors when the phone rang.

"Mr. Jackson?"

"Mr. Malone?"

"That name will do. I understand you want to talk with me."

▪ 22 ▪

It was a very ordinary-sounding voice, but it sent a little shiver up and down my spine.

"First, you should know that this line isn't tapped," I said. "Nobody's going to try to trace your call."

"Very reassuring. I can trust you, of course." A tone of almost amused irony.

"Actually, you can. I want to talk to you. I take it that you got this number from Wilma Skye."

"Yes. I told her that I was calling from the Durango Police Department and that we had some news that we wanted to get to John Skye. She said that you were trying to get in touch with this fellow they think is named Orwell and that we should give the information to you. I take it that Mrs. Skye is not a fool, that she realized that I am no policeman, and that she gave me a message you wished to give the man you call Orwell. What is it that you want to tell him?"

I didn't think I had much time to make my case. "It's simple enough. I've known John Skye for many years. I will swear to you on the sacred book of your choice that he had nothing to do with either the life or the death of Bernadette Orwell. He was one of her professors for one semester and nothing more. He was never her lover or anything like it. If she killed herself out of love, it was not out of love for John Skye."

There was a silence before the voice spoke. When it did, it was cool and detached. "Your friend has deceived you. The girl's diary tells a different tale. It says that she loved him and that John Skye used her and abandoned her and she could not bear it. In the modern liberal world, perhaps the idea of professors seducing their students is meaningless, the notion of abandonment hopelessly gauche, the idea of the girl afterward committing suicide laughable. Perhaps at Weststock College a professor so exploiting a young woman student is such a commonplace event that it means nothing to either the woman or the man. But in the world where some others live, it means a great deal. Those others believe that men such as Skye owe a debt, and they mean to collect it."

"Someone may owe you a debt, but it's not John Skye. John has been married to a woman he loves since before Bernadette was his student. He doesn't seduce students. You're after the wrong man."

"No sir, you are wrong. And now I fear I have no more time for this conversation. I only telephoned you in the first place because someone nearly killed you by mistake. For that he apologizes. He thought that you were Skye. You should count yourself lucky that he was thrice careless. He usually is not."

"You were wrong about me, and you're still wrong about Skye."

"You haven't seen the girl's journal. It's very clear." A note of fury entered his voice. "These Eastern colleges, these leftist dilettantes! So sophisticated, so liberal! They corrupt whatever they touch." Then the fury was gone as fast as it had come. The voice was cool once more. "Orwell women traditionally have gone south to college, Mr. Jackson, but Bernadette would have none of it. Weststock, only Weststock would do. Such irony. See what came of her attending that school. Drugs, loveless sex, betrayal!"

I wondered about the almost instantaneous changes in vocal tone. Did the anger come from conviction or from some other, deeper malaise? I was aware of an anger inside myself.

"I did see the journal," I said. "I found it on Martha's Vineyard and mailed it to New Jersey."

"And being an honorable man, you apparently did not read it first." I could see the twist in his lip. His voice rose. "John Skye was first her professor. A year later, he was her lover! 'Dear Jonathan,' 'sweet Jonathan.' Names of endearment. She was so happy . . . so trusting! Then . . . abandonment! Some other woman . . . !"

I had a growing certainty of my own. "I don't believe it. I've known John for years . . ." My voice sounded different to me.

His ear was sharp. "You're not telling me what you really believe."

True. "That's not so," I said.

"You know where he is. Someone wants to find him."

I thought of tomorrow. "John Skye is innocent. Besides, his wife and children are with him!"

"He has betrayed them just as he betrayed Bernadette Orwell. How many other women has he seduced and abandoned? How many more will there be? Where is he?"

"I'm his friend . . ."

"He does not merit your friendship. Where is he?"

"He's in the mountains."

"Take a certain person to him."

"I won't do that."

The voice became gentle. "Don't be afraid. The person only wants to talk. Perhaps John Skye can persuade him. Perhaps there is some explanation for the writings in the journal. If John Skye is indeed innocent, as he claims to be and you think he is, the person will walk away and that will be the end of it."

"He is innocent."

"Someone will listen to him," said the voice. "If you are concerned about his family, you need not be. His family is of no interest to this person."

There was a silence. My mind was racing. As long as Orwell was after him, John could know no peace. He could never know when the moment would come. If not here, then back in Weststock, or on the island, or abroad, should John travel there. Orwell would find him.

"I'll talk to him," I said. "I'll tell him you want to speak to him, to listen to him. I want this matter settled without any more trouble."

"Good. You're his friend. Arrange a meeting, if you can."

"No. No meeting. Walkie-talkies. There's a Radio Shack downtown. I can get them there. You can be in one place, and John will be in another. You won't see each other."

"You're a careful fellow."

"I don't want any violence."

"You don't want violence. What of the violence that Weststock professors impose upon the minds and bodies of the young women who are their students? Pah!" He paused. "Very well. Make the arrangements. Shall we say for the day after tomorrow? I'll be in touch."

The phone clicked and buzzed in my ear. I put it down. The half can of Coors was warming in my hand. I drank it. I did not like my anticipation of what was to come and tried to come up with alternatives. None of them seemed any better. I sat on the bed and thought about everything I knew having to do with the case. Then I called the desk and told them when to wake me up in the morning, brushed my teeth, and went to an uneasy bed. I was awake a long time and up early.

In the morning I shaved. Why? I wondered. It was a curious habit. If hair grew on your face, why not leave it there? Why did we shave some hair and not other? Women shaved armpits and legs; men shaved faces. Why not chests? Why not crotches? Certain exotic dancers did shave crotches, I knew. Why?

My level of intellectual activity was obviously not too high. I went out for a Colorado breakfast, then drove downtown to the Sheriff's Department. The sheriff wasn't in. I left him a message: call the Jackson, Wyoming, police and have them check automobile rental agencies to see if Gordon Orwell had rented a car, probably a four-by-four. If he had, get its make and number and put out a local APB for it.

Then I went to Radio Shack and bought two walkie-talkies and put them in my small backpack. I was waiting for Billy Jo when she stopped her pickup and horse trailer. She looked a little puffy around the eyes. My glands did a little dance anyway. I decided not to comment upon either eyes or glands. She had doughnuts and coffee, so she didn't intend for us to starve, however put out she might be about last night. I told her about my visit to the Sheriff's Department.

"Why did you ask them to do that?"

"Orwell set up an alibi for himself back east when he pretended to go into the Maine woods. He made sure there were plenty of witnesses to say he'd gone there, but he was actually down in Massachusetts having a couple of whacks at me. Last week, when he found out John Skye was out here, he told his mother he was going to hike in the Tetons. So I figure he did it for the same reason—to prove he was somewhere else when he was actually going to be down here. I think he probably went to Jackson, right where he told her he was going, and rented a car using his own credit card, probably a Jeep or some such machine, and told a lot of people that he was going to hike in the Tetons, and bought some camping gear and paid for it with the same credit card, then didn't go to the Tetons, but drove as fast as he could down here to Durango. He could have gotten here in less than a day."

"I never thought of that," she said.

There were rearview mirrors on both sides of the truck. I leaned forward and looked in mine. There were cars coming up behind us. I said, "Neither did I until last night, which may explain why I'm not head of the FBI." The cars passed us and went on ahead. I looked in the mirror again. More cars.

After a while, Billy Jo said, "What are you going to tell John? He can't stay up there forever. Sooner or later he has to come down, and this Orwell will be waiting for him."

"Maybe the cops will have Orwell by then."

"Or maybe Orwell will be back on duty. But even if he is, he'll get leave sometime, or retire. He can wait."

True. Revenge was not always an impetuous act. I thought of the old Beacon Hill political ethic: don't get mad, get even. It was a code that required action, but not immediate action.

"I'll tell John that Orwell wants to talk to him," I said. "He'll have to decide what to do. You and I can't solve his problem for him."

"I hate this!" she said in sudden anger. "I hate not being able to do anything!"

The sages have observed that to live is to suffer. Still, it is a bitter discovery when we make it ourselves, as most of us do sooner or later.

"Don't worry," I said. "It's going to work out. The bad guys don't always win these things, you know."

She thought about that for a while, then flashed me a wan smile. "I guess you're right."

All the way up the valley, I looked in the rearview mirror, wondering if any of the cars behind us were following us. When we turned off the highway at the foot of the cliffs, all of the cars drove right on toward the north. That was encouraging. On the other hand, if I'd been following us, I'd have gone right past too. And come back later.

Before noon we had topped the towering cliffs and were riding north toward John Skye's camp. Our horses had made a trail that only a blind man could miss, so I'd spent a good deal of time looking over my shoulder. I had seen nothing. That meant that Orwell either wasn't there or was there and was very good at his work.

23

There were a half-dozen white-faced cows grazing on the first meadow we came to. Two healthy spring calves were with them.

"You're a cowgirl," I said to Billy Jo. "Can you round up these cattle, or whatever it is you do, and drive them back down the trail we just rode up?"

"Sure. Why?" Then her eyebrows lifted. "Oh, I see. Wipe out our trail." She frowned. "Do you really think we might have been followed up here?"

"No, but I'd like to be sure."

"I'll take care of it. You stay right there and don't try to help."

I stayed put, and she swiftly had the bunch of cows and calves headed back along the trail. She and her mount seemed a single creature, graceful and lovely, sensual and efficient. I watched her and her little herd go out of sight into the trees.

After a while I saw her coming through the trees a considerable distance from the trail. She had ridden back where her horse's hoofprints wouldn't be easily spotted.

"No problem," she said, as she came up to me. "I booed them back to the drift fence gate. This Orwell guy would need a crystal ball to know where we went from there." She smiled. There was a glow in her face that made her look wildly beautiful. She liked the idea of danger. She would give some man fits, I thought. More than one man, probably. Me, maybe.

"Good work," I said. "I've been thinking. Too many people know that John's up here on the cliffs somewhere. I'd like to talk him into moving somewhere else. Not down out of the mountains yet; that's too dangerous. Somewhere else up here. Where?"

The games we were playing interested her, and her mind was quick. "Clear Creek. It's down on the other side of the Hermosa. You have to ford the river to get to it. Good camping ground, good water, good grass, good fishing. That's the place."

She rode ahead of me, her annoyance of last night washed away by her sense of adventure. My rump and legs hurt, but the sight of Billy Jo's graceful body swaying so easily atop her mare took my thoughts away from my discomfort.

When we rode into John Skye's camp, we found no one home.

"Fishing," said Billy Jo, after dismounting and having a quick look around. "Rods and creels are gone." She looked at the sun, then at her watch. "Probably down Dutch Creek. Be back in a couple of hours, most likely. Loosen the saddles and take off the bridles, and I'll get the fire going." She looked inside the black gallon coffeepot that sat on the grill. "Camp coffee. Best in the West. You never empty the grounds; just add more now and then. Eggshells to keep them down. More water when you need it."

"Terrific."

It was, too. Black as a politician's soul, but with a lot more character. I tasted it all the way down.

Billy Jo sat on her heels and looked at me sitting on mine. She had excited eyes. They flicked toward the big tent, then back at me.

"Is the rifle there?" I asked. I didn't really care, but I needed a distraction.

"What?"

"Is the rifle there? Your 30-30?"

"Oh. No. I guess he took it with him."

"Good. That means he took us seriously. I want him to take us seriously." She looked impossibly attractive. I seemed to be staring at her.

She flowed up onto her feet. "Let's go for a walk. It's too nice to just sit here." She put out her hands and I put up mine and she pulled me up. Pain. I gave a mighty, only partially feigned, groan.

"You just need some exercise," she said. "Come on." Hand in hand we walked out of camp onto the nearest meadow. The afternoon wind made waves in the meadow grass. It looked like a green sea. The sun was warm. Around the meadow, the spruce and quaking aspen moved in the wind. I felt about fifteen years old. I was excited and uneasy. Her hand in mine felt electric.

We reached the edge of the trees, and came to a fallen log. Suddenly she stepped onto the log, turned, and looked down at me with a hungry smile, her hands on my shoulders, pulling me close. My head came to her chin. Her breasts touched my face. I thought of how the Vineyard would be without Zee, and felt my will dwindle and fade and my passions rise. My arms went around Billy Jo's waist and I felt hers go around my neck and head, and then I lifted her off the log and let her body slip down until her lips found mine. I held her there, her feet not touching the ground, her body hard against me, her mouth searching, her breath short.

We were both gasping when I eased her to the ground. I saw a bit of blood on her lips, and touched it with my finger. She put up her own hand, touched the blood, and looked at her hand.

I tried to will my hunger for her away. It didn't want to go. My arms pulled her against me. I saw acquiescence in her eyes, felt it in her flesh. I put my hand to the nape of her neck and brought her face up to mine. When I let her go again, her eyes were wide and vague.

Some sound intruded upon us. I first brushed it away, then grasped at it. A voice, distant and high. I tied my tiny will to that voice, bound myself to it like Ulysses had himself bound to the mast while the sirens sang. Billy Jo looked dazedly at me.

"It's one of the twins," I said, my voice sounding strange to my ears. "Listen."

And indeed it was one of the twins, or perhaps both of the twins. And the voices were getting louder.

"They're back," I said. "They've found our horses in camp, and they're looking for us."

"Ah." Billy Jo, confusion on her face, stepped away. Her hands went to her hair, to her clothes, to her face. I handed her my handkerchief and she put it to her lips. I found her hat, which had fallen to the ground, and she put it on.

My heart was pumping and my breath was short. If desire at ten thousand was this exhausting, what would sex do to me? I remembered hearing that most people used up the same number of calories having sex as they got from eating one brownie. That was at sea level, of course.

I looked out into the meadow and saw a rider coming in the distance. I felt a surge of gratitude not unmixed with regret.

I took Billy Jo by the shoulders and sat us down on the log. "Look," I said. "This won't make any sense to you and it doesn't make much to me either. There is a woman back in Massachusetts who means more to me than I can tell you. She's gone away and she may not be coming back, but I am, by God, not going to fuck around with you or anybody else until I know for sure. Do you understand me? You are the loveliest thing I've seen since she went away. Worse yet, you have allure. You attract, you have the power to entice. If I were in any situation other than the one I'm in with this woman, I would be in your pants right now, twin or no twin. But I'm not going to get in them, so just keep them on while I'm around!"

I gave her a shake and she looked at me with astonished eyes. Then, unexpectedly, I heard myself laughing. I felt totally absurd.

"Jesus," said Billy Jo. "What's so funny?"

"Me. Not you."

"Hi," said the twin, galloping up. "So, here you are. We

saw your horses and Mom said you'd probably gone for a walk and she was right, as usual. What's so funny, J. W.? Are you telling her the Pig with the Wooden Leg joke again?" She looked at Billy Jo. "He always laughs when he tells that joke. He thinks it's great. Shall I bring you your horses, so you can ride back?"

Billy Jo adjusted her hat. "No. No, we'll walk back. Go tell your mom that we're coming."

"Catch any fish?" I asked, still smiling.

"We got enough for a good supper. Are you staying?"

"I'm afraid not. Next time."

"You never stay! Well, my sister is over the hill somewhere, looking for you, so I've got to go find her and tell her you're not lost anymore. See you in camp!"

The twin was off at a gallop.

"Here," said Billy Jo, handing me my bloody handkerchief. She looked at me. "You're a strange guy. I don't think I know anybody like you."

"And you're a woman and a half, and it's a good thing for me that I don't know many like you. Let's go find John and Mattie."

We walked across the meadows and down to the camp and on the way I knew something had genuinely changed between us. We talked like friends. I have had occasion to observe that in the absence of love, lust will do. Now it seemed that maybe the reverse was also true.

"What happened to your lip?" Mattie immediately asked Billy Jo.

"Branch hit me. It didn't even hurt."

"It's swollen."

"It'll be all right."

Mattie looked at me and then back at Billy Jo and said, "Hmmmph."

John, oblivious to this small drama, said, "Well, what's going on down in the real world?"

I told him what had happened out at the ranch, what I'd

learned about Orwell from the police, and about the phone call I'd received. "Orwell thinks John is responsible for Bernadette's death," I said. "Suicide after love betrayed."

"He's insane!" Mattie took John's arm in her own. She looked like a goddess protecting a mortal lover.

"He's wrong, at least," said John.

"He doesn't think he's wrong," I said, "but he wants to talk with you. Says he'll listen to your side. Whatever you decide about that idea, I think you two and the girls ought to break camp and go down to Clear Creek tonight." I got out the radio and told them about the walkie-talkie plan. "He wants it to happen tomorrow."

"Excellent. I think I will talk to him," said John, turning the radio in his hands. His tone was thoughtfully professorial.

"You will not!" said Mattie, astonished.

"I'm sure I can convince him that he's wrong."

"And what if you can't? What then?" Her tone was that of a mother speaking to a child proposing some wild idea.

John maintained his tone of academic detachment. "I'm sure I can. His idea is so completely absurd that only a madman could believe it once given the facts."

"That's exactly the point," said Mattie. "This guy is crazy!"

"Mattie could be right," I said.

"There! J. W. thinks I'm right. The twins will think I'm right. You agree, don't you, Billy Jo?"

Billy Jo hesitated. "Well, you'll be safer if you all go down to Clear Creek . . ."

"You see? Everybody agrees. This man Orwell is obviously disturbed. You can't reason with a disturbed man, and you know it. We'll break camp right now." Mattie squeezed her husband's arm. "Please, John, be reasonable."

He looked down at her in mild surprise. "Why, I usually think of myself as a reasonable man, Mattie."

"I'd be careful with this guy," I said. "He's pretty slick."

"He's dangerous, no doubt," nodded John. "But if we use

these radios when he and I talk, he'll have no opportunity to do anything foolish before I have my say. Afterward, he'll have no reason to pursue this vendetta."

Mattie snorted. "This man is a trained professional in the Special Forces or whatever, and you're a college professor! No contest! Be sensible!"

"Now, now, my dear, please be calm . . ."

"Calm!"

"Yes, calm."

"And what if he doesn't believe you? We have to go back to Weststock. What then?" Mattie naturally asked the right question.

John answered it. "We'll be no worse off than we are now."

"I want us to be better off!"

He patted her arm in that way men have of trying to calm the fears of the ones they love. "All I want is an opportunity to speak with him. I'm sure I can convince him of his error."

I was not so sure. "Where do you want to do it? Up here somewhere or down in town? Or somewhere else?"

He squinted at the sky, then swept his eyes over the surrounding meadows and trees. "Up here, I think. He may be younger and better trained at this sort of hunting game than I am, but I know this country and have acclimatized myself to this altitude, and that will be to my advantage. It will balance things out. Yes, we'll meet up here."

I looked at Billy Jo. She shrugged and looked at Mattie.

"We should leave this to the police," said Mattie.

"The police have had their try," said John gently. "If this plan fails, they can have another go. But with luck, we'll settle the matter before they need to."

"All right, then," I said. "You break camp and move down to Clear Creek. Tomorrow I'll bring Orwell here. I imagine he'll have that machine gun of his, just in case you and I are planning a double cross of some sort. Where will you be? Where do you want Orwell?"

John thought, and then pointed to the east. "I want him

yonder, on the cliff where the twins brought you the other day. The meadow runs right up to the cliffs there beside that grove of woods where the ledge goes down to the cave. I'll be watching from that ridge between here and the cliff."

"You'd better be hunkered down pretty good. I'll have to take him over the ridge, and this guy has good eyes."

John gave me a small smile. "He won't see me. Neither will you, even though you know I'll be there. Nobody's born a professor, remember. I was a kid playing cowboys and Indians up here, then I was a real cowboy, and then I was a hunter, and then I was in the army, all long before I became the effete East Coast pointy-headed intellectual I am today. I want Orwell in the meadow, in plain sight on top of the cliffs, before I'll talk to him. That way I'll know where he is, and he won't have any chance at monkey business, if he decides to try any. He'll have to come across a half mile of open meadow to get to where I am, and by that time I can either shoot him or be long gone."

Though I knew that people do things you'd never guess they'd do, I wondered if John could actually shoot somebody. I didn't want him to have to make that decision.

"I think being long gone is the best idea," I said. "After you talk, we'll wait on the cliffs for half an hour, so you can pull out. Then I'll take him back down the trail, and that will be that."

"And what if he doesn't buy John's story?" asked Mattie hotly. "What about that?"

"Why, I'll be gone," said John. "I'll make my way down to Clear Creek. I'll be quite safe, my dear. And if worse comes to worst, I'll have Billy Jo's rifle, after all."

"Wonderful." Mattie shook her head. "A middle-aged literature professor with a deer rifle against a trained soldier with a machine gun!" She obviously hadn't bought the macho image of John in his pre-professor days.

There were shouts from the meadow, and the twins came galloping over the waving green grass.

"What channel shall we use?"

"Thirteen," said John. "One of my many lucky numbers."

I looked at my watch. "About this time? That'll give Orwell and me time to walk up here and get out to the cliffs. I don't want him to have a horse, because that would let him move too fast. In fact, I want him to be tired when he gets here. I don't want him frisky at all."

John looked at his watch and nodded. "All right. When I see him out on the cliffs, I'll call him."

The twins rode in just in time to see Billy Jo and me climb into our saddles. They looked disappointed, which, compared to how Mattie looked, was not too bad.

"See you at Clear Creek," said Billy Jo.

We rode out as Mattie and John were extolling the virtues of Clear Creek to their questioning children. I didn't seem to be getting any better at riding. Everything from my hips down seemed to hurt. I imagined that meant that any hopes I had of becoming a rodeo rider had best be set aside. I was glad to let them go.

All the way down the trail I looked for signs that someone had come up after we had, but I saw nothing. There was no one waiting for us at the truck and trailer and there were no car tracks or footprints on top of those we'd made coming in that morning.

"You're the keen-eyed Westerner," I said to Billy Jo. "See any sign that we've had a guest?"

"Not a one, Kemo Sabe."

I had her drop me off at the north end of Durango, just in case Orwell was watching the motel. I didn't want him to know that she was involved in this matter. She raised a hand to her bruised lip. "If you ever change your mind about this other woman . . ."

"I don't plan to."

"But if you do . . ."

"Half the men in Durango will hyperventilate if you just bat your eyes at them. Believe me."

"I'm not interested in half the men in Durango. She must be some kind of woman."

"She is."

I shut the door and she drove away. I walked south along Main Street thinking about Zee and worrying about tomorrow.

▪ 24 ▪

By the time I got to my motel, I'd worked a lot of the kinks out of my bones. It was beer time, so I had a couple out of my cooler while I thought things over.

Both John and Orwell had said they wanted to talk. If they were telling the truth, John's plan might work. Of course, people with vested interests in issues didn't always tell the truth. I ran four scenarios through my mind: John and Orwell were both telling the truth about wanting to talk; John and Orwell were both lying about wanting to talk; John was telling the truth and Orwell was lying; Orwell was telling the truth and John was lying.

I thought some more. After a while, I decided to give up thinking, and went out for some food. I had stiffened up again and knew now why cowboys walk funny. I drove downtown past sidewalks full of tourists and had a steak at the Ore House. When in Steakland, eat steaks. I washed mine down with more Coors. Not bad.

I was home brushing my teeth and still thinking when the phone rang. I recognized the voice.

"I really don't think you're set up to trace this," said my caller. "But just in case you are, I don't plan to stay on the line. You want to talk to me, you go down to the Main Mall and go to the public phones there. When one of them rings, you answer it. Ten minutes." The phone clicked in my ear.

Ten minutes. I finished brushing my teeth, put on my straw hat, and went out into the neon night. I was in the Main Mall wondering if the guy wearing cowboy clothes and chatting on one of the telephones there was chatting on the one Orwell planned to use to call me when the man on the phone hung up and turned to me.

"Hello, Mr. Jackson," he said. "You're right on time." He gestured. "I thought this would be a good place for us to meet. Very public, no police that I can see, but a lot of civilians who might get hurt if either one of us tries to damage the other. Let's take a walk along the street, shall we?" He ran his eyes over me. "I don't see any sign that you're armed. Are you?"

I was looking at a young man with a drooping black moustache and the over-the-ears hairstyle seemingly favored by many young men in Colorado. He wore the hat, the boots, the denim jeans and jacket, and the plaid shirt that constituted the unofficial Durango uniform. I looked through the moustache and saw the face of Gordon Berkeley Orwell that I'd seen taken from the fax machine. If I were Max Carrados, could I have smelled spirit gum? Did people still use spirit gum to stick on false moustaches and the like?

"I have a pocketknife and fingernail clippers," I said.

"Ah. I, on the other hand, have a pistol tucked away, so I imagine that gives me an edge, should I need it. Will I?"

We walked out onto Main Street and turned right. The train depot was down that way a few blocks. "I don't think you'll need any firepower," I said.

"You must forgive me for telling you that I'd be calling on the mall phone. Tactics. Never let the enemy know your real plans. You understand."

"Yes. I talked to John Skye today. He's willing to speak with you tomorrow. He thinks he can persuade you that you're after the wrong guy. He thinks that once you are persuaded, you'll go away."

"If he persuades me, you may be sure that I will do exactly that. What scenario does your friend have in mind?"

I told him.

We walked down the street, two men in Western hats glancing briefly into windows filled with turquoise and silver jewelry as we walked and talked.

"So you plan to take me up there, eh?"

"I know where Skye wants you to be before he'll talk to you. I don't think you can find the place by yourself."

"I don't like going into places I haven't scouted. I'm never sure about what might be waiting for me."

"You have that Beretta machine gun. You can keep that in my back while we're hiking, if it will make you feel any safer."

He smiled. "So you know about the Beretta. Do you think your friend Skye will attempt to ambush us?"

"No, I don't think so."

"How about someone else? You, for instance. Or will the police be waiting for me?"

"I haven't told the police about this. They botched things pretty badly out at the ranch."

"I should believe you, of course." Two pretty girls came walking toward us. He stepped aside and they went between us. He never looked at them. "However, I make it a practice not to believe people too often. Tomorrow, you say?"

"Yes. We should start up the trail no later than nine or so in the morning, if we're to be out at the cliff in time."

"Where is this trail?"

"You can get a map of the San Juan National Forest from the Forest Service. You'll find the Goulding Trail going up the cliffs about halfway between Rockwood and Haviland Lake. They tell me that there are other trails going up, but that's the only one I know, so that's the one we'll use."

"I have one of those maps. Describe the trail to me."

I did.

"There's a cabin near the top?"

"Yes."

We walked. I thought that if I were Orwell, I wouldn't like the idea of coming up the trail toward a cabin where someone I couldn't see could see me and could be waiting. I remembered walking into villages in Vietnam and hating that very thought.

"And up on top there's another trail? Which way do we go?"

"I'll tell you that when we get there."

"Again, I must trust you, eh?"

I was suddenly angry. "Who are you to be talking about trust? You're the guy who almost killed me three times. I haven't done a damned thing to you. Do you want to do this thing, or not?"

"I don't plan to get my ass blown off by some wacko professor or his friends, I'll tell you that!" We came to the depot and pretended to look at advertisements for the Silverton train. After a while, he said, "Here's what I'll do. I'll meet you at the top. We can go the rest of the way together. You're going to start up about nine?"

I thought he would probably go up very early tomorrow morning, so he could scout the area before I got there. But I couldn't be sure, and because I couldn't be sure, he would be safe. He might even meet me at the bottom of the cliffs and go up with me, instead of going up earlier. He didn't like to let the enemy know his real plans, after all.

"I figure it will take me a couple of hours to hike up to the top. I'm not acclimatized to these altitudes."

"Nothing personal, but I'll expect to search you when we meet, so don't bring a weapon."

"Pocketknife and fingernail clippers. You, of course, will be dressed."

"Dressed," he said. "I haven't heard that expression since Jacksonville. The first time a guy told me he was dressed I didn't know what he was talking about. Yes, I'll be dressed. I will be a stranger in a strange land, after all, and if I'm going to have trouble, you're going to have more. Please wait here for a few minutes. I will see you tomorrow at the top of the Goulding Trail."

I watched him walk away up the street. After he disappeared beyond the nearest crowd of tourists, I went to my car and drove to my motel, brooding all the way.

25

Early the next morning, I got into my car and drove to the Sheriff's Department.

A deputy said the sheriff was in his office, spoke into a phone, and waved me through to the inner sanctum. The sheriff was chewing a matchstick. He pointed me to a seat. I asked him if they'd contacted the Jackson, Wyoming, police about Orwell renting a car there. The sheriff rolled his cigar to a corner of his mouth.

"As a matter of fact, we did. That was a good idea of yours. Orwell rented a Chevy Blazer. Blue. We've got the license plate number, but we haven't seen the car. Never knew there were so many blue Blazers in La Plata County until we started looking for this one."

"He might have changed the plates."

"We thought of that."

"You can't stop them all."

"That's right. Somebody back east said you were a cop once."

"A long time ago. Any other news from the east?"

"Some. Orwell was an actor in high school and college. Liked to play roles where he could try to look like somebody else. No surprise there, is there? He looks different every time anybody reports seeing him. Hell, we don't even know if all these sightings really are Orwell."

I had seen him close up. I knew.

"For all we know," said the sheriff, "the real Orwell may be up there in the Tetons, camping out."

"Yeah, that could be," I said. "But if it's not Orwell, I don't know who it could be. Anything else?"

"Yeah. This Orwell fellow is on special leave of some sort. Seems he got hurt on some job—down south of the border someplace, nobody's saying exactly where. His old man died a while back. The two of them were close, I guess. Then this summer, his sister pulls the plug on herself. Tough times for Orwell. Things seem to have piled up on him. His special leave seems to be for mental R and R. Could mean he's slipped a cog. Could also mean nothing." The sheriff shrugged his big shoulders, and a crooked smile played around his match-stick. "Ten-cent psychology. Worth a dime less than you pay for it."

I thought of Orwell's mother, who had suffered losses as great, but, as is often the case with women, had not decided to kill someone because of them. I got up. "Thanks for your help. I'll keep in touch. If I get any smarter, I'll let you know."

Out on the streets of Durango, the tourists were enjoying themselves. Beyond the buildings, the rimrocked hills rose in wild purity toward a bird's-egg-blue sky. The tourists did not know that a killer was perhaps walking among them, and the innocent earth did not care.

Back at the motel there was a message to call Billy Jo. I decided against it, but as I did, the phone rang. It was Billy Jo.

"My grandfather's old .45 Colt Peacemaker is out here," she said. "It must be a hundred years old, and it hasn't been fired in years, but it still works. I could bring it in to you."

"No, thanks. I don't want a gun."

"It's better to have one and . . ."

"No. There's not going to be any shooting."

"You're sure."

"I'm sure. I want us all to get out of this without anyone getting hurt."

"Be careful."

"Yes."

At eight o'clock, I parked at the foot of the Goulding Trail. There were car tracks leading farther ahead. I followed them on foot and came to a blue Chevy Blazer with New Jersey plates. It was tucked out of sight behind a clump of oak brush. I tried the doors. Locked. I tried an experimental call: "Orwell, come out, come out, wherever you are, and let's get going!"

No answer. Of course, the man I had decided was Orwell had never actually admitted that he was that person. If any of this ever came to trial, I could never testify that anyone calling himself Orwell had actually admitted to anything. Clever Orwell.

I looked up at the cliffs. Hawks were riding the winds like dots in the sky. I was wearing my very best hiking gear: shorts, a tee shirt advertising Papa's Pizza, my old combat boots, and my forest green Martha's Vineyard Surfcasters Association cap. I had a small knapsack containing the second walkie-talkie, a light jacket, a plastic canteen of water, and a ham and cheese sandwich. I delayed long enough to cut myself a walking stick, then, having no more excuses, and feeling empty and fatalistic, I started up the trail.

A bit after eleven, puffing like the little engine that could, I passed the Craig Cabin. There was a padlock on the door. I went on up toward the ridge, taking slow steps with many pauses, like the climbers you see in those movies of Everest. I got to the trail at the top of the ridge and sat down, sweating and breathless, my legs weak as Billy Beer.

To the east, between promontories covered with spruce and quaking aspen, I could see the mountains beyond the Animas Valley rolling away toward infinity in giant blue waves. Around me the wind sighed in the trees. At my feet the green meadow I had just ascended fell away to the tiny log cabin and on down to the stream that had, over a million years, cut the gap in the cliffs that made the Goulding Trail possible. It was all shining, it was Adam and maiden. The innocence of the wilderness. I stared at it with fascination.

"You came," said Orwell's voice from behind me.

I nodded.

"If you'll slip off that knapsack, I'll just have a peek. That's it. Ah. Lunch. Very good. Stand, please."

I stood.

"You will allow me," said his voice, and I felt his hands pat me down. "Thank you." The hands went away.

The knapsack landed lightly beside me. I picked it up, and turned. Orwell, wearing green fatigue pants and a green tee shirt and cap, was putting the walkie-talkie into a backpack. There was a pistol in a camouflaged cloth holster on his belt. There was a flap snapped over the butt of the gun. Orwell got his arms through the straps and hoisted the backpack up onto his shoulders. He noticed me noticing the pistol.

"No machine gun. I hope you're not disappointed, but they're hard to get through metal detectors at the airports. This pistol, on the other hand, goes through more easily. It's a Glock. A lot of it's plastic."

"I fired one once."

"Did you? An excellent weapon, I'm sure you'll agree." He gestured toward my scarred legs. "You are a veteran, I note. I recognize shrapnel scars when I see them. Asia?"

"The recent unpleasantness in Vietnam."

"I was too young, but my father was there. I was at Grenada and Panama. The men of my family attend all of the wars."

"I was an amateur soldier, not a professional."

"That is an important difference between us. Shall we go?"

I pointed north.

"After you," he said, with smiling mouth and icy eyes.

We walked north alongside the rail drift fence until we passed through the gate and came, a bit later, to the first of the great, rolling meadows that gave such fine graze to the cattle which summered there. Off to the southwest, the peaks of the La Plata Mountains pointed into the sky. On the far side of the first meadow, a few white-faced cattle grazed. It was a quietly pastoral scene, and I was struck by the irony of our tense intrusion upon it. The cattle lifted their heads and looked at us, then returned to their feeding.

Orwell seemed unaffected by the altitude that was making me pant. We came to the dark spruce woods that grew on the north slope of the vale where Skye's camp had been, and I found the trail leading through the trees. When we emerged on the campsite, Orwell said, "Stop."

I stopped and looked at him. He was standing half hidden by a tree, sweeping the terrain with field glasses. He took his time, then returned the glasses to his pack, and gestured to me to go ahead. I walked down into the campsite.

Orwell approved of it. "Water, graze for the horses, early sunlight, flat spots for tents. Good place for a hunting camp. Where's the nearest fishing stream?"

I didn't know. I pointed to the east. "We go that way."

We walked across the meadow Billy Jo and I had crossed only yesterday, found the trail leading out to the cliffs, and walked through groves of trees and over meadows under the warm nooning sun. We came to the ridge where Skye had said he'd be hiding. I'd seen no hoof- or footprints on the trail, and wondered if he was there. I didn't look to see if I could spot him. We passed out onto the last green meadow that led up to the cliffs and walked on.

We crossed the meadow, climbed the last rise, and were suddenly there, atop the cliffs. I felt the old familiar vertigo as I puffed for breath and looked across that horrible void to the magnificent mountains on the far side of the valley.

"This is the place," I said, tasting bile in my throat.

"Magnificent!" Orwell smiled and stared at the scene. "I've not seen anything like this since the Andes."

Now I knew why these heights were not affecting him. The Andes were even loftier than the Rockies. Seeing him smiling at the magnificent scene before him, I was acutely aware of the paradoxical truth that a sensitivity to beauty and the desire to kill can exist in the same person.

"It is amazing," I said, feeling the wind trying to push me over the edge, feeling the earth beneath my feet preparing to break off and plunge into the valley.

"An excellent spot for lunch," said Orwell. "You look a little green around the gills, Mr. Jackson."

"I am a little green. Acrophobia."

His eyes were sweeping the cliff top. "But before we eat, a little scouting, eh? Those trees off to the north will wait, but I think I'd like a look at this grove just south of us. Naturally, I want you to come along. Just in case you have someone in there waiting for me, you understand."

"Yes."

We went into the grove, Orwell behind me somewhere. I stayed away from the edge of the cliff and felt pretty good when I couldn't see it. We came to the far edge of the grove and turned back. We swept the place twice before Orwell was content that no one was there, and we returned to the spot where the meadows reached the cliff.

"I take it that we are being watched from some place out there," said Orwell, pointing to the ridge where Skye had said he'd be, then sweeping his hand north toward the trees on that side of the meadow. "A long shot with a rifle, so we're fairly secure. Still, I am putting a great deal of trust in you, Mr. Jackson."

"I want you to decide that you're after the wrong man, and then I want you to go back to the Andes, or wherever it is that you'll be going. I'm not interested in harming you, and I don't want you to harm anyone else."

"A romantic humanist, eh? How nice." Orwell had dug a can of rations out of his pack, opened it, and begun eating. I had no appetite. "I may not be going back to the Andes," continued Orwell. "This leg of mine. Infuriating, but not surprising. I may end up stateside, sitting at some damned desk!"

There were anger and despair in his voice, which surprised me. When I had gotten my million-dollar wounds, I'd felt only gratitude that I was still alive and might not have to go back into action. But then I was no career military man.

"For every man on the lines, there have to be a dozen supporting him," I said carefully. "You know that."

"The Orwells do not sit at desks!" He glanced at his watch, and got out the walkie-talkie. He switched it on and looked at me.

"Channel thirteen," I said. It was the first time he had admitted to being Orwell.

He put the walkie-talkie beside him on the grass.

"It's more than the leg," he said conversationally. "I'm home on special leave. Stress. My father's death, my sister's death this summer." He flicked his eyes at me. "I believe they think I've lost control. What do you think?"

"You're terrific," I said. "You're sitting there with a pistol at the top of the cliff, you've come two thousand miles to kill a man because you think maybe he seduced your sister, you already tried to kack me three times, and now you want me to tell you whether I think you're out of control? Forget it."

His laugh surprised me. "Don't contribute to the unbalance of the patient, eh? Very sensible. I withdraw the question. I apologize, as well."

Just then the walkie-talkie crackled. Orwell's smile went away. He picked up the radio.

"Dr. Skye? Yes, this is he. I'm listening. Make your statement."

He flicked his eyes toward me. They reminded me of the eyes of a snake. I made myself sit still.

▪ 26 ▪

I knew that my anger was a manifestation of fear, but the realization did not bring me calm. I listened irritably and watchfully while Orwell held the walkie-talkie to his ear. He said nothing. John Skye, as many academic types tend to do, was apparently making what he considered a reasonable argument. Intellectuals are inclined to believe that people are, ultimately, rational and that given certain facts they will arrive at proper conclusions. I was not so sure. I watched Orwell's face, trying to read something there that I could not read in his silence.

After a time, he suddenly looked at me. His eyes were without expression. He held up a hand, palm toward me, in that way people do when they are listening to something important. Then he spoke into the radio.

"Yes. Yes, you have. I am immensely grateful to you, sir . . . Yes, I understand. I will tell him . . . Yes. Would you like to talk to him? Yes, here he is . . ."

He held the walkie-talkie toward me, and I took it.

"Yes, John?"

"I told him everything, and he's agreed that he's been wrong. Thank God! I told him that I'm going back down to my family, but that it would be best if he doesn't meet them, since Mattie is pretty worked up about this whole affair. He understands that. He's agreed to stay with you for a half hour or so, so I can assure Mattie that I haven't been fooled and followed back to camp."

"Ah."

"It's all over then. I can't thank you enough, my friend."

"I'll take it out in beer. Best to Mattie. You'd better get going."

"Yes."

I thumbed the radio off and retracted the antennae. I turned to Orwell. He was staring at the ground and had a curious look about him.

"So John convinced you, eh?"

He raised his eyes. They were hollow-looking, devoid of feeling. His lips tightened, then one corner of his mouth flicked up. He nodded toward the west. "He's been out there watching us with field glasses. Now he'll slide away and go wherever he's going."

He rose and walked to the edge of the cliff. "This is unbelievable country! Look at those mountains. The hunting must be good here, too. Elk, deer . . . Do they hunt bear? They do in Maine. I hear that cougars and grizzlies are coming back to this country. That would be something, wouldn't it? To meet a grizzly up here." He turned back to me.

"Your friend Skye spins a fine web of words. The kind he spun to catch an innocent girl. He thinks he's caught me, too, but I listened to his silence as well as his words. He talked long of my poor sister's early affection for him, and longer still of his own innocence. But he said nothing of taking her to his Vineyard house this summer, or of abandoning her there and taking up with another girl! What a liar sweet Jonathan is! And what a fool."

"No!" I said, getting up. "John didn't take her to the Vineyard . . ." My voice trailed off, since if I insisted that John had not done it, I might be obliged to say who did, and thus put another life in harm's way.

But Orwell was not listening. He was carried away by his own convictions. "He'll go back to his wife and kiddies now, thinking that I'm going to go away forever and he'll never see me again.

"And he's right about that. He won't ever see me again.

But I will see him. Sometime when he least expects it! Damn him!"

This last was shouted, for I was already running into the grove of trees.

"You can't get away!" he called after me. "I know that grove from end to end! You can't hide! And if you try to escape across the meadow, I'll just run you down. You're not accustomed to these altitudes, but I am. Give it up! Make it easy on yourself!"

But I was into the trees by then, running, zigzagging, waiting for the thump of bullets. None came. I looked back. I didn't see him. I ran toward the cliff and came to it suddenly. My head swirled and I staggered away. I seized my fear and pushed it from me. I walked along the edge of the cliff. I heard Orwell's voice somewhere behind me, to the north.

"It's no use, Jackson. I babbled too much just now, so you've got to go. Nothing personal, I assure you. We sometimes have to do this sort of thing in my work. Today's friend is tomorrow's foe, or becomes a danger too costly to keep alive. Come out. I'll make it painless."

I worked my way along the edge of the cliff and came finally to the log that marked the entrance to the ledge leading to Skye's cave. I climbed over the log and found the ledge. I crept out onto it and lay flat, feeling the tug of the void, the suck of the vacuum, drawing me over. I clung facedown to the stone. I was condemned by my silence. I could not trade Jack Scarlotti's life for John Skye's. I tried to dig my fingers into the ledge.

Orwell's voice went away. I heard nothing. Then the voice came again, this time from the south.

"You're very good, Mr. Jackson. I was sure I'd have found you by now. Please step out and save us this trouble. I assure you that I'm better at this sort of thing than you are. The end of this game is certain."

The afternoon sun was slanting shadows toward the east.

Below me, the shadows of the great cliffs were already stretching across the valley floor. In not too many hours, it would be night, and not even Orwell could see in the dark.

The thought occurred to him as well. I heard his laughter. "I hope you aren't depending on the night to protect you. I have night glasses, as you should have expected from an old soldier like me. You won't see me, but I will certainly see you. Besides, you won't really last that long. Do come out, so I can shoot you cleanly. Otherwise you may suffer considerable pain before I can dispatch you." Then he said a strange thing: "Oh, God, I'm tired, I'm tired."

A half hour later I heard the brush of leaves and the sound of a snapping branch. He was moving just on the other side of the log.

I stopped breathing. To see me he had to come over the log and look to his left. There was no apparent reason to do so, and he did not. I heard him move on.

The next time, he *would* cross the log, because by then he'd have searched out all of the logical spots and would be doing the illogical ones.

I got up on my hands and knees, closed my eyes, and crawled down the ledge, brushing my left shoulder against the cliff face as I kept as far as possible from the abyss on my right. I came to a spot where there was no stone for my guiding shoulder to touch, and I opened my eyes. My stomach turned and my head whirled. I was looking a thousand feet straight down over the edge of the ledge, which narrowed sharply and cut back to the left around a corner of stone.

I brought my eyes up and around and saw the cave. It was a wide, hollowed space under a rimrock that made it invisible from above. The nearer corner went back out of my sight. Twenty feet of narrow, rotten ledge linked me to it. The ledge looked too narrow for me to negotiate on my hands and knees. I got up and plastered myself to the rock face and moved ahead.

A flat stone under my feet tipped. I cried out and tried to become part of the cliff. Small stones fell away into the void.

I shifted my feet and moved on, my boots uncertain on the ragged surface of the ledge. I stared at the cave and took coward's steps, feeling rather than seeing. Stones tumbled into the silence beneath my feet. And then I was there, scrambling with undignified haste back under the overhanging rimrock. I felt sweat on my brow and saw that my hands were trembling.

I heard a voice from above.

"Mr. Jackson, I do believe I heard your voice. Thank you. I knew you had to be somewhere near the cliff, but I didn't know where. If you'd like to jump, that will be even better. Please do! Meanwhile, I thank you again for that shout."

I didn't have much time or much to work with. I unlaced my boots and, with my pocketknife, cut a four-inch length of the tongue from one of them. I felt quite doomed and, curiously, quite detached. I punched a hole in either end of the portion of tongue and knotted a shoelace to it.

I now had a crude but serviceable sling. I was no David, and I was long out of practice, but there was nothing else. I tied a loop in one end of the shoelaces and hooked my middle finger through it. I held the other string between thumb and forefinger.

"Well, well," said Orwell's voice from beyond the bend in the ledge. "What have we here? Where does this lead? I believe I'll find out."

I would probably get only one try, but there were plenty of rocks for ammunition, so I took my time in selecting two: both squared-off pieces of sandstone an inch and a half by an inch and a half that fit pretty nicely into the sling. I said goodbye to Zee and wished her happiness in her new life, and stood up, the sling hanging by my side.

A hand appeared around the corner of the ledge. A moment later Orwell's face peeked around, jerked back, and peeked around again. He was a careful man.

"Ah," he said, "there you are." He swung up the Glock.

I stepped out of sight into the nearer corner of the cave. It was a shallow depression that barely hid me from him.

"You're making a mistake," I called. "Skye wasn't with your sister on the Vineyard."

"Such loyalty. Very commendable, I'm sure," said his voice. "But it's too late for such argument. Don't you agree? Won't you step out and make this easy for us both? No? Well, I should have known you'd not cooperate. I harbor no hard feelings, though, and I hope you feel the same."

I waited thirty seconds, then popped my head out. He was just rounding the corner. I ducked back, counted to ten, stepped out, and whirled the sling.

He heard the whir, looked toward me and swung the Glock up as the rock flew from the sling toward him. The stone did not hit him, but instead hit the cliff beside his face and shattered. Pieces of the sandstone hit his face and, as he involuntarily turned from the pain, he shifted his weight and the flat stone beneath his feet slipped.

As I fed the second stone into my sling, he teetered and swayed and the hand holding the Glock swung wildly. He groped in vain at the cliff, but found no hold for his hand. Then, quite slowly, it seemed, he leaned outward, and, even more slowly, fell. His eyes were wide and feral, but I thought he had a look of relief on his face. He did not cry out as he disappeared. I listened for a long minute and heard nothing of his passing.

27

As I crept back along the ledge to the safety of the cliff top, and felt the power of gravity tugging at me, I thought odd thoughts. Where had Orwell fallen? Into some black hole? Into some heaven or hell? I knew his body was somewhere beneath the ledge, on some outcropping of rock, perhaps, or at the foot of the cliffs, where it might be found or it might not. No matter. Orwell no longer needed that broken husk of what had once been a man. If he still had needs, they were of a different kind. As I climbed over the log hiding the entrance to Skye's cave, I realized that although I'd been careful coming along the ledge, I had not really been afraid of falling. It was as though such falling had no significance just then.

I walked down from the cliffs through the darkening night, and knew that I had had enough of violence, of revenge, of retribution. I found no place for it in my soul. I located my car and drove to my motel. I was tired. I had a Coors and thought about the bother which would ensue when I told the sheriff what had happened. I realized that the law had no more significance to me in this matter than the thought of falling had when I left the cave. What could the law do for Orwell or for me? Time enough to deal with that issue when the police learned, as sometime soon they surely would, of the blue Blazer at the foot of the Goulding Trail. I phoned the airport and, it being mid-week, got a space on the next morning's early flight to Albuquerque. Then I phoned Wilma Skye.

"It's all over," I said. "John convinced the guy that he was after the wrong man."

"Did he? Well, that's good. Where is the man now?"

"The last time I saw him, he was near the top of the cliffs," I said. "He told me he hoped I had no hard feelings about things."

"And do you?"

"None I can't live with. I'm heading home tomorrow morning. Please tell everyone goodbye for me. And when John comes down out of the hills, tell him I'll have a bluefish waiting for him when he gets to the island."

"If you go down to Francisco's you can tell Billy Jo goodbye yourself."

"Billy Jo and I are just friends, nothing more."

She sighed. "So she tells me. Well, I can't say I'm sorry about that. She's just a girl . . ."

"No," I said, "she's not just a girl. She's a beautiful young woman who makes my glands jump up and down. It just happens that I have a commitment to another woman who does the same things to my hormones and takes up all my thoughts too. Say goodbye to Mack. Thanks for everything."

But I couldn't let it go at that, so I drove down to Francisco's. Inside, I saw Billy Jo. She was smiling across a table at Grant Taylor. They looked like a pair. Maybe his boss would give her a job, as he'd said he would, and she would have a chance to compare her fantasies of adventure with the realities of law enforcement. And while she did that, she could search out the realities of Grant Taylor. She was at the right age for such explorations. I backed out the door.

In Albuquerque there was a seat available on a TWA flight to Boston via St. Louis. I landed in Boston a bit after five, and telephoned the hospital which told me that Geraldine Miles had checked out. After I identified myself as a policeman interested in her case, I was told that she had gone to Martha's Vineyard with her aunt and uncle. I ran to catch the bus to Woods Hole.

The bus and ferry people have an infamous schedule that seems deliberately designed to keep passengers from making connections. A lot of buses to Boston leave Woods Hole just before the ferries from the island arrive there, and a lot of buses to Woods Hole arrive just after the ferries have departed for the island. No one knows who sets up these schedules, or why, but there is no islander who has not, at one time or another, been victimized by them.

I was lucky. I caught the last boat to the island. I stood on the deck and felt the soft air soothe me. It was a far cry from the high, dry air of Colorado. I was glad to be breathing it. I was glad to be breathing any air at all.

I got into one of the taxis at the dock in Vineyard Haven. The driver stared at me.

"J. W. What are you doing in a cab? You never ride in cabs."

"I'll have you know I've ridden in several this very year. Take me home, Jeeves. I'm a weary traveler. Any bonito around yet?"

"I'm just a taxi driver. I don't have time to go traveling or fishing like you rich, retired types. How should I know?"

"Well, are there?"

"There are a lot of boats around the Oak Bluffs dock."

"Excellent news."

I had him drop me off at the top of my driveway. I got a week's worth of mail out of my box and walked through the Vineyard night down the long, sandy drive to my house. I never lock my door, so I never need to find a house key. So far, nobody has stolen the place. I was glad to see it again, and went inside and turned on the lights.

There was no message on the answering machine, because I don't have an answering machine. The only sounds were of the wind in the trees and a night bird I could not identify. I went to the freezer and got out some scallops I'd frozen the winter before and put them, Baggie and all, into some hot water to thaw. I found a Sam Adams beer in the fridge, and had some of that. Coors could not compare. I got a flashlight and went out to the garden and came back with some carrots and broccoli. I cut the carrots and broccoli into pieces and parboiled them while I got some rice started. I put the carrots and broc into my big wok with some olive oil. I had another Sam Adams and wokked the veggies for a while with just a bit of Szechuan stir-fry sauce, then added the thawed scallops. When the wok stuff was ready, so was the rice, so I loaded up a plate of both, laced it with soy sauce, and had at it. Delish! It was good to be home.

The next day, I was early to Collins Beach, where I keep my dinghy. I rowed out to the *Shirley J.* and found her well. There was only a breath of wind, so I motored out of the harbor and headed north across the shallows toward Oak Bluffs. One of the joys of a catboat is that she'll sail on water so thin you could make it into windowpanes. For the shoally Martha's Vineyard waters, no better boat has ever been designed.

There were already boats anchored around the ferry dock when I got there, but there was plenty of room for me. I dropped the hook and got out my gear. The water was like undulating glass in the morning light, and the sun was a giant grapefruit low in the eastern sky. It was going to be a hot one.

By noon, I was stripped to my daring bikini bathing suit and sweating. I had two nice five-pound bonito in my fish-box and was feeling pretty good. The wind was coming up from the southwest and the tide had turned so that the *Shirley J.* now swung in the opposite direction on her anchor line. It was time to go home.

In those light airs, it was a two-hour trip under sail, but I was in no hurry. I was, after all, one of those people out there in the sound in a boat about whom people on shore often said enviously, "Boy. Wouldn't it be nice to be out there on a day like this?"

I tacked in past a crowd of people on the Edgartown town dock, waved at some waves I received, slid past the yacht club, and fetched my stake with an eggshell landing. I looked around. No one was watching. There are hundreds of observers when I come in too fast or too slow or otherwise screw up my landings, but never anyone there to see me do it right. It's a law of the sea.

I rowed ashore and took one of my fish to the market. Bonito is a cousin of tuna, and is oily enough to be good for seviche, so I took the other one home just for that purpose. Bluefish is about the best fish there is for seviche, but I didn't have a bluefish, so bonito would do. The secret of a great seviche is using fresh, oily fish and adding hot peppers to the other veggies. The lime juice cuts the oil, and peppers give the dish a nice bounce. I have been known to make a meal out of my seviche alone.

Seviche was not the only thing on my mind. I needed to double-check something. I dialed Weststock College, told the switchboard lady that I had been told that a Dr. Jonathan Scarlotti was on the faculty and that I wanted to find out if he really was so I could interview him for an article I was writing. Yes, she said, Dr. Scarlotti was indeed a member of the faculty, and would I like to talk to him? I said no, that I was between planes, but would catch him later, thanks very much.

I hung up and had a beer. Jack Kennedy, Jack Scarlotti, Jack be nimble, Jack be quick, Jack of all trades. Jack of hearts.

I decided to think about something else, and got to work on the batch of seviche: cutting a couple of cups of half-inch bonito cubes; peeling and chopping a big tomato; chopping up a medium-sized onion, about a quarter of a big red pepper, and a couple of little chili peppers; crunching two small garlic cloves; adding about a half cup of tomato juice and not quite as much lime juice and olive oil; then tossing in some chopped parsley, a bit of thyme, and some salt and pepper. I put all this together and stuck it in the fridge to stand overnight.

Salivating in expectation, I then went out and weeded the remains of my garden, which was only a shadow of its earlier self, but still had plenty to offer. By the time I had reached my psychological weeding barrier, the sun was well to the west and it was martini time. I collected crackers and cheese, a pitcher of ice, a cold bottle of Stoli, and a glass, and went up to the balcony. The tempo of my island life, so interrupted by Orwell, was reestablishing itself.

There were still tyro surf sailors learning their game on the tranquil waters of Sengekontacket Pond. Beyond the pond, the highway on the spit of sand linking Edgartown to Oak Bluffs was busy with cars headed home from the beach. Beyond them, sailboats stood white against the dark sea and evening sky. I made myself a drink and cut some cheese and sat and ate as I gazed out over the serene beauty before me. I could not imagine a place I'd rather be.

If Zee were here.

I wished she were beside me. We'd been apart for two weeks, but a world of time had passed. If she left the island for good, could I bear to stay without her?

Could I bear to leave with her?

I had another icy martini and watched the night come down. The Cape Pogue Light began to shine. Across the dark waters of Nantucket Sound, lights on distant Cape Cod flickered into view. Stars began to appear. After a long time, I went downstairs, stirred the seviche, and went to bed.

The next afternoon I drove to Iowa's house to take his family some seviche and to see how Geraldine Miles was doing. Iowa was fishing with Geraldine, but Jean was home. She thanked me for the seviche. I thought she looked rather grim.

"Don't tell Iowa that it's raw fish, and maybe he'll eat it," I said. "How's your niece?"

Women are realists. "The bandages are off of her face, but she'll never look the same. She has more plastic surgery ahead of her. She may be pretty, but she won't be beautiful again. I could kill that man."

"How's the rest of her? How does she feel?"

"She's walking well. She has some trouble with one of her arms. It doesn't work just right, but she says it's getting better. She's in good spirits, but she's . . . fragile. I don't know what she'll do if she ever meets him again. And I don't know if she'll ever be able to trust any man again. It's a hateful thing he did to her."

Yes, it was. Instead of making Cramer whole, love had torn him apart. His center could not hold. His anarchical side had been loosed upon Geraldine.

"He's here, you know," Jean said. "Here on the island."

I felt a coldness in my soul.

"You've been gone," she said, "so you wouldn't know. He came four days ago. He phoned her. Can you imagine that? Said he was sorry. Begged her to forgive him. He got his car from the police and came out here to the house and just parked outside. We called the police and they came and he went away. We went to the judge and got a court order for him to stay away, and the police gave it to him. But I don't have much faith in court orders, if you want to know the truth."

Trouble in paradise. I'd had enough of it in Weststock and Colorado. "I'll be glad to bring over a sleeping bag and hang around," I said. "He probably won't do anything if someone's here. I don't have anything better to do for a couple of weeks, and by then he'll probably have run out of money or time or both, and be gone back to Iowa."

"We don't ever leave her alone," said Jean. "We're afraid he'll . . . I don't know." She put her hand up and tucked in some imaginary strand of loose hair. "The police are being very good about it. If we call, they'll come immediately. Still . . ."

"Do you have an extra bedroom? If you don't, I can sleep in my truck."

"I only worry when Dan's gone and Gerry is here with me. Look at what we've come to." She opened a closet door and showed me a shotgun. "It's loaded. Dan took us to the

Rod and Gun Club and made Gerry and me shoot it. I can't believe I have to have a shotgun in my closet just to live in my own house!"

She was right. It was a sorry way to have to live. "Dan just wants you and Geraldine to be safe," I said.

"Safe." The word was short and brutal, like a gunshot. Then she looked up at me and gave me a small smile. "No, dear, you don't need to stay with us. Dan isn't going to leave us alone anymore. We talked it over at breakfast. The three of us are going to stay together until that man leaves the island."

"Good." I tried to make light of it. "In that case, don't tell Dan that I got two bonito yesterday. If he hears that, he may change his mind about staying home."

"More likely, he'll make Gerry and me go fishing with him, and leave the house with nobody in it! That'd be just like him, bless his soul!"

"I'll come by now and then," I said.

"You'll be welcome."

As things turned out, the first time I showed up was nearly the last.

▪ 28 ▪

At dawn the next morning, on Dogfish Bar, where I was casting for bluefish, something very large took my Ballistic Missile. Almost certainly a large female bass. There is a thrill to catching a bass which is different than the one you get catching anything else, and I felt it then. The strength of the fish, the rising light, the loneliness of the beach, all combined to create a wonderful half hour.

The water is shallow at Dogfish Bar, and there are rocks on the bottom to snag your line if you're not lucky. My fish did not want to come in. It chugged away with my line, then reluctantly let me haul it back toward the beach. It swam up toward Gay Head and took me with it, over the rocky beach. I slowed it and led it in closer to shore. It turned and swam back toward Menemsha. I followed over the rocks and hauled it in even closer. I could almost see it. It was a major-league fish.

Then it was gone, and I was reeling in a parted line. I had no regrets except for the loss of the leader and lure since, after all, I was after bluefish and would have let the bass go if I had landed it. Now Nature would have to remove the hook and in time would do so, rusting it in two and allowing the lure to fall from the lip of the great fish so that no harm would, in the end, be done.

I re-rigged and fished some more. A dozen casts later I had my bluefish, a little guy who, as fish will, had mistaken my popper for something more tasty. He looked exactly the right size to fit into my frying pan, so I gave up fishing for the nonce, walked back to the Toyota, and drove out of Indian Country back down island for breakfast.

Juice, fried fresh baby bluefish, eggs over light, toast made from homemade bread, black coffee. The gods never had it so good.

It was a prince of a day. A new sun in a clear sky. Just enough wind to move sailboats over the water. A day for beaching and kite flying. Already the cars were lining up along the road across the pond, and young parents were hauling children, blankets, cribs, umbrellas, beach balls, and kites down close to the warm and gentle water.

I then mowed the lawn with my almost-as-good-as-new lawn mower, salvaged long ago from the Edgartown dump during the golden age of dump picking, before the environmental fundamentalists seized control of that once best of island secondhand stores and changed it into a neat, antiseptic place which soon, no doubt, will demand passports from its users. I am not one to mow my lawn any more often than it absolutely needs it, but it was getting hairy enough for me to begin to lose things in it, so a clipping was in order. I clipped it wearing sandals and nothing else, as is my occasional wont.

By the time I was through, I was sweating all over and in need of some beer and a swim. I got into my dinky bikini, put a couple of Sam Adams in a cooler, and drove to South Beach. A few hundred people were there ahead of me, but I got into four-wheel drive and turned east and got away from most of them. A half mile down the beach, I laid out my old bedspread on the sand, nailed it down with the cooler and my big beach towel, and plunged into the briny.

Perfect. I swam out and back in, floating on my back amid the mild breakers, wondered if there really were sharks just off shore, as some fishermen had told me there were, and finally came in over the thin strand of pebbles that hung on the sand just where the waves broke. I toweled off my head and hands and lay down on the bedspread with a beer. I felt good. If Zee had been there, I would have felt perfect.

In mid-August, the sun is in the same place in the sky as

it is in mid-April, so tans are hard to maintain. I gave mine two hours, then packed up. There were many kites still in the air, indicating that those who were vacationing on the island were not about to abandon the golden sands so soon in the day. I didn't blame them. If I had been paying as much to be here as they were, I wouldn't have left either.

At home, I showered off the salt in the outdoor shower, slid into more modest clothes, and went to Iowa's house to see how things were and to do some bragging about my bluefish. As I drove up, I saw a car with Iowa plates parked in front. Between the car and the house were Iowa, Jean, Geraldine Miles, and Lloyd Cramer.

Lloyd Cramer's arms were moving up and down in gestures of appeal and he was leaning forward. Geraldine Miles had Iowa's shotgun in her hands and was pointing it at Cramer. I stopped the Toyota, flicked my CB to channel nine, and sent out an SOS to anyone whose ears were up to get the police to Iowa's house. I repeated the message, but didn't wait for an answer. I got out and walked toward Lloyd Cramer through air thick with the sound of his voice. That voice was a droning plea, a series of promises. I thought the shotgun muzzle swung a bit toward me.

"Hold it, J. W.," said Iowa in a strained voice that spoke through Cramer's babble. "Gerry's not used to guns."

"It's me, Geraldine," I said. "Nobody's going to get hurt."

The gun muzzle wavered away. I walked slowly up to Cramer, my ears filled with the mad sound of his voice. He was begging to be taken back, swearing love eternal, promising to reform, admitting guilt, pleading for one more chance.

I looked at Geraldine. The shotgun was none too steady. "Point the gun at the ground," I said over the sound of Cramer's voice. I put what I hoped was a friendly smile on my face. "I don't think you want to hit me, but that's what might happen if you shoot. Please, Gerry, point the gun at the ground."

I was beside Cramer now, but he didn't notice me. He saw only Geraldine. He was pouring out his convoluted soul in a steady stream of words, asking her to forgive him and take him back. I saw the shotgun barrel drop and Iowa move carefully toward his niece.

"I think he's got a gun," said Iowa's flat voice.

"Mr. Cramer," I said, and touched his shoulder. He swung an arm as though to brush away a fly and his voice continued to fill the yard with pleas. "It's time to leave, Mr. Cramer," I said. "Geraldine doesn't want to talk to you now. Come along." I stepped around in front of him, beneath him and Geraldine.

He was a big man. His eyes were wild and full of tears and focused behind me on Geraldine. There was indeed something thrust inside his shirt that didn't belong there. I said, "Mr. Cramer," and the eyes found mine. "I know you love her," I said, "but she needs more time. Let's get you back to your car. You need some rest. I know you don't want to hurt anybody, so it's best that we leave."

He was crying. "I don't want to hurt anybody! I never did! I love Gerry!"

"I know you do," I said. "Come on. Let's go to the car. I'll go with you. We can talk. I'm sick of trouble and I know you are, too."

I put a hand on his arm and he blinked at me and we stepped back toward his car. For a moment I allowed myself to think that the situation was going to work out. Then he suddenly said, "I know you!" He pushed me away with a big hand and with his other groped inside his shirt. "You were there in her room! You're the one! You want to take her away from me! I won't let you! I'll kill you both!"

The hand came out of his shirt with a pistol in it. He swung it toward the people behind me. I got hold of his wrist with both hands and twisted it to one side as he squeezed off the first shot. Then his other hand was a fist as big and hard as a brick, beating at me, pounding me down. Another shot went off between our bodies. I got a knee into him, but that great thundering fist was making the world fade. Then I lost the wrist and he jerked away and swung the pistol toward me. I went for him again as the pistol swung into line and a shot boomed.

Cramer's face disappeared in a flower of blood and bone, and he went backward onto the ground. I turned to see Geraldine Miles with the shotgun in her hands. Her face was white as whey, but she was struggling to pump another round into the firing chamber and coming forward, her eyes fixed on Cramer. I turned back. The pistol had fallen from Cramer's hand. He wasn't going to use it anymore. In the distance I heard sirens coming. I put out a hand toward Geraldine as she stepped toward Cramer's body and raised the shotgun again.

"It's okay, Geraldine," I said. "It's all over. He's as dead as he's ever going to get."

Geraldine said a word which at one time would have been called unprintable, and shot Cramer again. I took the shotgun away before she could give him another round and thumbed on the safety. Behind us, Jean and Iowa stared at us, then came forward. Jean took Geraldine in her arms.

"It's all right, dear," said Iowa gently. "All of us are all right now."

Geraldine looked at her uncle. Her battered face was red and contorted. Her voice was like a knife. "He's dead! He's dead! The turd is dead!"

I had rarely seen such hatred on so young a face. I wondered if it would ever go completely away.

"I thank you," I said to her. "If it wasn't for you, I'd be lying there instead of him."

Geraldine stared at me and said nothing.

"And if it wasn't for you, J. W.," said Iowa in a shaky voice, "we might be lying there. What a world we live in."

The first police car came into the yard. The driver took one look at things and called for a lot of backup. Then he went to Cramer's body, felt for a pulse, stood up, and looked around in a confused way. We all waited in the yard for the rest of the police to come. It was a soft August afternoon. Overhead, the pale blue sky held a few gentle-looking clouds. At South Beach, the kites were no doubt still flying. On the green grass of Iowa's front yard, Cramer's blood soaked slowly into the ground.

· 29 ·

"You're always where the trouble is," said Corporal Dominic Agganis.

"I'm just not lucky, I guess."

"You'd better get out of the trouble business," said Agganis. "You've already used up eight of your lives."

"You've talked me into it. From now on, you can have all the trouble. If you're done with me, I'm going home."

"Oh, I'm done with you, but other people aren't." He nodded across the yard toward the house where Iowa, Jean, and Geraldine were talking with the Edgartown police, the sheriff of The County of Dukes County, another state cop, and some other cops I didn't recognize. The yard was full of them, too. "The girl will be charged. We got a hotshot DA with political ambitions, and you can be sure he'll bring her to trial if he can. There'll be a grand jury, at least, and you, my friend, will be on the witness list."

"Good. Self-defense. She saved my life and her own."

"So you say." He yawned. "We'll see what the grand jury says. I got to go talk to the lady in question. See you in court." He walked toward the house.

I drove home and poured myself a double vodka on the rocks and went up to the balcony. The view was as lovely as ever, but it meant nothing to me. I had felt this way before, and knew that in time I would feel better, that I would stop feeling empty and angry just because justice was rare and love elusive.

I drank my vodka and tried to let the beauty of the world flow into me. I had read that when the Navaho poets walk across the great, dry, brutal desert which is their home, they are not aliens to it. "Beauty before me," they say. "Beauty behind me. Beauty all around me." Martha's Vineyard, green and golden, surrounded by the eternal sea, was no desert, but rather a small Eden. Still I felt remote from it. I tried to let its gentle splendor enter my eyes and the sounds of its gulls and songbirds enter my ears and find my soul.

When it was dark, I went downstairs, still moody, knowing that I would have a bad night. Of all the earth's life-forms, only man wishes things were different. It is his bane, his absurdity.

But bad nights end, and the sea is a great restorer. It is indifferent to our fears and joys, merciless, beautiful, terrible, and nurturing. In the morning I went down to the harbor and rowed out to the *Mattie,* John Skye's lovely old catboat. She was beginning to collect some hair around her waterline, but was otherwise fine. Because he had chosen to spend so much time in Colorado, John had barely used her this summer. As I checked her bilge and bowline, I thought of Dr. Jonathan Scarlotti and his little band of graduate students, who had not had time to go sailing in the *Mattie.* I wondered if Dr. Scarlotti would ever know that he had perhaps indirectly been the cause of the deaths of Bernie Orwell and her brother, and what effect it would have upon him if he knew. I wondered if I should drive up to Weststock and make sure he at least knew his role in those deaths. The prospect appealed to part of me. I thought Dr. Scarlotti was exactly the sort of exploiter of women that Orwell had hated.

I rowed to the *Shirley J.,* put a bag of clothes and a cooler of food and drink aboard, and put to sea. I needed to sort things out.

I sailed on a broad reach all the way to Woods Hole, caught a fair tide through the narrows, and beat into Hadley's. I wound up the centerboard, found a shallow spot far from the other boats anchored there, and dropped the hook. I didn't want company. I took a swim, then sat in the wide cockpit and watched the yachts come in for the night. I was still there when the stars came out.

The next day I had a fair wind all the way to Newport, and the day after that to Block Island, where I anchored for two days while I walked that lovely little island from end to end, and ate my lunches on a long veranda overlooking the old harbor. On the third day, the rains came, so I stayed in the cuddy cabin and read again Childers' wonderful *Riddle of the Sands*, a required item in any ship's library. In the middle of the afternoon, it began to rain even harder. I put on my daring bathing suit, so no water-soaked sailors who might be looking would be shocked, got some soap, and went out into the cockpit and had a shower. The rain was hard and cold and felt good. It kept raining, so that night I cooked inside.

The following morning was gray and cool, with spats of rain blowing in on a southwest wind. I hauled anchor and beat out to sea, taking a bit of a pounding as I cleared the harbor entrance, but then having a better time when I headed north to clear Sandy Point, and finally having a fine following wind as I swung up toward Martha's Vineyard.

I sailed all day and into the night, because the *Shirley J.*, for all her many virtues, is not too swift. In the last of the light, I dropped the hook outside the entrance to Cuttyhunk, that tiny, westernmost member of the Elizabeth Islands. The people on Cuttyhunk live there partly because they like to be alone. I understood that desire, and did not go ashore.

At first light, I pulled anchor. In light morning breezes, I loafed along on the Buzzards Bay side of Nashawena and Pasque, then cut through Robinson's Hole, and caught the east tide past Tarpaulin Cove toward West Chop. The late morning wind came up and I had a fine sail. I rounded West Chop, crossed to East Chop, noted that the bonito fishermen were still at work around the Oak Bluffs ferry dock, and headed for home close-hauled.

I was back on the stake by mid-afternoon, and ashore a half hour later. I put my gear in the Toyota and walked down to the Navigator Room for a beer. When I came out, the chief was drinking coffee across the street in front of the Dock Street Coffee Shop. I walked across.

"Home is the sailor, home from the sea," he said.

"As the general said, 'I have returned.' "

"Your millions of fans will be greatly relieved," said the chief. "Your boat's been gone for eight days."

"My, Grandma, what big eyes you have."

"The Law never sleeps. I've been trying to get hold of you for a couple of days. The harbormaster told me the *Shirley J.* was gone. Where you been?"

"Sailing, sailing, over the bounding main. Block Island and points between here and there. Why do you want to see me?"

"The DA is going to convene a grand jury."

"I figured as much. I guess I would, too, if I was the DA. A man's been shot to death, after all."

"I imagine he's going to make as much as he can about that second shot after Cramer was down."

"I'll testify that Cramer seemed alive to me and that I was in fear of my life."

"The doctors will testify that he was probably dead."

"I'm no doctor and neither is Geraldine Miles. I thought he was still alive."

"Geraldine told us that you said he was dead."

"She was confused. She only wanted to save my life. His pistol was still in his hand."

"When we got there, it wasn't."

"I kicked it out after she shot at him the second time. I was in fear of my life. I'll testify to that."

"You spent a lot of that time in fear of your life. You got a lawyer?"

"No. I don't trust lawyers."

"Maybe you'd better get one. Perjury is a bad rap."

I spread my arms. "Perjury? Me, commit perjury? What are you talking about? I'm a fisherman! Would a fisherman lie?!"

The chief stared up the street. His mouth was kinking, almost as if he wanted to laugh. Instead, he drank some coffee.

"I don't think a grand jury will bring an indictment against her," he said, "but you never know."

"They won't, if I have anything to say about it."

"So I gather. There's another thing. The Sheriff's Department in La Plata County, Colorado, say they've found a car rented in Jackson, Wyoming, by one Gordon Berkeley Orwell, but carrying the New Jersey plates that are supposed to be on Orwell's New Jersey Jeep Cherokee. They wonder if you know anything about that."

"I'm the one who told them to look for that car. Where'd they find it?"

"How should I know? At the foot of a trail that goes up some cliffs or other. They want to know if you know where Orwell is. Seems that they talked to John Skye and he said he saw you and Orwell at the top of those cliffs. The sheriff hasn't talked to anybody who's seen Orwell since. Wonders if you know where he is."

Where was Orwell? Was he smiling down at me from heaven? Frowning up at me from hell? Floating disembodied in the primal fluids of the universe? Had he been reabsorbed into the World Soul? Had he seen the white light of Truth? Were the energies that once had taken the form of his earthly life been recycled into some new shape? A flower? A fish? A cancerous cell in some smoker's lung?

I told the chief about how I'd taken Orwell up to the top of the cliffs so he could talk with John. Then I said, "After he and John talked, I talked to John on the walkie-talkie. John told me that he had convinced Orwell that he was after the wrong man. I stayed there on the cliffs for a while, then came down. The last time I saw Orwell, he was near the top of the cliffs. The last thing he said to me was that he hoped I had no hard feelings."

"You didn't toss him off the cliff, then?"

"I have acrophobia," I said. "I get sick if I get too close to the edge of high places. Ask John Skye. Ask Mattie. Ask the twins. Ask John's niece. They'll all tell you."

"He was scheduled to return to duty, but he didn't show up. Apparently very unlike him. Do you think he was suicidal?"

"I think you have to be a little off center to do some of the things he did. I don't know if he was suicidal."

"They say he was on special leave. Stress syndrome, or some such thing. Do you think he might have jumped?"

"I don't read minds."

He finished his coffee and dropped the paper cup into a refuse disposal container. Edgartown is a neat town, and the chief would never drop his cup in the gutter.

"I don't read minds either," he said. "Glad I don't. I wouldn't want to know what a lot of people are thinking."

"How's Geraldine Miles?"

"Women are tough. I just hope this doesn't make her too tough. It's not good to be too tough." He walked up Main Street.

I went home, showered, shaved, brushed my teeth, and dressed up in my fancy clothes—Vineyard Red slacks, a blue shirt with a red anchor over the pocket, boat shoes without socks, my belt with little sailboats on it, and called Iowa's house. Jean answered.

"I want to take your niece out on a date," I said. "Do you think she'll go?"

"I don't know, J. W. Why don't you ask her?"

"Put her on the line."

Geraldine's voice said, "Hello?"

"J. W. Jackson here," I said. "I want to take you to dinner. I just got back from a week at sea, and I need to look across the table at a real, live girl and talk to her instead of to myself. Can I pick you up at six?"

"I don't know. I'm not sure . . ."

"Great! I'll see you at six. You have a white dress?"

"Well . . ."

"A white blouse will do. You look terrific in white. See you at six. Wear your dancing shoes."

I rang off and made myself a martini, wondering if I knew what I was doing.

At six, I picked up Geraldine. She was wearing low heels, a dark skirt, and a white blouse. Her hair was combed so that it partially covered the side of her face that was most hurt.

"Very nice," I said. "The Veronica Lake look."

"Who's Veronica Lake?"

"A woman in my father's world. Let's go." I gave her my arm.

We ate at the Navigator Room, which not only has excellent food, but also has the best view of any Edgartown restaurant. She ate with little bites and had white wine. Afterward I talked her into having coffee and a cognac. Everything went on my plastic card. I had so much on there already that a bit more didn't hurt at all. When we were through with our cognac, I walked with her down to the town wharf and we went up to the balcony and looked at the boats. The stars were just beginning to come out. There was a soft wind from the south.

After that I took her to Oak Bluffs.

"What are we doing here?" she asked, with a small smile.

"We're going to dance," I said.

"Oh, I don't know. I . . ."

"Anytime before last year, you'd have been taking a chance if you danced with me," I said, "because I was terrible. I never knew where my feet were, or what I was supposed to do. But Zee Madieras has made me into a new man. She showed me how to dance any kind of dance, and now I'm going to show off with you. Come on."

We went into the Atlantic Connection. It was crowded and the music hurt my ears, but the dance floor had space for two more, and I led her there. I put my arm around her waist, took her right hand in my left one, and stood there, holding her gently against me.

After a while she looked up at me. "This is it? This is the way you dance?"

I smiled down at her. "Great, isn't is? As long as I don't move my feet, I can dance any kind of dance."

"And this is what your friend Zee taught you?"

"A terrific teacher. She changed my life. Isn't this fun? God, when I think of the years I was ashamed to step out onto the floor!"

Geraldine put her head against my chest and began to laugh.

We danced until pretty late, and then I took her home. That week I took her fishing and clamming and quahogging. I took her out dancing two more times. We danced at the Hot Tin Roof and again at the Connection. Toward the end, I began to shuffle around a little, just to show I was willing to experiment. When I took her home that night, she pulled my head down and kissed me.

"Thanks," she said. "Uncle Dan says that Zee Madieras is due home tomorrow. I guess that means you won't be taking me out anymore."

"There are a lot of nice guys who'll want to take you out," I said. "Just give them a chance."

That night I didn't sleep too well.

Zee's ferry came in mid-afternoon. I had spent the day doing things that needed doing around the house. I was under the Toyota trying to find an irksome little oil leak when I heard a car coming down my driveway. I suspected that I needed a new gasket for my oil pan. On the other hand, maybe I could get away with just tightening a couple of bolts that had loosened up. The car stopped and a door opened. I slid out from under the Toyota and looked up at Zee.

My heart turned over.

I brushed at some grease on my shirt, then looked up again. Zee was walking toward me. She was wearing a pale blouse and skirt that emphasized her dark loveliness. She walked in beauty, like the night, right up to me.

"Well," I said. "You've come back."

"Yes."

"Were your conferences enlightening?"

"Yes."

"Have you made any decisions?"

"Yes."

"Do you have a lot to talk about?"

"Yes."

"With me?"

"Yes."

"I have a lot to talk about with you, too," I said, "but first things first. Will you marry me?"

"Yes," she said. "Yes, I will."

Enter the Wonderful World of Philip R. Craig's Martha's Vineyard Series

Martha's Vineyard is home to ex-Boston cop J.W. Jackson and his much-adored family. Yet this idyllic vacation spot offers no escape from danger—and from the peaceful beaches to the quiet towns, murder sometimes rears its ugly head.

Turn the page and get a glimpse into the world of J.W. Jackson, and see why "Spending time with Craig on Martha's Vineyard is the next best thing to vacationing on the island itself."

—*Minneapolis Star-Tribune*

During his career as a cop on the back streets of Boston, J.W. Jackson saw enough evil to last a lifetime. So he retired to the serenity of Martha's Vineyard to spend his days fishing for blues and wooing a sexy nurse named Zee. But in **A Beautiful Place to Die,** *when a local's boat mysteriously explodes off the coast, killing an amiable young drifter, Jackson is drawn reluctantly back into the investigative trade.*

■ ■

Now the *Nellie Grey* was in sight, moving smoothly out with mild following waves, the wind at her back. She came past the lighthouse and we could see Jim and Billy. They waved and we waved back, and they went on out beyond the shallows that reach east from Cape Pogue. Beyond the *Nellie Grey* the long black boat altered her course to hold outside the *Nellie*'s turn as she swung south beyond the shallows to follow the beach toward Wasque.

"Come on," said George, lowering his binoculars, "let's go back to Wasque so we can watch them fish the rip. The east tide will be running and there may be something there."

Susie, looking sad, nodded and turned to the Wagoneer.

"We'll follow you down," I said, "but then we're going on into town. We want to sell these fish."

"And I've got to get some sleep," said Zee. "I've got duty again tonight, and right now I'm frazzled out."

Just at that moment the *Nellie Grey* exploded. A great red and yellow flower opened from the sea and expanded into the air. Petals of flame and stalks of debris shot up and arched away as a ball of smoke billowed from the spot where the *Nellie* had been. A moment later the boom of the explosion hit us, and the sea around the *Nellie* was one of flame. I thought I saw a body arc into the burning water.

A university professor visiting Martha's Vineyard has fallen in love with the island's gently lapping waves and whispering island breezes. But on a warm June day, she's swallowed up by a dark and merciless sea, never to be seen again. And in an attempt to preserve his beloved home's peace, intrepid sleuth J. W. Jackson dives into the investigation of this mysterious and "accidental" **Death in Vineyard Waters.**

■ ■

She gave a small smile. "Of course not. I believe a salesman would say it comes with the territory. Besides, there may be something to the idea. Why should flesh and spirit be separate, after all? D. H. Lawrence thought that the separation of the two was the major malaise of Western civilization, you know." Her fingers played on my arm and then suddenly withdrew, as if she had just become aware of them being there. "Dr. Summerharp is just an old . . . woman without a good word for anyone. She needs love and understanding, not hatred."

"Dr. Hooperman was not so generous in his feelings."

"Ah, well, he must be forgiven, too. Momentarily done in by gin, I believe. I recall that my husband invited you to visit us at Sanctuary. I echo that invitation. Please do come up." Her eyes looked up at me from beneath hooded lids.

"Thank you." I was suddenly sure that her husband would never leave her no matter how involved she might sometimes be with some other man or woman. I looked at my watch. "I'm afraid I must go and save my car," I said.

She offered her hand. "A pleasure seeing you again. Do come and visit us."

I went down the library walk. Glancing back, I saw that she was watching me. We exchanged waves. Three cars behind mine a meter maid was scribbling out a ticket. I just beat her to the Land Cruiser, thus thrice escaping the clutches of the law in a single day. Not willing to press my luck, I left town and went home, where I worked at things that I'd been meaning to tend to but hadn't because I'd been occupied with Zee. Now I had the time. Too much of it, really.

That evening, I looked up "moldwarp." I learned that it was a name for the common European mole. I had now pulled even with Hotspur on one word, at least.

Precisely one week later I read that Marjorie Summerharp was dead.

When J.W. Jackson foils an attempt to terminate former mob boss Luciano Marcus on the steps of Boston's Symphony Hall, it puts a definite damper on his newlywedded bliss. But **Death on a Vineyard Beach** *promises more than just off-island danger, for the mayhem follows J.W. and Zee back home to Martha's Vineyard, and keeping the circling sharks from the kill may just be more than J.W. can handle.*

■ ■

Later, in bed, I listened to the sounds of the night: the odd calls of nocturnal creatures, the swish of leaves, the groans of tree limbs rubbing together. Once or twice I thought I might be hearing unusual noises in the yard, but when I slipped out of bed for a look, there was no one there.

The next morning, when Zee was home from her graveyard shift and asleep in the bedroom, another car came down our driveway. I didn't recognize this one, or the two guys who got out of it. They were young, bronze-skinned guys with dark eyes and muscular bodies.

"You Jeff Jackson?" the first asked.

I had the garden hose, and was watering the flowers in the boxes on the front fence.

"That's me."

"I have a message for you," he said, coming up to me. "Stay out of Linda Vanderbeck's hair!"

And so saying, he hit me in the jaw with his right hand and followed with his left.

At first, the girl J.W. Jackson encounters strolling alone along South Beach seems like your typical teenager. But there's nothing typical about young Cricket Callahan, the spirited only daughter of the vacationing President of the United States. What Jackson can't figure out is why the feisty First Kid is so intent on eluding the Secret Service, or why the Chief Executive himself wants J.W. and Zee to watch over the errant sixteen-year-old. In **A Deadly Vineyard Holiday,** *the answer unfortunately comes in the form of a dead body . . .*

■ ■

I put another basket and rake into the Land Cruiser, and we drove out to the pavement and turned toward Edgartown. There was a car parked beside the bike path a hundred feet or so up the road in the direction of Vineyard Haven. I thought there was someone in the driver's seat.

The car was still there when we came back with our quahogs an hour and a half later.

I pulled into the driveway and stopped and looked at the car.

"What is it?' asked Zee.

"I'm not sure," I said.

As I got out of the Land Cruiser and crossed the highway, I thought I saw the driver taking my picture. Then, as I walked along the bike path toward the car, its driver started the motor, made a U-turn, and drove away.

I thought the car had a Massachusetts plate, but I couldn't make out the number.

I walked back to the truck.

"What was that all about?" asked Zee.

"I don't know," I said. "Probably nothing."

But I didn't think it was nothing.

In **A Shoot on Martha's Vineyard,** *J.W.'s idyllic summer hits a snag when a movie scout from a land called "Hollywood" invades the beaches—and takes a liking not only to the island locale, but to Jackson's lovely lady Zee as well. And when a longtime nemesis turns up dead—and J.W. is the prime suspect—the ex-Boston cop will have to cast his line to find the real killer.*

■ ■

I liked having Zee's hand in mine. I liked being married to her, and having Joshua making us three. I didn't want to do anything to unbalance us.

One of the things I liked about our marriage was that it was stuck together without any coercion of any kind. There was no "We have to stay together because we said we would" or "You owe me" or "You promised me you'd love me" stuff nor any "Think of the children" stuff, either, even though we had said we'd stick together, and we did owe each other more than we could say, and we did love each other and, now, we did have Joshua to think about.

Basically Zee and I were married because we wanted to be married, and for no other reason.

I wondered why I was thinking such thoughts, and suspected that it was because of two things: the first was a sort of restlessness that had come over Zee since Joshua had made his appearance. Her usual confidence and independence were occasionally less pronounced, occasionally more; her normal fearlessness was sometimes replaced by an uneasiness that I'd not seen in her before, and at other times she became almost fierce.

A postpartum transformation of some kind? I didn't know. Maybe she saw the same things in me, and all that either of us was seeing was the fretting of new parents who didn't really know how to do their job and were worried that they were doing it wrong.

The second thing bothering me was more easily identified. It was Drew Mondry.

Him, Tarzan; Zee, Jane.

They even looked like Tarzan and Jane. Both were suntanned and spectacularly made, with his blond hair and brilliant blue eyes contrasting well indeed with her dark eyes and long, blue-black hair. Golden Tarz; bronze Jane.

And there was that little charged current that had run between them this morning.

May I call you Zee? I'll phone you later.

In **A Fatal Vineyard Season,** *the arrival of Julia Crandel and Ivy Holiday, two actresses staying on the Vineyard for the summer, has incurred the wrath of local gangsters. Worse still, a deadly stalker from one of the ladies' pasts has found out where they are hiding, and it looks like it's up to J.W. Jackson to follow his conscience and protect two frightened, helpless off-islanders . . . and put himself in danger as well.*

■ ■

The two young women exchanged looks, then put smiles on their faces. "Yes," said Julia. "You're right. We'll just be vacationers like everybody else."

"We'd love to have you up for drinks before we go," said Julia later as they got into their car.

"Tomorrow I'm off with the kids to see my mama over in America," said Zee. "I'm afraid I won't be around for a while."

"Too bad," said Ivy. She looked at me. "Maybe you'll come by, J.W."

"I've been known to have a cocktail," I said.

The car drove away.

"She has great come-hither eyes, doesn't she?" said Zee.

"Who?"

"You know who."

"Oh, her."

Martha's Vineyard is a magic place that can isolate you from the real world for a while and cleanse your soul, and I hoped that it would do that for Ivy Holiday and Julia Crandel. But as the old Indian medicine singer said when his spell failed, sometimes the best magic doesn't work. Two nights later, someone kicked in the front door of the Crandel house, took a knife from the kitchen, and went upstairs after Ivy and Julia.

A surprise visit from a dear old friend only adds to the joy of good weather, great fishing, and loving family for J.W. Jackson this idyllic island summer. But his elation turns to dread when a rundown summer shack burns to the ground, and an unidentified corpse is discovered in the ashes. Fearing it may be that of his friend, J.W. dives into an ugly mass of arson, extortion, and secrets—and in **Vineyard Blues,** *the ex-Boston cop may just be headed down a road toward murder.*

■ ■

That night, sometime after Zee came home, climbed into bed beside me, and we both snuggled to sleep, I was awakened by the fire whistle in Edgartown calling to the volunteers. Then I heard sirens and more sirens, and I was disturbed by the direction they seemed to be headed. I listened, then eased out of bed and went into the living room and turned on the scanner. Voices and static crackled from the speaker. I heard the name of the street where Corrie had been staying, and had an almost irresistible urge to go there. But I knew that the last thing the firemen needed was another citizen getting in their way, so I remained where I was.

In time I heard someone say that the place seemed to be empty, and I felt a surge of relief. Apparently, everybody had gone to a party at another house, said the voice.

That would be the party the twin had mentioned, where the college kids would combine fun with charity as they tried to help those who'd gotten burned out earlier, and where Corrie had been asked to do some singing for the good cause.

Another bad fire, but at least no one had gotten hurt, in spite of the arsonist who I now believed was pretty clearly at work. The fire marshal could handle it. I turned off the scanner and went back to bed.

It wasn't until the next morning, as I made breakfast and listened to the radio news, that I learned I was wrong about no one being hurt. A body, as yet unidentified, had been found in the ruined remains of the house.

J.W. Jackson abandoned Boston, hoping to leave the violence of the big city behind. But in **Vineyard Shadows,** *when the past comes looking for him in the guise of two brutal thugs, the former cop knows it's time to put down his fishing pole and start opening doors he'd hoped were closed forever.*

■ ■

I got the details by talking with the survivors, since I wasn't at the house when it happened. Instead, I was on the clamflats in Katama with my son Joshua. When we came home, there was a cop at the head of our driveway, and an ambulance was pulling out and heading toward the hospital in Oak Bluffs. I turned into something made of ice.

The cop recognized my old Land Cruiser and waved us in. I drove fast down our long, sandy driveway. The yard was full of police cars and uniforms. Sergeant Tony D'Agostine met me as I stepped out of the truck.

I was full of fear. "Stay here," I said to Joshua, and shut the truck's door behind me.

"There's been some trouble," said Tony.

"Where's Zee? Where's Diana?!"

"Take it easy," said Tony, "it's all over."

"Where are they?!" I pushed him aside, and went toward the house. He followed me, saying something I wasn't hearing. I saw what looked like blood on the grass. Jesus! Cops stood aside as I came through them.

That was the beginning of it for me.

With the arrival of warm weather and good fishing, everything should be just fine for J.W. Jackson and Zee. But something's wrong. A mysterious man named Mahsimba, who is on the Vineyard searching for two priceless soapstone eagles missing from his African homeland, has embroiled him in problems both personal and professional. And in **Vineyard Enigma,** *J.W. couldn't have known that helping Mahsimba would pit him against powerful figures in the Vineyard's art world, including some who would stop at nothing—even murder—to add forbidden objects to their collection.*

■ ■

"In any case," continued Mahsimba, "with the discovery of the ruins came European treasure hunters and so-called experts on ancient cultures. One of the treasure hunters was a man named Willi Posselt. In 1889 he discovered four eagles carved from soapstone and traded for what he considered the best of them. Over the years, a total of ten eagles were found in Great Zimbabwe and shipped elsewhere, to museums and private collections. The whereabouts of eight of them are known, and my country is working very hard to have them returned to their homeland. I'm here on your island in search of the two missing ones. I think they may be here, and Stanley Crandel thinks that you may be able to help me find them."

*In **Vineyard Deceit,** a Middle Eastern potentate and his entourage are descending on Martha's Vineyard—and chaos is in the salt air. Ex-cop Jeff "J.W." Jackson would rather be fishing with his lady Zee, but the island's overtaxed police force needs his help to control the madness their visitor's arrival has stirred up. But when Zee vanishes, Jackson becomes a frantic investigator and suddenly stands to lose everything that he dearly loves.*

■ ■

"Are you all right?"

"Yes. You?"

"Yes."

Beyond the gut, the cigarette boat slowed and swung around and came back. There were three men aboard. They eased up near us.

"Are you all right?" This from the dark-eyed helmsman. There was a British intonation overlying an accent I didn't recognize.

"You missed us by at least a foot, you stupid man!" Zee was furious.

The helmsman darkened even more, and his mouth tightened. An olive-skinned man with a hatchet face frowned. A blond young man dropped a ladder over the side. "Come aboard," he said, leaning down and putting out a hand.

"I don't want to ride with a maniac," said Zee, coughing. "Get away from us before that fool at the wheel really does kill us both!"

"Please," said the blond man.

Zee waved her fishing rod at the helmsman. "I had a good fish on, you dunderhead! You cut him off! People like you shouldn't be allowed to drive! My God!"

The helmsman glared, and the man with the hatchet face spoke to him in a language I didn't know.

The water was warm, but we were still slowly being carried out to sea. I swam to the cigarette boat and climbed aboard. "Awfully sorry," said the blond man, giving my hand a fast shake. "Please, miss, come aboard."

I reached down a long arm. "Come on, Zee."

Spitting water, she swam over and handed up her rod, then climbed the ladder and glared at the helmsman, dripping.

"Just to make sure I've got the right man," she snapped, moving toward him, "it *was* you who nearly cut us in two, wasn't it?"

The helmsman lifted his chin and looked first at each man on the boat and finally at her. "It was indeed, madam. And what were you doing there, anyway?"

"You incredible jerk! I was fishing there, but this is what I'm doing here!" And before he or anyone else could move she hit him in the nose with her fist.

He gasped and raised his hands to his face.

"There, you wretched man!" cried Zee.

He staggered back. His legs hit the side of the cockpit and he went overboard backwards. Zee looked slightly abashed. The man with the hatchet face looked suddenly deadly. His hand dipped under his light summer shirt and came out with a flat semiautomatic pistol. He was very quick. He swung the pistol toward Zee, and I barely had time to step between them.